BOLSHEVIKS
AT THE
BALLET

Also by Robert Wilton

The Gentleman Adventurer
Death and the Dreadnought
Poison in Paris

The Comptrollerate-General novels
Traitor's Field
Treason's Spring
Treason's Tide
Treason's Flood [*projected*]
The Spider of Sarajevo

Shakespeare & Sherlock
Sherlock Holmes and the Adventure of the Distracted Thane
Sherlock Holmes and the Case of the Philosophical Prince

With Elizabeth Gowing

No Man's Lands: Eight Extraordinary Women in Balkan History

BOLSHEVIKS
AT THE
BALLET

Robert Wilton

Published in 2022 by Elbow Publishing

© Robert Wilton 2022

Robert Wilton has asserted his rights under the Copyright,
Design and Patents Act, 1988, to be identified as the author of
this work.

Cover design by Sally Ellis-Rudd.

A catalogue record for this book is available from the British
Library ISBN 978-1-9163661-2-1.

Extract from *Le Figaro*, 16th November 1968

Extract from *Le Figaro*, 16th November 1968

DOSSIER DU AVENTURIER GENTILHOMME

A curiosity is reported in Biarritz

M. Tretiot recounts that a charming oriental trunk, sold at auction as 'the property of a lady', was found to have a false bottom. Concealed within this space was a dossier of papers. These proved to be the work of an English Gentleman, Sir Harry Delamere, who in the years before the First World War was a renowned traveller, adventurer and libertine. His later years remain a mystery, and indeed rumour and scandal attached to much of his life, so it is thought that this dossier may be enlightening. The Minister of Interior has directed that the papers shall be first reviewed by his Department before any further steps are taken with them.

1.

The execution was beautifully managed.

The doomed man, standing noble and defiant. The five members of the firing-squad at an elegant diagonal, so those of us watching could see each of them and admire the discipline as the rifles came level as one. The tension rising to its unavoidable climax, the volley of shots, noise and smoke and the man gasping, staggering and dropping.

I don't know if you know the opera *Tosca*, and if you don't I'm the wrong person to introduce you. Broadly-speaking, the chap's been condemned for some political business - I didn't get that bit; something about Italy and Napoleon, all rather a muddle - and the chap's lover - Tosca, hence the name - makes a deal with the Chief of Police, who's a brute, that if he replaces the firing squad's live rounds with blanks then she'll let him have his filthy way with her, he being a toe-rag as well as a brute, albeit one with good taste, for Tosca's damned handsome. Chief of Police agrees, and makes the arrangements, and comes back with his tongue hanging out, at which point Tosca stabs him to death, which is hardly playing fair but serves the dirty old so-and-so right. She watches the boyfriend's execution feeling rather pleased with herself, but when she sneaks back later to compliment him on faking it so well and lead him to safety, she finds that Chief of Police double-crossed her while she was double-crossing him, they were real bullets after all, and so the chap's dead, and for her this really puts the tin hat on a trying day and she chucks herself off the battlements. General message seems to be that you shouldn't trust policemen, Italians, or women.

In this case, it was all happening against a unique backdrop. Old friend of mine has done very well for himself, and he and his wife like to annoy the rest of us by organizing evenings of opera and the like so they can show off their enormous garden. Tosca's life and death and a bit of the other melodrama was sung among the gloomy old evergreens of a December evening in Surrey, flaming torches for light and braziers for heat. I pretend to be unimpressed, but it's very lovely.

I should add - and here you really shouldn't take my word for it, for I have no artistic taste whatever - that the music is wonderful. You never know what's going on story-wise, but the sound is magnificent.

Much of the story I had to get afterwards. I got the execution, and Tosca's impatient wait for the firing squad to pop off for their tea, and her discovery of the cruel trick, the body lying there really dead after all; and finally her defiant shriek to the enemy she killed but whose posthumous revenge she could not avoid, a shriek to a cruel God, and then she was gone over the castle walls. Or, in our case, sort of crossly flinging herself away behind a rhododendron. Dramatic musical climax and we all clapped. It is grand stuff, as I say.

We were still applauding, and the singers began to gather in front of their audience, forty or fifty of us in best evening wear. Then things broke down. There was hesitation on the grass stage, confusion, and then a scream.

I was wondering what I'd misunderstood, and some of the audience were still clapping and others were rather giving up, and now there was obviously trouble on the stage area, the performers gathered in a huddle. A few more moments of raised voices and everyone looking around uncertain and then our host was getting up from the front row of the audience and walking to join the discussion.

Almost at once he was walking back and beckoning... to me.

I've always had a horror of this. At the music hall, which I visit more often than I do the opera, they usually pull some chump out of the audience; and I'd throw myself off the battlements rather than go through that. But the look on my friend's face had me out of my seat and following him back to the huddle of singers.

He turned to me. 'He's been shot', he said, very quiet.

For one stupid moment I stared at him, still not sure how much of this was normal business at the opera and not wanting to show my ignorance. 'Well, yes…'

'Really shot. Real bullet.'

Now I looked at the chap on the ground. I bent down beside him. The crimson stain in the middle of his white shirt looked very real; the sickly grey complexion on that empty face was unmistakable.

And the brilliant madness of it - the trick in the opera become the trick in reality - struck me only then.

The execution really was beautifully managed.

2.

My host took my arm and pulled me aside. 'What do you say, Harry?'

I looked at him sourly. 'You want me to unmask the culprit, or confess?'

'You can't manage either?'

'Let me toss a coin, at least.'

'It must be some sort of accident, but I suppose we have to have the police here, don't we?' I nodded. 'Harry, you're handy with this sort of thing; the police, I mean.'

What he meant was that I am usually in or stumbling around the fringes of trouble, making the police a persistent blot on my landscape. It was why he'd pulled me out of the audience. If there's a to-do, ask Harry; probably turn out to be his fault anyway so you'll save a bit of time.

'Cover the body but don't touch it', I said. 'Impound those rifles and any ammunition. Police'd prefer you keep all the guests here, but that'd start a riot, so you'll have to let them go and accept a grumpy policeman; if you've a guest list, grand. All these singers will need to stay, and the musicians. But the excitement's going to wear off and they'll start feeling damn' cold. So let'em get coats, and something warm to drink.'

He beckoned the butler, and within fifteen seconds servants were bustling around according to his instructions. Then he turned back to me.

For one of the brief periods when my ruin of a father was in the funds and aware of my existence, I was at school with Andrew Tucker. He was always a fresh challenging intellect and good company, and I think he finds me sort of reliably entertainingly odd, and I play along because his wine is so good. Now Sir Andrew, he's something to do with politics - all terribly clever and influential and I don't remotely understand it, my political awareness being on a par with my opera. I'm not sure even he knows what he's talking about, but he was always good with the chat, and he makes lots of money so it must be all right.

He was looking less assured. 'Bit grim', I said. 'Sorry it's put a dampener on the evening. But one way or another the business'll be confined to the performers.' It was only the first of my many misjudgements in this affair, but perhaps the most spectacular. 'You'll have an hour or two of constables trampling the herbaceous border, then it'll go away.' He absorbed this doubtfully.

Then a handsome woman was taking his arm. Lady Philippa Tucker is her husband's equal in intellect and influence. She's an excellent and charming hostess, but to me she behaves like a hospital matron with a patient who might be contagious, or barking mad. Sort of benign alarm. I like to pretend she's fond of me, but it's probably just disapproval.

I think I'm even Godfather to one of their unsettlingly

brilliant daughters, though she and God are keeping it quiet.

Andrew murmured to his wife, and turned away to go and give the guests their marching orders. Philippa was watching me with her usual wary affection, ever alert to the moment when I would succumb to the urge to say something ungodly to Miss Ellie or start filching the spoons.

I gave her the potted version of what I'd said to her husband. She seemed no less sceptical.

Another female voice came over her shoulder. 'You in trouble, Harry?'

'Probably', I said. One handsome woman had become two. Lady Victoria Carteret, who'd had the increasingly dubious honour of being my companion for the evening, had appeared instinctively to support her friend and hostess, slipping her arm through Lady Philippa's.

Victoria Carteret's the one woman I shall ever truly love, but that ship sailed a long time ago, or passed in the night; or sank. She occasionally borrows me for an evening because everyone in her circle knows the score and I scare off all the obnoxiously eligible men who'd otherwise be pestering her. My disreputability makes me a useful social bodyguard; or eunuch.

I let myself be borrowed because she's beautiful and brilliant and it really annoys her father.

'Harry's been reassuring me', Lady Philippa said.

'Oh dear.' Victoria tutted at me. 'I didn't realize things were so desperate.'

'They're not,' I said.

'Daddy's going to be thrilled when I tell him you invited me to a murder.'

'He's welcome to his own, anytime.'

'Harry, shouldn't you be off doing something terribly important and... you know, male? I must help Philippa with her guests.'

Off they glid, two swans, and I paddled away into the shallows.

Someone had thoughtfully laid a coat over the dead body, but when I got there a woman was bending down beside it and the coat had been pushed aside. She was rummaging at the body.

'Excuse me', I said, and she gaped like a cornered animal. She stood quickly and stuffed something into the front of her dress.

3.

Standing, she was above average height, full-figured. It was a darkly handsome face, big round eyes and strong features and almost certainly foreign; not more than mid-twenties. She looked angry, and defiant, and afraid.

I tried to go gentle. 'Best not to fool around with the body.'

She said nothing. She glared at me.

'I need to know what you're hiding.'

She clutched both arms around her chest. 'You cannot force me!'

I glanced around. Plenty of servants managing things, and any time now the police would arrive. 'Honestly,' I said, 'I probably can. But I'd rather not.'

I took a step towards her. Her eyes darted round for options. I was a yard away from her and her hand plunged back into the dress and then lunged at me. Something brushed across my face and I flinched and she'd turned away and then tripped over the body.

It was all getting a bit daft and I was in no mood for any of it. I started to speak but she turned away and collided with a man coming towards her.

He grabbed ineffectually at her shoulders to steady her. 'Oh gosh, Nina…' His voice was English, a bit breathless. 'You poor thing. I say, this is ghastly, isn't it? You go and join the others. Keep warm - try to keep warm, please.'

And off she went, hurrying into the darkness.

'Nicely done', I said. 'But I do need to speak to her.'

He considered me, a bit anxiously. A little younger than me, and well dressed, except that in place of an acceptable necktie he'd wrapped some atrocious green velvet business up in a loose bow.

'Pardon me', he said, and for an instant I thought he was apologizing for the tie. 'But, er, you are… ?'

Wondering if you're the first of my Christmas presents, was the real answer; instead I said who I was and that our host had asked me to keep an eye on things until the police arrived.

The chappy nodded, and looked appropriately grave at the thought of the police, and I waited. 'Oh!' he said at last. 'Sorry. Yes. Humphrey Erskine.' It wasn't a hand-shaking sort of moment, but we nodded the courtesy to each other. 'Foreign Office, actually. But temporarily detached' - he made it sound like a mental condition - 'as liaison officer for the visiting artistes.'

I was more confused than before. 'The visiting -?'

'The troupe. The performers.' Everything Humphrey said seemed hurried and anxious. 'They're a group of Russian artistes - terribly famous - modern, you know?' - I didn't - 'here with a programme of ballet and opera. Cultural diplomacy, that's what we're calling it.'

I glanced at the shrouded figure lying beside me. 'And what would you call it now?'

He swallowed uneasily. 'It's… This is horrible.' The word itself came out horribly. He looked genuinely shaken, poor chap - emotional. 'He was such a - such a fine man, you know? Physically, and… and musically.' He was gazing down at the body.

'What was his name?'

'Kyril. Kyril Vassillev.'

I nodded. It had felt wrong to be talking about him so impersonally.

'I say, what do you think actually happened?'

I shrugged. 'Always a tricky business, fooling around with firearms.' I glanced after the woman. 'You know who she was?'

He looked uncomfortable some more. 'Her name's Nina. Vassilleva.'

'Vassill-?'

He nodded. 'The dead chap's sister.'

'Ah. Listen, if you're their escort you can talk to them, can't you? The police are going to fuss around, and it's going to seem a bit rough and heartless. But if they keep as steady as they can - not too operatic - just answer the questions - they should come through all right.'

He nodded, and was turning to go. 'Erm, you've got a bit of…' he touched his cheek.

I felt my face, and my finger came away sticky, and red. The girl Nina hadn't slapped me or scratched me; she'd… wiped something on me.

'Everything under control, Harry?' Victoria again.

Blood.

'Not in the least', I said. 'You?'

'Oh yes.' Behind Victoria I could see our hostess and another woman, about the same age and general poise, dark hair with a flash of white in it. There was no sign of the rest of the guests; by some routine miracle of womanly efficiency they'd all been packed off into the night.

'We ought to get you off home now', I said. 'Not the best of nights out, I'm afraid.'

Then a voice behind me, heaviest London, said 'Bloody hell…' And I knew my night had just got dramatically worse. 'Guess we know who the chief suspect is, don't we?'

4.

Wearily, I gathered my strength and turned.

9

Yes indeed, there he was.

The horrendous heavyweight suit, the red hair, the face of grim triumph.

'Victoria', I said, 'let me present Inspector Ernest Bunce. Bunce, this is Lady Victoria Carteret.'

Perhaps because I was looking for it, I saw something twitch in the Inspector's face when he heard the title. But he managed to nod politely and swallow a 'M'lady'.

Victoria nodded graciously and said: 'I take it you're old pals', which was about the worst possible thing she could have said. I looked away into the darkness, knowing I didn't want to catch Bunce's eye.

'Absolutely', I said to the undergrowth. 'Due to an… unfortunate misunderstanding, the Inspector briefly thought me guilty of murder. Well, four murders. Well, I was guilty of one of them, but it wasn't murder.' Now I looked at him, and said intently: 'But it was all straightened out in the end, wasn't it?'

He just gazed at me.

'Is that blood on your face, Sir Henry?' The usual tortured emphasis on my title; he's about the only person who ever uses it, and he only does so for hilarious ironic effect. His evening kept getting better and better.

'It is. And on my finger.'

The eyes were bright and hungry. 'Whose?'

'The victim's.' Big, satisfied smile. 'That's right, Bunce: I poked him to death. Very very hard. Seriously, this isn't one of your regular evenings, when you fit me up for whatever you've got spare then we go and have a pie and a pint. You're with the quality tonight. You have to pretend to be a proper policeman.'

As ever, my brilliant sarcasm washed off him. The heavy smile spread up his face. 'I'll be sure to get a proper statement from you, then, eh?'

'You'll have all the co-operation we can offer, Inspector.' Victoria was determined to do the decent thing, just like her ancestors when they came over with William the Conqueror or Julius Caesar. 'And I can start by reassuring you that you need have no doubt about Sir Henry's integrity. Should you need reinforcement of this, my father will be very pleased to confirm the point to the Commissioner.'

I winced. Having managed a moment earlier to say the worst thing possible, she'd now managed to find something even worse. Even leaving aside the fact that her father would rather have put the noose round my neck than put in a good word.

Bunce just stared at her. Then he contrived another respectful nod. 'Much obliged, your ladyship. Assistant Commissioner Puddlepuff will be eagerly waiting my report, and I'll be sure to advise him to seek his Lordship's counsel.' He turned to me. 'I… humbly hope' - thunderous emphasis - 'Sir Henry' - ditto - 'that we can presume on you to stay and assist us, and not do a bunk. Mean to say, if I've to be a proper policeman, you ought to be a proper gentleman. Fair's fair, eh?'

I nodded. 'Fair's fair.' And he was gone.

Victoria stared after him.

'Gosh,' she said. 'Your friend's quite… er…'

'Yes, he is rather.'

'Harry, there isn't an Assistant Commissioner Puddlepuff, is there?'

'I fear not.'

'Oh.'

She went to say her farewells, and I trudged round the scene of the macabre incident. I took it for granted Bunce would keep me kicking my heels for as long as possible.

There were signs of life on the edge of the garden - someone in the doorway between terrace and house; policemen marshalling opera performers in another corner - but most of it was deserted. It had the strange desolation that follows any performance - the empty chairs where a busy audience has sat, now uneven and scattered with forgotten glasses or papers. And it had the strange desolation that follows tragedy. The body - Kyril, wasn't it? Vassillev - was still lying in the middle of the stage area, under its makeshift shroud. A policeman was keeping an eye on it from a respectful distance.

I stood an even more respectful distance away, trying to replay the business. That moment of anticipation: for the characters and for the audience, all watching the doomed man, all waiting for the rifles to fire, all wondering what would happen. The music building, building, and the climax, the explosion of music and intensity.

I wondered about the rifles. What type they were; where they'd been picked up. Were they real weapons? Deactivated? Just props?

Could I remember smoke from breech or barrel, or was that fancy, conjured out of the drama? If yes, had it been ball-less cartridge, or some cruder business of flash and bang?

I wondered about the noise. Had I heard rifle fire, or drums and cymbals?

What, in all this madness of make-believe and melodrama, had been real?

One thing, certainly. In front of me there was a real man, and he'd taken a real bullet in his chest. And now he was really dead.

A shout from behind me, and I turned. A figure racing away from the house and across the garden and into the trees, followed by two policemen. Shouts from them and the performers, and somewhere ahead of his pursuers the man was disappearing into the night.

5.

There was a lull for a few moments, and then Bunce appeared from the house, striding hard after the chase. He was refusing to run - good officer never flaps in front of the troops - but clearly straining to.

The far end of the garden, hidden by the greenery and the night, had gone quiet. Then Bunce must have reached it, for it got very noisy. He'd control enough not to run, but not to hold back his feelings on the subject of ungodly word policemen who couldn't keep an ungodly word eye on ungodly word derogatory word foreigners.

Soon he appeared again, moving at the same furious tramp back towards the house. I made the mistake of being in his vision and he glared.

I hadn't been about to say anything. Even an indomitable brute like Bunce has his breaking point, and his evening had been difficult enough even before witnesses started lighting out. But something about my face or his frustration was too much. 'Not a word', he said hoarsely, barely seeing me. 'Not a bloody word.'

I resumed my consideration of the garden.

After a while, my rather unsatisfactory reflections on the rifles led me off in search of them. To one side of the garden, concealed from the performance area by thick bushes, I found the space where the singers had waited. A shed, which I supposed they'd used for changing or keeping warm. A few wooden chairs. A brazier, now dying to the faintest glow of embers. A lantern hung from the shed, yellowing a pool around it. Standing by the shed was a policeman, watching the death of the fire a little sadly.

Propped beside him were five rifles and a few swords.

'Evening', I said.

My arrival had prompted him to stand straighter: nothing about respect, just not wanting to be caught slouching. He nodded, and then pointed a thumb towards where he'd heard shouting. 'Trouble, sir?'

'One of your witnesses got bored and did a flit. Inspector's a bit disappointed.'

He looked more uneasy.

'If in doubt,' I said, 'tell the Inspector you felt obliged to keep a close watch on me. He'll like that.' I found a few sticks and threw them into the brazier. It began to flame, and the constable's face warmed up a bit too. 'I'm just curious about the kit there.' I nodded towards the weapons. 'What are they, d'you say?'

He shrugged. 'Look pretty basic.'

I nodded. Staying an unthreatening couple of yards away, I peered more closely. 'Might be old Enfields, from the look. Forty or fifty years since the Army used those, and we were always the last to get anything new. There were still a few floating around in the Cape, ten years ago. Better as a club or a crutch. Working, you think? Not mock-ups?'

He glanced down a bit longer. Shrugged. 'Breech looks real enough.'

'You serve, Constable?'

He shook his head. 'Too young for the war, sir. My elder brother.'

'He come through all right?'

'He did sir, thanks be.'

'Thanks indeed.'

'Delamere!' A hoarse growl from behind me. 'What in hell you up to?'

'Oh, hallo Bunce. Hoping to pinch one of these rifles and run amok in Dulwich, but your man stopped me. Pretty imposing, these constables.'

Bunce considered his constable for a moment, then: 'Come along.'

I wasn't too keen on being ordered around the garden by him for the rest of the night, but I felt obliged to try to co-operate with a policeman doing his job, however charmlessly.

He stopped suddenly. He glanced around, as if concerned that someone might see him talking civilly to me. 'All right, I know it's unlikely you shot a man, unseen, from the front row of all those nobs,' - I looked like I was reviewing the logic of this brilliant insight - 'but it's an unholy bloody mess, and it's all very political and you're mixed up somehow and I'm buggered if I'm letting anything more slip away. So I want you to hang around, yes?'

I nodded, and followed him towards the house.

I was wondering what he meant by 'political'.

I was shepherded into a corner of the garden where the surrounding wall abutted the house. I was one of half a dozen, with three policemen watching us closely.

This was not, I realized, hanging around. Just a handful of performers were being kept back; and me.

Not good. But a free ride back to the civilized side of the river, perhaps, and that's hard to come by after tea-time.

A bit of light was reaching us from the house, and I could make out the woman Nina, standing with her arms wrapped round herself and gazing into nothing. One-two-three-four others, and they were all wearing simple stage versions of a uniform jacket. The Delamere intellect accelerated to ramming speed, and I worked out that these had been the firing squad. And now they were a man down, one of their number having made a break for the wide open spaces of south London.

I tried to produce a friendly nod, for all the good it did in the gloom.

The champion garden wall clamberer was putting himself fairly and squarely in the frame, wasn't he? Lighting out like that was a desperate gamble. Chummy obviously had something he didn't want to talk about.

There was more. I'd been assuming that the death had been an accident. Wrong sort of round, too much powder, all very unfortunate. But if it had been an accident, would the man who fired the fatal shot have known he'd done so? With five of them firing at the same time at the same target?

The runner was looking like the culprit, and it was looking like deliberate murder.

Bloody elaborate way to do it, though.

I'd got this far when our three policemen suddenly stood straighter. A moment later we heard the heavy feet and voice of Bunce. 'Right lads, stir yourselves. We'll have this lot back to - Oh, Christ on a bicycle…'

First the policemen, and then the rest of us, turned to see why he'd run out of steam.

Bunce was staring towards the terrace. A figure had emerged from the house, and was looking around the garden. Natty check three-piece, bowler hat set at a very dashing slant. He addressed the garden in a brisk nasal drawl: 'Now, what have we here…?'

Bunce was looking disgusted. 'Bugger me, that's all we need', he muttered at the undergrowth.

The dandyish figure was striding across the terrace towards us. 'Well now, it's old Bunce, surely!'

'It ain't Prince Albert and that's a fact.' Bunce glowered up at him. 'You tell me, Faversham: who were you expecting?' Faversham smiled down at him, pretending to find this amusing. 'Best stay up there on the terrace; wouldn't want to get mud on those fancy shoes. You've missed all the action, sadly. Still, pity to interrupt your tea.'

'The action, as you well know Bunce, doesn't start till I get here. I'll need a full report.'

'Best be up bright and early for your morning paper then. Regulars have got it all tidied.'

'Imagine my relief. Good news is that Special Branch are taking over now.'

'Like hell.'

'Have taken over.'

'Says who?'

'Says anyone you like, Bunce, from the Commissioner to the boy who shines your shoes.' Bunce didn't answer. His three policemen were staring into infinity. His guests - my operatic friends and I - were listening in with diverse levels of indifference. I was hearing enough to know it didn't bode well. I was either going to be dealing with an angry Bunce, or his rather unappealing Special Branch pal. 'The Branch have overall supervision of all matters relating to the visit by the

Russkies, and when one of them dies by violence I don't think anyone's going to be surprised when we exercise that. Now then, as I understand it he was performing when...'

He'd turned as he was speaking, and begun to pace along the terrace. Bunce was obliged to walk beside him - and slightly beneath him.

I happened to meet the gaze of one of the policemen, and tried to show both sympathy and frustration. He probably thought I had wind.

Bunce and friend were back at our end of the terrace again, and as they turned Bunce was describing his actions since getting here, and then I heard the friend ask who we were. I didn't get Bunce's reply. I wondered, without optimism, how fairly he was representing me.

By this time I was rather bored and not a little chilly. I knew it would be the worst possible thing to ask how long we'd be.

'He what?' Bunce and Faversham were halfway along the terrace, but Faversham's incredulous sneer came loud. Poor Bunce. Having to explain how he'd lost one of his suspects over the garden wall really wasn't going to help his claim to superior competence.

I was working out how long, worst case, it would take them to interview us all, whether they'd have the genius to allow this to happen somewhere warm, and how long it would take to find a cab. And I was starting to wonder whether I might not be better after all playing the snooty gent: must dash but let's have lunch at my club sometime.

At which point Faversham announced: 'Soon as our wagon's here you lot will accompany us for questioning. You'll be spending the night as guests of the Special Branch of the Metropolitan Police.' And I knew I was too late.

6.

My poor host was looking more embarrassed than ever. Quite right too: bad form to let your guests get arrested, especially before offering the brandy.

I reassured him that it was very much routine for me. I did urge him to have his man immediately contact my man, Quinn, to let him know what had happened. It's easy enough - for me, anyway - to fall into the hands of the authorities; important thing is not to get forgotten about.

It took Faversham's crew another half an hour to whistle up a Black Maria.

Very dull; very cold.

Despite diverse exchanges with the police, I think this was probably my first journey in one of their cell-carriages. Can't recommend it. Experts tell me I was lucky to be by the back grille, but fresh air was the last thing I wanted that night.

The door of the Black Maria slammed behind us, and the wagon swayed and eventually re-settled.

No lights in there, of course. My companions were the faintest outlines in the darkness. Half a dozen people squeezed into a wooden box perhaps eight feet by five. Bare wooden benches. From somewhere around us the clanking of metal, and there were odd bits of metal sticking out here and there, no doubt for when prisoners had to be chained.

Opposite me was a police constable, to stop us damaging the luxurious fittings or singing dirty songs. By chance I was next to the girl Nina, still in her frilly costume frock.

One of the other rifle men muttered something to one of his comrades, in a lingo I couldn't get. The comrade snapped something back, and the first shut up.

The wagon had settled to stillness again. We weren't moving yet; Special Branch probably trying to work out which way up their map went. I realized that my young neighbour was shivering badly.

I took off my coat and slipped it around her shoulders. At

the first touch she flinched and started to resist what must have seemed, in the darkness, like unwanted attention. I felt her shoulders stiff under my arm. And then she was wrapping the coat tight around herself.

After a minute she said softly: 'Thank you.'

'Forget it', I said. 'I stole it anyway.'

She didn't laugh. I wasn't sure I was joking; it had been pretty dark in the garden when I'd grabbed it up.

There was a flurry of shouting and chatter from outside, moving to the front of the wagon. Then someone slapped the side a couple of times, and at last we were moving.

I don't want to seem rude to the road-layers of south London and the makers of police carts - sure they're doing their best - but between them they deliver a shocking ride. The cart had suspension enough to sway and bounce, but not enough to cushion the constant jolts and drops in the road surface. Crammed into our dark box, our journey was an endless shuddering, interrupted by the moments when we'd be thrown up to the roof or flung against each other or impaled on one of the metal protrusions.

It didn't help me work out where we going, either. I assumed that Special Branch had digs of their own somewhere; so we weren't just going to the nearest police station.

Another great heave, and I slammed against the back of the wagon and then into the girl beside me.

As we settled again, I said: 'He was... your brother, I think. I'm very sorry.'

She turned her head to me, and I saw the big eyes pale in the gloom. Eventually I think she shrugged, though the gesture was lost amid the general juddering. 'It is nature of our life. But he did not deserve. He was good boy.'

I looked sympathetic. Also lost in the circumstances. 'You're... Russians?' I asked.

Again the eyes. They seemed sharper this time. She glanced towards the others, then back at me. I got the sense of a general edginess. 'We are subjects of Russia', she said. 'We are citizens of the world.'

I gave her a respectful 'ah' to suggest I knew what she was talking about. Then back to the shuddering and the guarded silence.

Another great lurch as the wagon took a corner, and then we stopped.

The wagon stopped. Everyone inside it carried on, toppling sidewards into their neighbour and all crushing the two sitting nearest the front. Someone hissed something angry in foreign, and even the policeman opposite me muttered a curse.

There was a muffled shouting from in front of us. 'Oi! Move your doings, chum, or we'll have you in the back an'all.' Silence, and we could only wonder at what had blocked our way. 'It's late and it's bloody cold! Don't make me get down there!'

Then an explosion, and the world was deafened and stunned.

7.

All is darkness. All is chaos.

I've been too close to an artillery barrage - and you never want to get too close to the Royal Artillery; clever chaps all of them, but average wine, tedious technical conversation, terrible lumbering jokes and it doesn't help that they're all deaf as posts. And I've been knocked about by the occasional enemy shell. And once by one of our own shells; allegedly an accident, but it's unwise to be rude about the jokes of a man with a Vickers 15-pounder cannon.

What had just blown up - apparently right in my ear - was smaller than all that, but staggering. In our cramped black box the noise was thunderous and we were thrown every which way.

A second explosion: had I heard a second? Blindly, clumsily, we were clambering over each other and collapsing back into our seats.

I heard the third explosion, certainly: a pistol shot, and it really was right beside me, and the wagon door was wrenched open.

When your hearing goes, your balance goes; and then your balance takes much of the rest of you with it. It was all happening in my dream, a weird wallowing underwater sort of dream, my fellow-prisoners and I bouncing and flailing. I saw one of them rising and his mouth opening in a command and he was lunging for the exit. I saw the policeman opposite yelling too, and then he had a pistol and it was looming in front of me and aiming at the escaper and he couldn't miss. I saw another hand outside the wagon and this one had a gun too and that meant the policeman was a goner unless -

I joined the silent yelling and lunged forwards and knocked the policeman's arm up and if he fired the bullet must have gone into the roof. And I kept on moving, throwing myself out through the door and so stopping the attacker getting at the policeman.

I was half out when someone grabbed my shirt-front and pulled me the rest of the way. I was trying to recapture my balance on the cobbles and there were other bodies tumbling beside me and then a man was shouting at us. I guess he was shouting at us: his mouth was wide and strained but all I could hear was the faintest whine, as in the nightmare when you scream for help and no sound comes and you cannot move. I couldn't move now, except that someone had grabbed me again and I was stumbling forwards and we were all jostling and staggering away from the ruined wagon and into an alley.

Odd thing: I'd seen the mouth, but I hadn't seen the eyes; they were hidden in some woollen mask business covering the top of the chap's head. There were two or three of them like it.

Bewilderment and unstoppable stumbling carried us a couple of dozen yards down the alley and round a corner. We stopped, gasping.

If this is where you're expecting me to have used some terribly clever unarmed manoeuvre to escape, to have applied my ice-cold intellect to take control of the situation and turn the tables, gosh is this account going to be a disappointment. Do by all means buy me a whisky some time and flutter your eyelashes and invite me to share the lessons of my many years hanging around fate's anus, and I'll surely find some bright things to say. But lesson number one is that none of the lessons matters a damn when the world goes bang.

Oh, and for the record: those very rare people I've known who could actually muster the self-possession to freeze the moment of crisis and think clearly and exercise their advantage as a member of the reasoning species, they've all got one thing in common. They're dead. The chap who can stop in the heat of the skirmish and use his brain is liable to get a bullet in it. It's the brutish panicking beast who ducks and runs and hides - and survives. Ask any old soldier; politely.

The leading mask stuck his head round the next corner, and then he was back and gesturing with his pistol and he and his mates were grabbing at us and off we trotted again.

Lest you think too badly of me, I should say that by this point it was reason as well as instinct carrying me along. These were some very excited individuals and they had explosives and at least one of them had a pistol: as a general rule, such people are best avoided, but if you can't avoid them it's best to do what they say. I was also very aware of my predicament vis-à-vis the police. At the start of our journey I'd been an innocent bystander, confident that two minutes of suave conversation when everyone had calmed down would get me released promptly and probably with deferential thanks for my patient co-operation. As soon as that damn' bomb went off and we ducked down our alley, I had become

- however accidentally and unfairly - party to a very serious crime. Any minute now this neck of the woods was going to be over-run with very angry policemen, all dreaming of the interrogation they were going to inflict before the judge put on his black cap. Any attempt at suave conversation would get my teeth kicked out. I needed to be far and fast away from this place, and as my new companions seemed to have a plan for managing that very thing it was worth sticking with them. So, as I say: where they trotted I trotted.

Oh, and during our brief pause I'd snuck a coin out of my pocket and used it to scratch a sign in the brick behind me. Now you're impressed, surely.

At the far end of the alley the leading bandit hardly hesitated. An instant to check that there wasn't a squad of coppers lurking, and then he was gesturing furiously and as we all came up there was a box-bodied motor car in front of us: the door swung open and in we all piled and none of us had found a seat when it lurched forwards.

And so off we set, my new pals and I, armed and dangerous fugitives from justice on a little motor excursion through south London.

8.

Motor cars haven't got much acceleration, especially when weighed down by half a dozen sweating criminals. And from the undramatic movements of the vehicle I got the impression we had a sensible driver too. Veering through the evening traffic and hooting at everything would have been no kind of escape at all. Instead we were proceeding with stately speed and steady course, and that was our best chance of disappearing. Which was good, wasn't it?

The chap who'd been waving his pistol was in with us; his mates must have jumped in up front. He was still at highest anxiety, eyes wide and gazing hard all around. But he'd pulled his mask away, he was getting his breathing under control, and he was holding his pistol well below the window sill.

Experienced fighting man. Or at least intelligently furtive. It made it less likely he'd put a bullet in my gut by accident; but also less likely I'd be able to do anything he didn't want, such as sneak away. Rather handsome, in his way: elegant moustache, well enough trimmed.

They're roomy outfits, the big touring cars. We were seven in there. The pistoleer and three of the operatic firing squad squeezed across the back seat like the grimmest-looking sardines you ever saw. Me facing them on the flip-down, between the girl and the fourth of the singing riflemen. The fifth, of course, had done the bunk over the garden wall, and was looking wiser for it every moment.

I glanced at the pistol again. Hard to be sure in the gloom, but it looked like a Mauser: slender, with the short straight magazine under; there'd been a fashion for them among officers in the Cape who found the Webley too heavy. The finger was held straight, along beside the magazine: again the professional, not going to shoot himself in the foot yet ready for action.

The motor car stopped suddenly. Those of us facing backwards thumped our heads against the driver's partition, and the others lurched forwards on their seat. Mr Pistol was immediately alert, eyes darting around, finger onto trigger.

The car didn't move. Chummy was gazing ahead now. Obviously some obstruction or threat. Instinctively my eyes went to the door handle, and part of me was just wondering, and I glanced up... And he was watching me. And slowly, madly, he was smiling at me. And then he raised the finger of his free hand, and waggled the negative.

With a swerve the car set off again.

Around us, through the steamed windows, ghostly glimpses of south London by night: house-fronts, horse-cabs, passers-by, all oblivious to my little gang.

I've never bothered much about the social niceties, as

they'll tell you in Belgravia and all the other bits where I'm unwelcome, but I can't think of an occasion where conversation has been harder to strike up. When you're kidnapped, the form's a lot clearer: head down until the excitement wears off, then a couple of funny stories and try to give the impression you're a lot richer than you are so they take good care. But I hadn't been kidnapped - had I? Scooped up with them by the police largely by accident; rescued with them because in the rush they weren't going to start checking tickets.

I was assuming it was rescue.

What I wanted to ask, of course, was which of them had fired the fatal shot - and whether it was accident or design. But you know how it is: you can't just blurt out to perfect strangers the suggestion that one's a murderer.

Something touched my cheek. I turned to find it had been the girl's finger. The big eyes were looking up at me.

'Sorry I attack you', she said.

'Don't mention it', I said. 'I thought you were... interfering with the body. But you were... saying goodbye, yes?'

The eyes hardened. 'I carry his blood now. It cannot be washed until the crime is washed.'

I thought of my cheek, wondered whether it still showed where she'd smeared some of that blood across it. I didn't say so, but I was planning a wash regardless of the state of the police investigation into poor Kyril's death. Quinn - my valet - wasn't going to let me wander round with war paint on.

And yet... I was feeling the blood on me, in more ways than one. And, like it or not, I felt the obligation.

Her exchange with me, and our progress, seemed to ease the tension a bit. One of the men opposite - big lad, thick in shoulders and neck and fleshy face - leaned forwards. He was glaring at me, rather stern. With a bit of a twist he managed to extricate his arm from where it was being crushed against his mate, and pointed a big finger at my chest. Trying to hide my alarm, I met his gaze calmly.

His words came out with the same difficulty as his arm. 'You - save - my - life', he said heavily.

It took a moment to get what he was talking about. He was the chap who'd jumped for the exit when the bomb had gone off, to find himself staring at the policeman's pistol.

The bandit chief beside him was looking interested. He said a few words, in their foreign language. The other chap replied enthusiastically. After a moment I saw he was re-enacting the key elements of the escape from the wagon. The chief considered me with more calculation, while the other held out his hand for me to take: not pleased-to-meet-you style, but arm-wrestling. I clasped it; rude not to. 'You are brother', he said. I nodded at him, grave, and tried to look brotherly. His fingertips, I noticed, were oddly gnarled.

It was terribly nice of him, but I really wasn't sure I wanted to be the brother of a man who was on the short-list for devious killer of the month and whose pals were prepared to dynamite police wagons to get him out of trouble. He thought I'd been saving his life, while I thought I'd been saving the policeman's.

While I was stuck in their company the misunderstanding was convenient. But in case I ever managed to re-join mainstream society - a distant prospect, perhaps - it was more dubious. Rather than admitting he'd acted recklessly and been within a second of getting shot for it - even if he realized as much - the policeman was far more likely to say he'd been about to stop the escape single-handed but bloody Delamere had attacked him.

Re-joining mainstream society was looking less likely. And now I had to wonder, as the man with the pistol was surely wondering, how closely the police were tracking us, and how aggressively they'd try to stop us.

At which point there was an ugly mechanical clanking and the motor car began to slow and our compartment was shrouded in steam and smoke.

9.

That's the trouble with the engines on some of the big tourers. Underpowered for a full load, and liable to pop a valve when the going gets too heavy; like a fat man with a dicky heart trying to ride a bicycle uphill.

There was a moment of silence, and wide-eyed anxiety all round. I'd been startled, but I wasn't as upset as the rest of them: I rather wanted their plans to go awry, at least enough for me to oil out, and any little re-adjustment that didn't involve me getting shot was fine.

There was a figure at the window, looming out of the smoke, and the door was flung open. Fast unhappy words, in what I was assuming was Russian. A single word from the Mauser man, vicious and probably best not translated.

But again: he thought on his feet, and he kept his unit moving. A word of command and he was pushing the girl Nina out and following himself and reaching in for me and then wrenching the rest out. Another word, a gesture, and they set off walking. I'd made a point of staying close and looking bewildered and co-operative and all the time my head was turning slowly and considering the alleys, the shadows, the obstacles I could put between me and them. I started following, exactly as ordered, nothing to see here, and if I was already moving it would make a sudden acceleration even easier. Then I felt a hand heavy on my shoulder.

I turned to find the chief. He came in close, big smile on face, hand still gripping my shoulder. To the few passers-by in the night we looked like old friends stopped for a jolly chat. His coat was over his forearm, and it thrust forwards into my gut with a sharp and very uncoaty prod.

Still smiling, he leaned even closer. 'Nice you are his brother', he said quietly. 'Nice you are her gentleman. If you try funny business I put bullet in your spine, ok?'

'Right you are', I said.

'Don't think I worry about making scene, kill a few more

people.' He looked slowly around us, the typical south London nightscape, with its idlers and strolling couples and late traders. 'I live to make scene. And… When I have to make scene, I have to make it big as possible, ok? You try funny business, better I shoot many people not just one, ok?'

I matched my expression and voice to his. 'As soon as I punched that policeman,' I said, 'I became one of you - whatever you are. We're stuck together now, however little either of us likes it.' It wasn't strictly true, but I wanted him thinking I wouldn't try to run off. My turn to smile: 'Now take your damn' hands off me.'

He clapped me on the shoulder, pretend congenial and sincerely malicious, and we walked off together. He stayed just a fraction behind me. The coat was still over his arm.

The whole business showed extraordinary organization. This chap and his mates hadn't just knocked off our police wagon by chance - happened to be passing, bit of a lark. And we were only in the Maria and in that place because of the very particular way the evening had developed.

The impression was getting stronger that the death of the singer was no accident. Some plan had been afoot. This chap had been ready to react.

Except… really? I'm all for contingency planning, and on this evening's form I'd cheerfully have replaced the entire British Army planning staff in the Boer War with this one shifty foreigner. But do you really set up an assault on a Black Maria as a just-in-case? Bit far-fetched, and hellish reckless.

So what about the chap who'd got over the garden wall? Had he got word to chummy, now walking so companionably at my shoulder, that something was up at the opera? There'd been a fair bit of hanging around after his escape. While Bunce and the Special Branch chap had been waving their little truncheons at each other, had this gang been making the arrangements to spring the rest of the team? Fast work. Rustle up men and guns and fireworks. (Bombs, was it, or grenades? Army had basically given up on grenades as more dangerous to the home team, but maybe these chaps were less picky.) And inside half an hour they'd been on the spot - or, more likely, following - and ready for a spree. Damn' fast work.

And it all brought me back to another question. The not insignificant matter of who the hell these lads were, running around London waving pistols and blowing stuff up. Russian, from the accents and the impenetrable grumbly lingo? The papers these days were full of the anarchist threat, and I'd always discounted most of it as nonsense. Editor can't get a seat on the train because of some chap with darker skin or a funny hat, and suddenly London's drowning in blood-thirsty foreigners and civilization ends by Tuesday week. But maybe this boy, with his explosives and his discipline and his kill-them-all banter, was the real thing.

In which case, what on earth had he been up to at my old friend's opera party? And what on earth was he up to with me now?

I felt a subtle but solid shove. 'Hurry, my friend.'

Thirty yards ahead I saw an omnibus, the standard horse-drawn double-decker.

'You're not serious?' I growled over my shoulder. 'This is the master-plan? All London's police after us, and we're hopping on the bus?'

He called something ahead to the rest of our group, and they began to clamber aboard. The hand was on my shoulder again. 'So useful, your omnibuses.' Again the malicious amusement in the voice. 'So efficient. So anonymous.'

As we got closer he swung round in front of me. The face was in mine, and the Mauser barrel was in my gut. 'I repeat. Better for me I kill all these people than none. Your choice.'

I pointed over his shoulder. 'You're about to miss the bus, old lad.'

We just made it, with a scowl from the conductor and the pistol hard in my back.

10.

'Well now,' I said, looking at my new pals, 'ain't this jolly?'

Brisk tour of the back-streets plus a ride on the omnibus: big night out for the league of dynamiters. We were sat facing each other, squeezed in much as before. I was between the chief and Nina, with another comrade beyond her; opposite us were the other five.

That included, I now saw, the chap who'd got over the wall. He'd been one of the gang who'd sprung us from the Maria. He was at least as dapper as the leader, with an even finer 'tache. They had thus re-united the full firing squad from the opera.

The firing squad was facing me.

The omnibus rolled and bumped through the night. I reckoned we were heading north now, for the river.

The conductor was squeezing and kicking his way up the aisle, occasionally coughing out a 'Fares!'

He nudged the foot of the first of our team, who looked startled, and then uncomfortable. The standard pantomime of patting pockets and shrugging and he was looking desperately at his mates.

They all went through the same routine, and the conductor grumbled something impatient. The firing squad, of course, were all still essentially dressed as the firing squad: they'd taken off the costume hats and jackets, but not been allowed to re-gather their own clothes or, it appeared, their own wallets. Nina was shaking her head likewise, and they were all looking desperately at the chief beside me.

He started to shift his arm, and then stopped. For the first time, I saw discomfort on that disciplined face. Even when his car had blown up he'd been more assured. Sub-consciously he touched two pockets, but already he was turning to me.

'Oh, you are surely bloody joking', I said.

Again, challenge sparked his confidence, his defiance. The

hard smile - and the subtle jab of pistol barrel into my side: 'A contribution to our funds', he murmured, 'is always welcomed.'

I found some coins and gave the conductor what he wanted, pointing out the members of our party. 'Big day sight-seeing', I said. 'Spent it all on postcards and sticky buns.' He grunted and moved on.

'Best not to carry your wallet when you're on the job, eh?' I said to the big cheese.

'We depend on the generosity of the people.'

'And the people end up paying the price.'

He patted my knee. 'Do not worry', he said. 'Now you are certainly brother.' He was looking out the back of the bus. I couldn't see anything, except a distant figure on a bicycle disappearing and re-appearing under the street-lamps.

Although I was still itching to learn more about what had happened in that garden, my mind was on escape again. We'd made a clean getaway from the ambush of the Black Maria, so the police were less of a concern now. My new companions presumably didn't want me hanging around. I couldn't be any use to them - apart from paying their bus fare, obviously. If they took it into their heads to ransom me for the Delamere family fortune they were going to be sore disappointed. I was an inconvenience, and they ought to be pleased if I found a moment to drop off the back of the bus.

Once we were north of the river, perhaps. No sense in a long walk home. And still the pistol in my side. I could assume a certain amount of bravado in pop-gun Percy's threats, but if he was prepared to set dynamite in a London street - to risk killing a policeman or three - he was more than serious enough for my taste. Perhaps it really would suit his purposes to shoot a few innocent bus passengers, if I made a nuisance of myself.

Then again, if he was such a hooray - and if he felt the need to carry out a spectacular like this evening's - I was going to be an increasing burden. He must figure I'd seen too much of him and his group. He'd surely have no hesitation about leaving me face down in a ditch.

I was only assuming they were a group. They'd none of them seemed surprised to be sprung from the Black Maria and chivvied away through the back passages of London. And chummy had gone to a certain amount of trouble on their behalf. You have to know someone fairly well to start blowing up police vans for them, don't you? I couldn't believe my pal had gone through all that business just on the off-chance - see who he ended up with, lucky dip. Rough old way to make new friends.

On we rattled, through the night. A bit more kerfuffle when a woman called out for the omnibus to wait and then added her considerable presence to the squeeze, baby in arms and husband in tow. She tried wriggling a step forwards down the aisle, red and rather out of breath.

Buffalo Bill kicked the leg of the firing squad member opposite, and nodded up at the woman. Immediately the chap stood, and his mate beside him, and made way for her to slump down. I do like a well-behaved anarchist; courtesy costs nothing, even in the cause of international revolution; if it did they'd probably have touched me for it. I noted that however good his manners were, my neighbour himself wasn't going to move the pistol away from my side.

The important thing, I was thinking to myself, was not to let them know who I was. My only knowledge of anarchists - the Army Pay Department aside - is through the newspapers, but I suspect they're the type to hold a grudge. If by some chance I did escape before they cut my throat, I didn't want to spend the rest of my life in hiding.

'Why goodness me!' said the woman with the baby. 'If it isn't Sir Henry!'

11.

'Fancy seeing you on the bus, sir!'

She was delighted. My companions were not: unease, suspicion. I could feel chummy rigid with alertness, and his pistol sharp in me. I was still fighting for words. Who the hell was she, anyway? 'Still, you never was a one for fancy airs, was you sir? We always used to say you was as happy having a natter in the kitchen as at table.'

'Company was usually better in the kitchen', I said. Just in time I had her. And when the dining table in question is headed by Victoria Carteret's father, Magnus Lord Aysgarth, you can be sure the chat's better - and the welcome for Delameres warmer - in the kitchen. Or in the outside privy.

'Mott, sir. Genge as was. In service with-'

'Yes', I said hastily; 'of course I remember you.' It was essential she didn't mention Victoria and her family: bad enough me being number one on the anarchist death list; I wasn't having Victoria dragged into this madness. 'Janet, I think?' She beamed. I turned to the husband, trying to look roguish: 'Seem to remember you were settling down with some promising young chap on the staff there.' My best genial aristo impression.

It went as well as ever. The husband looked like I'd punched him in the nose, and Janet Mott-née-Genge started to babble about some things not being serious and not what the Lord intended and then the baby started screaming, and now the whole bus was looking at me with the same expression as the husband.

The slightest murmur from beside me: 'Her, her child, all of these people.'

The good Janet was pressing on. 'Who're your friends, sir? Cricket club outing is it?'

The idea was so atrocious it made me glad I'd been kidnapped by revolutionaries instead. 'No,' I said; 'these are... friends of mine. Visiting.' My friend next to me smiled a greeting at her, dark charm, and poor Mr Mott looked even more grumpy. 'They're, er, Russians. Russian noblemen. Wanted to see the sights, and, ah, no way better than the good old bus, eh? Still, don't let me butt in. Think this is our stop.'

I turned hopefully to my neighbour, and felt the pistol barrel harder in my side.

'Funny, funny man,' he murmured.

Mercifully, it looked like it really was our stop: or at least the big cheese was also feeling that Janet Mott was a tourist experience best enjoyed in small doses. He barked a word, and our party shuffled silent towards the back of the bus. A courteous and pistol-less gesture: 'After you, Sir Henry.' He emphasized the name, and again the charming smile. I left, babbling farewells over Janet's so she didn't have a chance to ask to be remembered to Lady Victoria.

The bus had brought us through the heart of the old city, near Liverpool Street Station. The firing squad were standing, empty-faced, in the shadow of a shop entrance. The girl Nina was looking at me, rather sadly. Our liberators were standing as if guarding us.

For a moment their chief stood watching as a cyclist overtook the bus and disappeared, and the bus pulled away. Then he turned to me. One hand was still under the coat. 'Soon we talk', he said. 'Maybe you see dawn. But not here. If you run, I shoot you in back. Yes?'

'Yes indeed.'

A single word of command as usual - clearly not a man for the inspirational speech - and we were off down an alley to the east.

12.

This was a London I had never known.

I don't mean geographically. When forced to be in town, I

like to get about on foot; bit of a crowd on the bus, and always the risk of a foreign dynamiter on the lam trying to touch you for the fare. And I tend to go east rather than west: the Janets of the world have always seemed happy to chat to the Delameres, when their employers have been slamming the door on us. The shacks and shadows beyond Liverpool Street were not unfamiliar to me.

But this was the first time I'd seen them through the eyes of the people who find shelter there; the ones for whom these alleys and slum houses are sanctuary. Apparently the only Anglo-Saxon in the party, I'd have seen myself as home team for this event. And yet it was chummy with his Russian accent and German pistol and habit of blowing up police wagons who moved through the darkness so surely and naturally, while I was uneasy and stumbling. All the shop signs I now saw seemed alien, Hirschheims and Giovanellis and Kaczyńskis. The expressions of wariness that watched me from doorways were on faces darker than my own. My escort knew every turn and every loose stone. I heard murmured exchanges, greetings, respects; men nodded acquaintance, or turned away to forget more quickly.

And then we were into an alley off an alley, and then a tiny courtyard that had never seen the sun, and there was a knock at a dilapidated door, and murmurs in an unrecognizable accent, and a bolt was drawn back and we were inside. Just a few minutes' trot from all the lights and amusements that the centre of London offers, and I might as well have been on the moon.

An old man fussing around us and we were hustled up flight after flight of narrow creaking dirty wooden stairs, and then into a room and the door behind us shut out the world.

It wasn't the worst place I've ever lodged, but my man Quinn would have never have got so far behind with the dusting. A shabby attic room, just like ten thousand others within a mile of it. Bare boards, a moth-wrecked rug, some shreds of mouldy wallpaper clinging on - it had once had rather a lively stripe to it, by the looks, but like everything else in that room the paper was faded now, and stained.

All this by the light of a lantern that the caretaker downstairs had given one of the team. In its glare we were pale and wild.

It showed a diversity of seating: a mattress, a horsehair sofa that seemed to have come through an artillery barrage, an armchair with a bit of rag covering the more uncomfortable of the protruding springs, a couple of wooden contraptions.

Having been pushed in among the first, I took the opportunity of bagging a relatively sturdy looking wooden chair under the one window. I wanted to look like I was comfortable and confident, however much of a lie that was. The other options looked like they'd collapse or never let me up again. And I wanted to be near that window.

It wasn't much of a window but, well: always the opportunity, even if it be of the smallest. It looked like it gave onto the roof, and it was the only other way out of the room.

The attitude to seating gave me a new feel for the people I was with. There was the chap I was thinking of as the leader. Two who'd helped him spring us from the police wagon - one of them the dapper rifleman who'd leapt the garden wall to summon assistance. The other four of the firing squad, and the good Nina. Now that they were in relative safety, a couple of the firing squad seemed more relaxed - throwing coats off and settling into the comfier chairs - while the others were looking as fidgety and out of place as I was. Nina was neither one thing nor t'other: she sat quickly and instinctively, but she wasn't relaxed.

So perhaps this wasn't a coherent group. So - and I was really guessing now - perhaps Don Quixote and his grenade chums had felt the need to liberate a couple of the team, and been obliged to drag the rest along. And found themselves with a rather confused baronet by way of bonus. 'Buy the set, get one free' sort of arrangement, like at the wine merchant's.

The big cheese closed the door behind him and stepped to the middle of the room like he was about to make a speech. It turned out that he was, but first he raised the Mauser and pointed it at my face.

13.

'Comfortable?' he asked. 'Who are you?'

I considered him. The bright steady eye; the neat moustache.

'After you', I said.

He pulled the safety lever back; nasty little click.

'Well done', I said. 'Necessary pre-condition for operating the weapon, but doesn't make it more or less likely you will. How d'you find the Mauser, by the way?'

'Adequate for task'. Each word came soft and sharp. 'I want to know your name.'

'I can think of many good reasons why you might shoot me. Disappointment at not knowing my name isn't one of them.'

'Perhaps I use bad reason instead.'

'If you wanted to find out my name, you could very easily. If you're not shooting me out of hand, then you're really trying to find out how co-operative I am. Or just showing off your stripes in front of the platoon; but I think you're a cooler bird than that. If you want to find out how co-operative I am, then try co-operating with me.' I sat back, a pose of relaxation. The chair creaked alarmingly. 'I don't care who you are or what you're doing. If you've harmed one of those policemen, or a horse, then damn you for a brute; but I can't and won't get in your way. I will not, however, be threatened into conversation. If you're seriously interested in a model of this night that lets us both live, then you go first.'

The pistol was steady in his hand. The barrel was a long tunnel in front of my eyes.

I glanced to Nina, on the chair a yard away. 'Mind out for the bang', I said. 'Bit sharp, the Mauser, specially in a confined space.'

I forced myself to focus on the eyes behind the pistol.

'I am… known as George', he said.

'Hallo George. Nice to meet you. I'm known as Henry.'

'Sir Henry, that woman said.'

I glanced at the pistol. 'I guess we're skipping the formalities. Call me Harry, if you prefer.'

'Surname?'

'I'll make one up if you will.'

The pistol firm in front of my face. Once again, despite the evening's madness this man at the centre of it seemed so very calm.

Nina began to talk foreign at him; not loud, but passionate, urgent.

He didn't look at her. 'She says you not threat', he translated. 'She says you good man.' He murmured a few words back to her. 'I tell her that is exactly problem.'

She went on in English. 'He was only in audience. Not official, not escort, not police. Just audience. When Kyril is shot, his friend ask him to look. He is respectful man.'

George's eyes hadn't moved from mine. No loss of focus for this chap. Now the eyes widened. 'But what you respect?' he asked. 'British justice, or pretty foreign girl, or German pistol?'

'Police don't like him. They argue. They arrest him with us.'

Again the eyes narrowed. Behind them, calculation. In front of them, the trigger finger ready.

I could see his problem. Although calling me good and respectful was more of a stretch than I'd have ventured myself, she was right I was no threat. But I was confusing. And George was chap who wouldn't like - couldn't like - confusion. I was guessing - bad form to ask a chap how he votes - he he was some kind of foreign radical, some political outlaw. He'd be wanting to stay in the shadows, and he'd be suspicious of mysterious Englishmen popping up in the middle of his revolutionary dynamite jamboree. However generously they subbed him for the bus fare.

Calculation: could I help the authorities track him and his chums? Calculation: was this billet a one-time doss, or somewhere they'd want to use again? Calculation: had I heard any detail this evening that made him vulnerable?

If I was him, I'd have shot me.

'You are our guest', he said. 'You stay. Welcome.' A handsome and very fake smile. 'We decide later.'

He'd already decided. He was going to kill me.

He snapped a couple of words to the others, and the two who'd been his companions in the assault on the Maria and in chivvying us through town looked more alert.

If they were lying low here for the night, he'd not want to kill me right off: the shot, or the shouting if he came at me with a knife, would draw attention; and no one likes to while away the hours with a dead baronet in the corner, blood everywhere and starting to go green and rancid.

But I'd put good money on the fact that when they moved on in the morning, it would either be via a deserted bit of riverbank - 'ooh, look down there Sir Henry, is that a penguin?', thump, job done - or I'd be held back for a quick question on interior design, and my body would be left to gather dust with the rest of the furniture.

I smiled at the company, like a chap who was being made to feel welcome. Somewhere out in the night, someone was whistling. It sounded like 'The boy I love is up in the gallery'; fairly sure it wasn't Tosca.

George stowed his pistol, and popped out. I wondered if he might rustle up a whisky and soda. One of his watchdogs shifted closer to the door.

My smile settled on Nina, and was briefly sincere. 'Thank you', I said. 'You didn't have to speak out like that.'

She shrugged. 'Enough killing tonight, maybe.'

'Thanks anyway. Was your brother a... a professional singer? He had one of the main parts, and he was jolly good.'

She nodded. 'He love music very much. We all... we all need to escape. Some of us must use guns. Kyril used music.'

I didn't try to reply. She gave a little smile, embarrassed at the intimacy. 'Group make visit to England. Some are professional dancers, for when they give ballet. Some like Kyril: professional singers for when they give opera. Dancer who can sing is in opera chorus; singer can be on stage for ballet if does not have to dance. But also they need helpers: for moving stage, for roles with no singing or dancing. Too expensive to bring from Russia, so they ask community here.'

'And Kyril got you involved? You're living here, and he got you a few weeks' work?' She nodded.

It explained the overlap between the relatively professional world of the opera, and good old George and his explosives.

It didn't explain the evening's extravagant excitement. You don't dynamite a Black Maria and bust your mate out just because he's got tickets for a show or might miss his train. George wasn't a Russian consular official unwilling to have his fellow-citizens inconvenienced by the Metropolitan Police.

The song-and-dance troupe had hired a few spear-carriers and stage-hands from the émigré community. Made sense: get people who speak the language, keep it in the family, throw a few shillings in the right direction. And if this lot were like any other semi-closed community, the relatively big chiefs like George would get first dibs when some tasty bit of work on the side came along. Same in the labour unions, same in the British Army General Staff.

Did Nina herself have a day job in the revolution?

'The boy I love' seemed to have got into my head; now I was whistling it.

Nina had subsided, eyes wide and far beyond the tatty wallpaper. Poor kid. She'd shown vulnerability this evening, sure; but also fierceness, and toughness. She'd been calm during the escape. She knew George well enough to interrupt him when he was shooting people.

Had to be a rough old life, living in poverty and exile in the arse end of London. I wondered what you'd have to be prepared to do, to survive. I wondered what happened if you mixed that resilience with some political belief.

George was what happened, obviously. George with his Mauser and his explosives, committing outrages and then slipping through the cracks of the city, his excesses and his familiarity with the streets both beyond the comprehension of most Londoners. Far from home, and yet utterly assured. George, and Nina.

Still she gazed into infinity, after her brother.

Behind me, barely perceptible, I heard a tap at the window.

14.

I've never had to advertise for a valet. So the idea of trying to summarize my needs and expectations in that line has, thank God, never arisen.

What's one supposed to say? 'Wanted: iron-willed suit-brusher and courteous thug with strong inclination to moral borderlands and the spirit of volunteerism; sense of humour an asset'?

I'd been too young and too poor to think about that sort of thing before going into the Army. And when I came out of the Army after the peace of '02, I found that I had acquired - besides sun-leathered skin, some alarming scars and an antipathy to authority and group activities - Quinn.

By that point we'd got used to having each other around. I because I'd been sharp enough to work out quickly that a steady sensible Sergeant is the single most important bit of kit for a young officer. He because I would, as he once put it, 'always share a fag with the sentry before sodding off for oysters and champagne', and because I tended not to get him and his youngsters killed. I knew I needed a chap to do the logistics and stop me going about too scruffy. He, I imagine, had weighed the attractions of returning to his god-forsaken Cornish fishing slum or becoming a house-breaker, and decided that keeping me up to scratch might be as adequate in civilian life as it had been in southern Africa, and with fewer mad Dutchmen shooting at us.

I say 'I imagine': none of this was ever discussed, of course. Back in England for the first time in a couple of years, Captain Delamere and Sergeant Quinn had stood on the dockside and realized themselves incapable of any kind of meaningful farewell. So I'd paid for his train ticket to town, and then I'd offered him a drink, and eventually I'd found rooms, and he was... still there. I must at some point have popped the question, and he must have heard a proposed salary and assumed I was joking, and then found I was serious, and accepted anyway; then when end-of-month came due he found I'd been joking after all. One gets used to a thing, I mean to say, and we've never had to debate whether or not my rather rootless ramshackle lifestyle constitutes contractually-sound employment under English law.

Anyway, some brief version of that lot ran through my mind in the moment after I heard that tap on the window. I'd had a flicker of it as I'd watched the figure on the bicycle pedalling past the bus.

I didn't jump, or turn, and I knew he wouldn't expect me to. A casual glance around the room suggested no one else had noticed the noise, or thought it significant.

I waited a bit longer, and stood slowly. I made a pantomime of stretching uncomfortably, and then of feeling hot. I said something to the same effect, and before anyone could reply or move I was opening the window and taking the revolver from Quinn's hand and turning, and I had them; boot very much on other foot.

I was watching the two guard-dogs in particular; both

were halfway to their feet, their eyes moving between my face and the big barrel of my Webley revolver and making their calculations. 'Live through this night!' I said quickly. 'I am not police, I am not any kind of threat to you. But my mother warned me about accepting invitations to stay from people you've not had tea with. Your guns down. Now.' They weren't sure. 'If I can pluck a revolver out of the midnight sky, I've gumption enough to use it. Be smart, and tomorrow you'll be singing your arias and blowing up policemen like none of this happened.'

Slowly they laid their pistols on the floorboards, and then as instructed they kicked them under the old sofa.

'Thanks for your company this evening', I said. 'My regards to old George and' - I turned to her - 'once again, Miss Nina, I'm sorry about your brother.' She gazed at me, anger and wonder.

Then I had one foot on the chair and my free arm through the window and Quinn was pulling me up and out and I popped into the night sky like the cheerfullest of corks. I followed Quinn along the roof a few yards, across to the next, in through a window and then down another creaking dusty stair.

At ground level, in a doorway, he gestured silence. Then he beckoned me slowly forwards.

Careful to stay in full shadow, I moved until I could see out. We were in an alley, which gave onto the little courtyard.

A dozen yard away I could see half a dozen figures outlined. By the way they were standing, it was clear they were trying to stay hidden. But there was enough light sneaking down from somewhere to show that the front two, at least, were in the distinctive helmets and uniforms of policemen. The light also showed what gleamed in their hands.

I tapped Quinn's shoulder, and beckoned him the few yards back to our staircase.

'Forces of righteous anger', I murmured into his ear. 'Except those ain't policemen.'

I saw the frown. He moved back to the doorway, looked, and returned. A brief nod, and he murmured: 'Boots are wrong.'

'Carrying a damn great knife is wrong too. Police budget isn't that limited.'

It was quite the insight on hidden London I was getting. One group of armed lunatics was bad enough. Now there were rival groups. I had no doubt the new arrivals - armed to the teeth and furtive - were here for my pals. Two unrelated armed gangs up to no good in the same tiny courtyard would be too much of a coincidence. The police uniforms were an elaborate business, though. Perhaps this was the Gilbert & Sullivan mob; no doubt things were bad between them and the serious opera boys.

Quinn shrugged. Bad men will tend to rub up against other bad men, and the results are often ugly. Perhaps this new lot felt they'd been unfairly excluded from slots in the chorus.

I pointed back up the stairs. I mouthed: 'I have to.'

Quinn's an emotionless sort of chap - life on a fishing boat in the North Atlantic'll do that - but he knows how to show what one might politely call 'dismay', and what one might more accurately call 'my employer has gone off his rocker'.

'They're not bad…' I murmured; 'well, they probably are bad, but… I can't - and… there's a girl…'

This was not, I confess, the first time Quinn had heard me say those three words. In the gloom I saw him giving the same snooty reaction he usually does. I grant you, things don't always go smoothly; but his reaction only stiffened me.

Trying to keep the creaks to a minimum while moving as fast as I could, I set off back up the staircase.

15.

I tapped on the window.

I guess they were more alert now. Everybody turned to look. One body strode towards me, pistol rising as he came.

I'd made sure both my hands were visible. Big smile. I waved.

He stood glaring at me, Mauser steady as ever.

I pointed urgently, mimed opening the window.

Still he glared.

Well, for God's sake… I guess my exasperation showed. At last - the pistol carefully towards my head - he stepped forwards and opened the window.

'You forget your top hat?' he said sourly.

'Bunch of men downstairs, dressed as policemen and no doubt coming for you. That's bad, but these ain't policemen and I suspect that's worse.'

There was a hammering downstairs.

'What mad trick is this?'

'All right', I said, 'let's play a game of How Stupid Is George? You go first.'

George was not stupid. But he was confused, and understandably so. I knew that my insane reappearance was proof of my *bona fides*. He might think it proof of my insanity.

From downstairs, we heard a ghastly scream. 'You could ask your caretaker's advice,' I said, 'but I think they've just cut his throat. Come along!'

George had heard, and George knew that it was bad. Venomous, he hissed one harsh word. Immediately he was looking around the room, and I knew he was marshalling his resources for the defence.

'Quickly, man!'

Thumping footsteps on the stairs, rising in volume and nearer.

'We fight here! They do not come in small door so easy.'

'No, but setting a fire outside the door, that would be

easy. Miss Nina,' - I gazed at her, urgent - 'we're going to find out who killed your brother. But you need to be alive to see it.'

I think she was already doubting the 'dying pointlessly' model, and this clinched it. She pushed past George, reached out an elegant wrist and I pulled her up into the night. She came a damn sight more gracefully than I had. That got the rest of them moving, and they all clambered out, and Quinn and I guided them across the roof and down through the adjacent building. Credit to old George: he saw the rest of the team safely out before he followed.

The main party hadn't got to the ground floor when we were stopped by Quinn coming back up. He shook his head: courtyard still infested with fake policemen, no doubt. I motioned the team to stop and, while Quinn guarded the rear, retraced my steps to the first landing. A greasy sash window gave onto a sloping roof. I liked the look of that, and led them out onto the tiles and down into another alley.

Further credit to George: he took orders as well as he gave them; once he accepted he was coming with Quinn and me, he did so silently and smartly, and between us we managed a rapid and unseen escape through the maze of night-time back-streets, picking up Quinn's borrowed bicycle en route. Three minutes later we were in the shadows opposite Liverpool Street Station again.

'Who were those bods, anyway?' I said.

George said a word - spat it, rather, or gargled it. It was the word he'd said earlier, but I still didn't get it. Frustrated patience, he tried again: 'Okh-ra-na. Russian secret police. Always they torment we poor exiles.'

'What the hell are they doing here? Pretending to be bobbies, I mean, and slaughtering doormen?'

The smile had no life in it now. 'Oh, poor English. So much happen in London, and you all so safe and ignorant.'

I offered him my hand. 'Not to be rude,' I said, 'but I rather hope we don't bump into each other anytime soon.'

He shook my hand and smiled. 'Thank you for coming back. Oh, and for bus.'

'Not at all. Thanks for busting me out of the police wagon.'

'Anytime.' He turned to go, paused, glanced back. 'You very strange man.'

'You're not so dull yourself, George. Try not to blow anything else up tonight, eh?'

The roguish smile reappeared - he wasn't making any promises - he threw me a casual salute, and then he led his merrie men and woman away into the darkness of this new unfamiliar London. A final glance over the shoulder from Nina, handsome and wondering.

I watched them away for a few moments, turned to Quinn, and shook my head.

'Grand job tonight, Quinn. Thank you.'

'Bit of phys. last thing, sir; good for the digestion.'

'I was fairly sure it was you on that bicycle, but I wasn't certain till you turned up at the window.'

'I was waiting when you set off in the Black Maria, and after that you were easy enough to track.'

'Bit of an improvisation, leaving my monogram like that, but I knew you'd spot it.'

'Monogram, sir?'

'My initials. Scratching them on the wall while the bandits were distracted. Bit of a risk, but-'

'Didn't... didn't see it, sir. Luckily with all the Russian lads running around with pistols-'

'You must have! Scratched in the brick in that alley for you, easy-'

'In the dark, sir?'

I gave it up. We set off westwards. Quinn had his bicycle to return; I needed a drink.

16.

Several hours sleep and a good breakfast, and the night's events seemed even more fantastical and happily more remote. I was slouched in my armchair - about as ancient as the furniture in George's flat, but smelling less peculiar - and reading the racing pages, when there was a heavy knock at the front door of the flat.

I half-heard Quinn going into the hallway to open it. I half-heard voices. I definitely heard the shouting, the banging, and a faint choking.

Newspaper in hand, I stuck my head into the hallway.

The front door of the flat was open, and a man in a rather nasty brown suit was sprawled up against it, Quinn's forearm crushing his throat, Quinn's other fist raised ready to punch him in the head.

I glanced briefly at the face, wide-eyed and gasping, and then at my valet. 'Everything all right, Quinn?'

'Under control, sir.'

'Right ho. Let me know if you need a hand.'

I turned away towards the racing news.

'Delamere!'

The voice was familiar. Sadly. I went into the hall.

The man being crushed against it had gone rather pale now, and was struggling less. Beyond him, on the landing, I could see two men. One I had met only briefly, last night; he was in a different suit now, but again three-piece and again very natty. Now he had a pistol up and pointing at my valet's head. The second man - suit equally appalling, but in a different way - I had met too often.

'Morning, Bunce', I said. 'Collecting for the benevolent fund, or you delivering the milk now?' Behind him, on the stairs, there was a policeman in uniform.

Inspector Bunce nodded a sour greeting.

Three-piece suit's turn to shout: 'Delamere! Tell your man to release my sergeant.'

I looked at Quinn, at the man he was throttling, and back at three-piece.

'Why?' I said.

He produced his best sneer. 'Because assaulting a police officer is a very serious offence.'

'Gosh', I said. 'It's always the fun stuff they bar, isn't it? Ten Commandments, and so on. This building is private property. This apartment is private property, and your man is just inside it. You've shown no warrant, you're not in uniform, you've offered no formal credentials, and your pistol says you attacked first. I reckon we might just get away with it, you know?'

He cocked the pistol.

'You're... Faversham, I think.' I considered him. 'You ever pulled the trigger, Faversham - for real?' He glared at me. 'I'm not sure you have. You see it in the eyes, especially the first time: that moment, that fragile courage, eyes a bit wider and a bit more desperate, just before the trigger finger trembles.' Still glaring; still uneasy. 'To avoid any misunderstanding, Faversham, let me be clear that if you touch my valet I'll kick you down the stairs. And if I think I see that look in your eyes, I will kill you first.'

The expression started to open: the bravado of the official on duty, the bravado of the man with the gun. Then he heard the click.

That's one of the benefits of the Webley revolver, over things like the Mauser: lovely loud click from the hammer.

He looked down to see my pistol pointing at his stomach. And when he looked down I was able to slap his pistol aside, grip the stock and twist the weapon out of his hand. 'Right,' I said; 'let's all calm down now, shall we? Quinn, release that person please.'

Quinn pulled his forearm away, and the plain-clothes man in the brown suit slumped gasping against the door.

Inspector Ernest Bunce is a miserable sod at the best of times, but now there was something twitching at his lips as he looked at Faversham's anger. 'Go easy, Delamere', he murmured. 'Need a chat about last night.'

'Oh!' I said. 'Of course. Come on in; what'll you drink?'

I hung both pistols up on the hat-stand by their trigger-guards, and they swung there companionably. I saw Faversham eyeing the arrangement and not liking it. 'Old Albanian custom', I said. 'Once you accept my hospitality and cross my threshold, it is a point of honour that I can do you no harm.'

Faversham eyed me like I was half-witted, and Bunce eyed me like I was lying. 'Last time I called here, Delamere, you'd just shot a man to death in your sitting room.'

'Oh, that was quite different. He hadn't let me hang up his pistol. Besides, he wasn't Albanian.' I ushered them in; Quinn stood back respectfully. He and the uniformed policeman seemed to be old pals - an exchange of grumbled 'hallo mate's - and then brown suit had struggled upright.

Quinn considered him, and said eventually: 'Wipe your feet.'

17.

'Look, Faversham', I said, trying to do the genial host act, 'I do hope you'll excuse the fuss. Bit jumpy after last night's excitement. Never cross my mind to stop the police going about their lawful whatnot. Soda with that?'

He and Bunce and a recovering brown suit were established in my sitting room with drinks, and Faversham had deigned to accept a cigarette too. The uniformed man had disappeared into the kitchen with Quinn for a cup of tea and a natter.

Faversham was trying to work out if I was serious; he didn't know me like Bunce did. Eventually he sneered: 'Bit of a shambles last night.' He looked at Bunce and then at me as if it were our fault.

'Shocking business', I said. 'Any of your men badly injured? Horses?'

'They'll all recover, mercifully.' He took a long drag at the cigarette, expelled the smoke from his nostrils and crossed one elegant leg over the other. 'Face facts, Delamere:' he said down his nose, 'you're in a deuced dicky position vis-à-vis last night. In with that gang, I mean to say.'

I considered this. Partly the revelation that someone was still saying 'deuced' a decade into the twentieth century; partly the dickiness of my position. 'To be fair,' I said, 'I was only in with them because you put me in with them.'

'Being in with them was one thing', Bunce said in his usual London scowl of a voice; 'busting out with them was another. Very embarrassing for Special Branch, that incident.'

He didn't look at Faversham as he said it, and Faversham didn't look at him. The truculent slouch of the one and the suddenly harder glare of the other screamed their mutual hostility. Most amusing to watch, of course, and occasionally stir the pot a little, but I knew there was only one direction in which they would each vent their feelings.

'Oh, it was horrifying!' I said, trying to look like someone who'd been horrified. 'I've been under fire, but... The surprise, and the noise in that confined space, and the smoke, and everyone panicking. Don't know if you've ever been blown up, but you lose your faculties completely. Utter chaos.'

Bunce tutted. 'Heart-breaking', he said heavily. 'And you such a sensitive man. We've one policeman says you attacked him; he reckons you were crucial to the escape.'

'On the contrary, I tried to stop one of the others attacking him.'

'By hitting him yourself?'

'Of course I didn't hit him.' I did hit him, of course. This was the snag, as expected: I hit him, but for his own good. Couldn't see the judge going for that one. 'God's sake, I defy anyone to describe individual movements in that bedlam:

stuck in that damned box of yours, pitch black, deaf, blind and choking. If he got lamped by me or Doctor Crippen or Marie bloody Lloyd he couldn't have told the difference. Probably just banged his head in the scrummage.'

'Let's assume, shall we, just for a moment, that you're not guilty of assaulting a police officer?' Faversham did enjoy his pose of sneering disdain. He had the voice, the posture, the suit for it; even the way he held his cigarette. 'What happened after that?'

'God knows. I fell out, or was pushed out. Collapsed on the cobbles. I remember worrying about more explosions. Got myself upright. Couldn't hear anything, couldn't really see anything. I guess I sort of staggered away out of the smoke and collapsed. When I came to I was lying in an alley. God knows how far I'd got or how long I'd been out.'

'Hang on', said Bunce. 'You didn't go off with them?'

'What, the others in the Maria? The opera lads? Lord no. Why, where did they get to?'

I'd thought about this bit. I really didn't want to admit to the later stages of my mad journey. Even if I had gone at gunpoint, and even if I could convince anyone else I'd gone at gunpoint, it was still too compromising. Bunce was just itching for an excuse to feel my collar, and the fact that I'd spent the evening with George and his dynamiting chums and not got my throat cut was very suspicious indeed.

Oddly, I also had the faint sense that I didn't want to make it too easy for the police to get to Nina.

'We've witnesses to the gang escaping', Bunce said. 'By motor car, and maybe by bus.'

'They broke out of your wagon and then hopped on the bus? Don't be daft.'

Faversham jumped in, shaking an elegant finger. 'Forget the bus; ridiculous suggestion.' Poor Bunce. 'These are bad men, Delamere. Anarchists. Revolutionaries.' He got twice as many syllables into the word as I'd have managed. 'Dynamiters. And you were seen with them.'

'I and a hundred other music enthusiasts were seen with them. Then you forced me to be seen with them. And then everything blew up and no one was seeing anything.'

'We can get you' - Bunce again - 'on consorting, aiding and abetting, conspiracy to murder, attempted murder, take your pick.'

'You can try, Bunce,' I said, 'but you'll look bloody silly when it comes up in court.'

'I really don't care what happens in court, Delamere. Fairly confident what'll happen in my cells, though.'

Genial smile from Faversham, the elegant mediator. 'Let me - ah - put you in the picture, Delamere.' He did love those 'p's. Puff of smoke, flick of ash off trouser. 'You can leave with me, or you can leave with Bunce.'

'Any chance of you both going to hell? No?'

He tried again. 'You're not going to end up in Bunce's cell. Because you're co-operating with Special Branch.' He leaned forwards. 'This thing is Po-litical, d'you see?' Definitely political with a capital P, for Faversham. Behind the pose of chummy manipulation I saw a new earnestness. 'Visiting Russian high-ups, revolutionaries lurking in the shadows. We're taking it all damn seriously. Last night's outrage…' He shook his head.

Yes, I thought, you are taking it seriously. I didn't know what he was talking about with his visitors and his revolutionaries, but I knew there was anxiety behind the flippancy.

He licked his lips and pressed on cautiously. 'Bunce said he'd had trouble with you in the past.'

'No trouble', I said suavely.

'No trouble', Bunce said, less suavely and with a different emphasis.

'Hoping that we can - ah - count on you to do your bit. Play the game, eh?' Some of Faversham's poise was back. No doubt he was also hoping to imply that he and I were more similar sorts of chap, very different to Bunce and his shabby concerns. Next he'd be asking what school I'd been to.

I was beginning to understand why they'd turned up like this. Two relatively senior policemen popping round for a drinkie was far more courtesy than my very doubtful status required; for all I'd scoffed at the idea, Bunce wouldn't have had much difficulty lifting me on any of the charges he had in mind. Clearly there was something bigger going on, behind the shooting and behind the attack on the police wagon.

I assured them that I'd only be too pleased to play my part, anything for the old country, and do have another, and they said they better not, and they'd be in touch, and I showed them out - the uniformed bobby hurrying after and putting his helmet on and wiping tea off his moustache.

They lingered for final pleasantries on the pavement. A closed carriage was parked on the other side of the street, a couple of dozen yards off. I noticed that it was in better shape than the average - less battered, and the driver up top smarter than a regular cabbie. I noticed that there was a hook and some discolouration on the side of the door where an emblem might be hung, though no emblem was hanging there today. I noticed a hand briefly on the window-sill: someone inside, waiting, or watching.

Faversham was making his farewells - glad to have you turning out for the home XI, trying to remember if I might have bumped into you at school, and so forth - when one of his plain-clothes bods hurried up. A quick salute and: 'We bust into one of the regular hang-outs, sir. Can't be sure if our pigeons had been there, but we found a body. Throat cut, within the last day.' That would be the poor caretaker who'd opened the door to us last night, and then opened it to his murderers in their police disguises an hour later. 'Seems too much for coincidence, sir.'

Faversham nodded. 'Turn the slum upside down; the whole district. That sort of rumpus, the gang toing and froing, someone's bound to have seen something.' The policeman saluted and bustled off.

54

Not good. Someone was indeed bound to have seen something, and among a gang of scruffy immigrants in a district of scruffy immigrants, the most likely something to have seen was the chap clambering in and out of windows in full evening wear and his substantial Cornish valet on a bicycle. I nodded soberly, trying to suggest how awed I was by Faversham's efficiency.

And off they toddled, Tweedledum and Tweedledee, two rather different paragons of British policing.

The closed carriage was still parked up. As I watched - because I watched? - it lurched into movement.

I turned away, but made sure to follow its reflection in the front window of my building. As the carriage rattled off behind my back, I distinctly saw the ghost of a figure, very fair hair and a veil, leaning forwards to look at me.

18.

The previous evening had left me uneasy. My little excursion with George & Co. had given me an insight on a London I didn't know, and that was leaving aside the bit where they'd blown me up. And before that, of course, the shooting during the opera. A mad incident - bizarre - and all very unsatisfactory. Unfinished business.

I got a cab and went south again. Our hosts of the previous evening had, understandably, gone away for a couple of days while things blew over. But the butler knew me and I burbled of my lost coat and he let me in for a poke around.

Like a morning-after dinner table, and a morning-after lovers' bed, there's something distinctly sour and seedy about a morning-after murder scene. They'd carted away the body now, along with the chairs and all the other bits and bobs from the performance, but pale dead Kyril and his bloodied shirt-front still seemed very present. The garden felt chilly, and rather desolate, and the scuff-marks on the grass marked the movements of last night's ghosts.

I stood a while gazing at the stage area, to no great purpose or effect. I prodded around the shed where the performers had waited, thinking about the rifles that had been propped there. I considered the stage from different angles, from behind the umpteen bushes that fringed it, concealing the shed and much else. I wandered down the garden to where the chap must have scrambled over the wall, to go and warn old George and prompt the assault on the Black Maria.

I had looked into his eyes across the omnibus aisle. According to the simplest logic, that chap from the firing squad had shot poor Kyril and done the runner to escape justice. Did that make the killing a bit of radical business?

But if the killer had got away over the wall, then by definition it wasn't him being busted out of the police van. George had to have had some other motive for that: either he couldn't have one or more of the team being interrogated, or he was just a sentimental sort and felt sorry for them.

Or - if the shooting was some radical revenge - perhaps more than one of them was in it. Only one wound, though, one fatal shot.

Not for the first time in those dozen hours, my thoughts turned to the girl Nina. Not a superficially beautiful woman: handsome rather; dark-wild appealing. Appealing in her grief; appealing in her calm amid the chaos.

How could she be both? How could she be comfortable among the gang, and also grieving at the death, if the killing had been some gang business?

I wandered back again, up the garden towards the house.

A figure was standing in the centre of the stage area, where the body had been. Silent; solid; buried in thought.

'I didn't know anything about *Tosca*,' I said. 'Not until last night.' He turned, surprised but controlled. 'You know anything about *Tosca*, Bunce?'

Inspector Bunce let a smile across his face. Somehow, he felt it was good news that he'd found me here.

'I got a bit lost in the details,' I went on, 'but one of the main players is a policeman. Bloody awful fellow.' He'd stopped smiling. 'Question seems to be whether he's the loser because he got murdered at the end of Act II, or the winner because he does for Tosca and her boyfriend in Act III.'

I stopped a little way from him. You never quite know, with Bunce. 'What do you reckon, Bunce? Worth getting stabbed by the heroine, if your own plan triumphs after all?'

He was silent. Not one for the parlour games and operatic banter.

It's one of the things I find annoyingly admirable about Inspector Ernest Bunce. He's a pain in the arse, irrationally prejudiced against Delameres and determined to see me banged up for something; and he will not, ever, be stopped or distracted or pushed off balance for long. Like the punching-bag in the gymnasium: in the end it'll always swing back and thump you.

'Wondering if I've got the murder weapon about my person? Wondering if I've tossed the vital clue over the garden wall?'

He smiled again, almost surprised. 'You don't get it, Delamere, do you?' The rough London voice was low and slow and steady. 'Doesn't matter if you've a blood-stained dagger up your sleeve or not, doesn't matter if you're guilty of this crime or not, doesn't matter if you win the prize for smart-aleck comment of the day or not. You're a wrong'un, Delamere, and one of these days I'll have you.'

I considered this.

'Yes,' I said. 'I guess you will.' He smiled more cheerfully. 'Meanwhile, has your solitary thinking got any farther than mine did?'

He shrugged; looked rather sourly around the stage area.

'I guess your lads had a proper look at the rifles. All of them were working weapons?'

He considered me a moment, then nodded.

'Any difference in the condition of the breech?' He looked

unsure. 'I mean: anything to show that only one had fired a live round?'

He shook his head. 'Expert says all the same.'

'So: fullish charge in each, but only one with a real bullet.'

He nodded. 'Because otherwise there'd have been more than one wound, right?'

'Seems likely. They weren't aiming perfectly, but still. So, only question is whether the chappy knew he had a live round up the spout and was shooting to kill, or didn't know and was as surprised as the rest of us.'

'Not as surprised as the dead lad.'

'Indeed. In fact, if all the rifles were firing full charges they'd all kick to the same extent. If the killer hadn't known it was a live round beforehand, he still might not know now.'

'Bit of a chance, isn't it?' Bunce's natural scowl suited the question. 'If you want to kill the man. Slipping a real bullet into one of the rifles and hoping he's aiming properly.'

It was a good point.

The scowl twisted his face even more. 'One of them's done it, bold as brass in front of a hundred people. And now they've all hooked it I can't find out which of them.'

'What's the point of them being guilty if you can't beat it out of them, eh?' He didn't find it funny. Perhaps it hadn't been a joke. 'Poor Bunce.' He glared at me; he might very briefly tolerate my hilarious commentary, but he wouldn't swallow pity. 'Trying to do a basic job of policing and solve a crime, and the brass are only interested in what the Russian Embassy think.'

The scowl threatened to cover his face completely, and then subsided. 'What about you then, eh?' he asked. 'Whatever you did or didn't do last night, you got well out in the end and slept all sound in your own bed. Why aren't you on your second bottle of champagne or off to Monte Carlo or something?'

'How well you know me, Bunce.' Now it was my turn to scowl. 'Like you say: bold as brass it surely was. Right under my nose. Sort of insulting, you know? And an insult to my host, my friend, who asked for my help and all I've done is get Shanghaied by you and blown up by the Russians. And…' - I shrugged - 'there's a girl. Russian girl. Only got involved to earn a bit of pocket money and have a chance to mix with her own kind. I don't know how she fits in to any of it, but her brother's been killed right in front of her and she's hurting and no one wants to help.'

'Funny', he said, the old hungry look in the eyes, 'how much you suddenly seem to know about these Russians.'

19.

Fortunately a policeman interrupted our performance before we could explore that uncomfortable point. A salute and a note for the Inspector.

The Bunce scowl was getting quite an outing today.

'Waste of bloody time', he muttered. 'Right. Better shift.'

Then the constable said: 'Sir, is this gentleman Mr… Delamere?'

'Yeah. This gentleman' - Bunce hit the word with distaste - 'is Mr Delamere. Nothing we can do about it, unfortunately.'

'Sir, it's just they're looking for him too. Same meeting.'

Another notch for Bunce's weary frustration. 'Oh, lucky old him.'

'That's handy', I said. 'You can give me a ride, Bunce. Tip for you if we don't get blown up this time.'

We were bustled in through the Home Office tradesmen's entrance. Then we were bustled up stairs and along corridors and up more stairs and around and about a bit, and everywhere was dark wood and tiling, like the better type of Victorian lav., and occasional dusty young men looking vaguely around for their chins. Eventually a vast polished door was opened with painstaking silence and a frown, and

Bunce and I were pointed to seats against the wall.

The whole outfit was bog-standard imperial: panelling all round, portraits of great men now forgotten, bust of the king, imposing conference table, upright chairs with upright men in them. There must have been a dozen at the table and as many lurking with us on the touchline. There were suits and facial hair that hadn't been seen outside Whitehall for twenty years or more. At the junior end of the table I saw Faversham; outfit smart and sober today.

'...living outside most recognized social frameworks,' someone was saying, 'and in many cases wholly outwith the systems of record-keeping and monitoring intended to manage the flow of foreign immigrants into this country.'

'That's not anything new though, is it? Is there some new trend that we should be aware of?'

'Well, Chairman, we've been, so to speak, waiting for the Big One for too long. These people - these anarchists, these so-called Bolsheviks - have two motives in being in England. First, they want somewhere less risky than their own countries to lie low and gather their strength. Second, they look for opportunities to advance their interests by attacks on our institutions. Thus far we've managed, by God's mercy and efficient policing, to avoid anything significant in that line. But it's long overdue. As for the recent trend: Faversham?'

Faversham followed on suavely. 'Thank you, sir. Our reporting, monitoring and undercover work show a definite surge in activity levels among the more radical elements, and in anxiety among the immigrant communities. Pardon me, sir, but like a spider's web: when there's movement somewhere, the tremors can be sensed all the way through the system.'

The chap at the head of the table - winner of the Best Kept Bureaucrat award, 1870 - looked very sceptical about the spider's web thing. 'Well we simply can't be having that, ah... Faversham. We're relying on the police and the, ah, Special Branch to keep these ghastly people on a tighter rein, most especially at the present period. The visit from St Petersburg is a matter of national strategic interest; the alliance system that knits all Europe together. We cannot give our guests the impression that their undesirables are living lives of ease and luxury here and free to plot mischief. This nasty little incident is precisely why they're such a menace.'

'Pardon me, sir.' Faversham again. 'Fully agreeing with your strategic assessment, sir; but it's not yet clear that the events of the last twenty-four hours are anything other than score-settling within the radical community.'

The big cheese looked uncertain, as well he might. 'If we tolerate these kinds of people, this is the kind of thing we must expect them to get up to, eh? One fellow with his throat cut, another shot down in front of an audience of civilized Englishmen trying to enjoy an evening of culture.'

'Ladies too, I gather', someone added, and there were murmurs of outrage.

'I don't like it', said the chairman. 'But as far as last night's incident is concerned, I presume for now we must pass it off as - as how did you put it? Something about spiders?'

'Score-settling, sir. Within the radical community.'

'Such is our analysis, I take it.'

Faversham spoke for a good three minutes without apparently stopping for breath or articulating a single clear idea in any direction. None of us was any the wiser about our analysis; but the chap had a sound pair of lungs on him and a fine speaking voice.

There were some approving murmurs.

'Charming theory if it keeps you warm,' I said. 'But it's pretty daft, isn't it?'

Every face in the room turned to me: surprise, indignation, anger. Apparently they didn't encourage heckling from the cheap seats at these shows.

There was a heavy creak next to me, as a heavy policeman sat up with fresh interest in the proceedings. I'd managed to make both myself and Faversham look foolish, and Bunce's day was looking rosier.

The worthy ancient at the head of the table began an 'Errrr' that promised to last well into the evening, capturing his unease about who I was, what I was talking about, and what the world was coming to when lesser mammals interrupted the big beasts.

'Delamere', I added. 'On special attachment to the Metropolitan Police.' That'd wipe the smirk off Bunce's face. 'Couple of snags, if I may. Three. First: if the killer was one of the opera firing squad, he couldn't possibly have expected to get away with it.'

'He seems', said someone, 'to have got away with it all too easily.'

'It's a fair point, sir, but he couldn't have expected to. Everything about the shooting says it was planned. Everything about the assault on the Black Maria - including the chap bolting beforehand - suggests improvisation or some other objective. I can't find a way that links them.'

They were watching me with cold interest. They didn't like me chipping in, and no one was rushing to agree with me. But they didn't have answers or alternatives. I claim no great brilliance, I should make clear: I was just the only one of them who'd been on the spot, and I'd had rather longer to think about it.

'Second: if the killer wasn't one of the firing squad but just rigged one of the rifles, successfully killing the chap was one hell of an unlikely prospect, with the squad singing and dancing and more concerned with looking artistic than with aiming; he'd be lucky if there was even a serious wound.'

'What if he fixed all five of the rifles?'

'Then the probability switches round: you'd have expected more than one wound. Instead there was just the one fatal shot and otherwise not a scratch. I had another look around the scene this morning, and the shrubbery the chap was standing against didn't seem to have sustained the damage I'd have expected if four or five live rounds had gone into it.'

'And, ah…' - patronising indulgence from the head of the table - 'your third… notion?'

Delamere going down as well as ever with the senior staffers. 'Well,' I said, 'I'm no kind of expert on these radicals and revolutionaries-'

'No.'

'-But it seems an unlikely way for them to go about their business. I suppose you might do something spectacular and sacrifice the trigger-man and make sure he didn't have too much to give away to the police, but surely only for a really high-profile target. Make a statement, so to speak. Yet this dead chap wasn't anything in particular, and so all that melodrama seems absurd.'

'Well, some element of speculation may be productive,' said the big cheese, managing to avoid looking at me. 'But for working purposes we're best not having too many hares running. The most likely scenario, and thus the main line of approach for Special Branch, seems to be a deliberate act by one of the gunmen in the squad. Wouldn't you agree, ah, Faversham?'

Faversham hesitated. Whatever one thought of his taste in suits, he was not a stupid man. Not stupid enough to ah agree. But not stupid enough to disagree with the top brass. 'Thank you, Chairman', he said carefully. 'Special Branch will stick to facts not speculations, and we shall chase it down.'

This was a natural and positive conclusion to the meeting, assuming one cared about rhetoric and protocol rather than foreigners getting shot in south London gardens. The chairman thanked everyone, and that was it.

As I was leaving, I saw Faversham in intent chat with someone: little chap, round-rimmed spectacles, and a suit that was somehow unusual - old-fashioned or foreign.

The round-rimmed specs were gazing at me.

I arrived back at my rooms at the same time as Quinn. As we tramped up the stairs I gave him the gist of the discussion I'd sat in on, and his expression showed the respectful scepticism with which the Sergeants' Mess always treated pronouncements from the Officers' Mess.

'So we can stay well out of it, can we sir?' He didn't sound optimistic.

'Dearly love to', I said. He was opening the door. 'Wouldn't mind knowing what happened at the opera. And Special Branch clearly need help understanding foreign radicalism in this country, as well as how to do up their own boots. What's essential - if I don't want the Russian secret police cutting my throat - is that I avoid any suggestion I've been familiar with the radical mob.'

Quinn had got as far as the hat-stand and the door into the sitting room, and stopped.

'Any chance you lost your overcoat last night, sir?'

I'd been hoping that this aspect of the night's foolishness would pass unnoticed: it's a good coat, and Quinn takes good care of it, and he gets very ratty about unnecessary household expenditure.

'Did I? Wouldn't say I lost it, exactly. Sacrificed. Cost of war.'

'I understand, sir', he lied. 'Just that... it seems to have turned up again.'

I looked into the sitting room, and sure enough there was my coat, draped elegantly on the upright chair.

The elegance, I should say, was mainly down to the body inside the coat. Sitting alert, looking up at me with a guarded smile, was Nina.

20.

'Hallo', she said.

'Hallo', I replied.

That was about it with the diplomatic niceties. Still the guarded smile.

'Well this is nice', I said. 'Isn't this nice, Quinn?'

Quinn failed to smile. 'Yes indeed, sir. And there was you just saying how you hoped to bump into your friends from last night again.'

That was exactly the kind of hilarious insight we didn't need. God knows I wasn't happy at London's most wanted woman inviting herself for a visit, but I didn't want to annoy London's most dangerous woman and her even more dangerous friends.

'I return coat', she said.

'Very thoughtful. Hope it kept you warm.'

'You were very kind to give it.'

'Don't mention it', I said, really wishing she hadn't. It had been bad enough Quinn thinking I'd merely lost one of my few decent garments. Behind the stony expression I could see what he thought of me making a present of it to a woman who blew up policemen.

'Any chance of a cup of tea, Quinn?' I said, too quickly. He grumbled something and turned to go. 'And very clever of you', I went on to Nina, 'to, er, find your way in here.'

'You leave your front door key in pocket.'

Quinn stopped still. I could tell his expression from his shoulders. He cleared his throat, and set off for the kitchen.

A sudden clattering stopped him, and we all turned.

Nina looked irritated.

I turned back to her. 'D'you think your friend would like to join us now?'

She called something, and the door to my bedroom opened. A woman was standing there and, after a quick glance to gauge the atmosphere, she strolled in looking pretty relaxed. Early twenties, like Nina; a bit fairer, a bit more solid. She was playing cool, but her eyes were moving quickly between me and Quinn and her friend.

'We keep the money in the biscuit tin,' I said, 'but it's a bit of a thin month, I'm afraid. Think we'll need another cup, Quinn.'

Quinn was watchful: too many uncertainties. He nodded,

half-paying attention.

'Sara was curious to see what is life of English gentleman. No stealing. Is not our way.' She glanced at Sara. 'So? You want life of English?'

Sara shrugged. 'Is not so much luxury. Comfortable yes but simple. And extra tidy.' She'd been keeping an eye on Quinn, as alert as he for what might happen next, and now she looked at him more directly. 'This is you, I think. You run very disciplined house.'

If she'd stood him a pint and sat in his lap and started being rude about Devon, she couldn't have found a straighter way to Quinn's heart. The tension was out of his face and shoulders, though he was still ready.

'And the two characters?' asked Nina. 'What you think from rooms?'

Another shrug. 'One live like aristocratic farmer in Siberia.' The 'a's were long and rich, in the Russian way. 'Money all gone but sentimental feelings. Other is like… like gladiator.' She hit the word with a fruity awe.

'And what does that make you, Miss?' said Quinn, the slow Cornish drawl and a smile breaking over the rocks. 'You a roman queen or a lion?'

'All right, Quinn, all right. Let's have the damn' tea, shall we?' Off he went. He may even have been whistling. 'I don't mind you pillaging my sock drawer,' I said to the girls, 'but don't go unsettling the staff.'

The friend accepted a chair, which meant I could relax and stop wondering what she was going to pilfer.

Then we sort of sat there, listening to the faint sounds of Quinn and the teacups.

'You ask why we come', Nina said. 'You expect we steal coat.'

'Not at all. Anytime. Door always open. Especially if you've got my key.'

'Also I return key. If we want, we make copy already.'

'The thought had occurred.'

The smile died. 'Also, last night I feel you serious about Kyril. You are kind. You want to help find who kill him.' Didn't leave me much choice. 'Police do not care. Police happy when poor foreigners kill each other, they go home early for tea.'

With the angry phiz. of Inspector Ernest Bunce in my mind, I made a pathetic effort at tutting to pretend she was wrong. She just went on gazing it me.

'Sorry to ask,' I said, 'but are you really sure this wasn't... revenge, radical politics, whatever you call it?'

She shook her head slowly. 'This happen, but' - she shrugged - 'Kyril is not like this. He live only for music.'

She looked very alone, perched on my upright chair and mourning her brother.

'And the men in the, er, firing squad - any of them have a reason to kill him?'

Another slow shake of the head, another shrug. 'Some are political men. And dangerous. But: why poor Kyril?' The eyes widened, lost in the memory. It was a moment for tears, but they didn't come. Instead she sniffed in one enormous breath, of revival, of resolution.

Quinn came in with the tea, and we all faffed with that.

'Also,' Nina said, suddenly brighter - good cup of tea'll do that - 'we have invitation for you.'

'Invitation? Er, another-'

'Do not worry.' Smile. 'Not opera. Tomorrow is arranged for foreign ballet and opera visitors' - she gathered herself for the next word - 'excursion. Is public demonstration of flying machines.'

'Flying machines?'

'So foreign peasants can see twentieth century. You have seen flying machine?'

'In the papers, of course. But...' The idea was so unexpected, and it only made the morning more bizarre.

'We discuss. We think you should come.'

That was when we heard the knock at the door.

The two women were immediately glancing at each other, at the door, at me, at Quinn: suspicion, concern, threat, possible betrayal. Sara was immediately on her feet, Nina stiff in her chair. I don't pretend I was any less edgy. Not for the first time I was in the worst possible company.

But I made a sort of calming gesture to them, and put a finger to my lips, and nodded to Quinn to go and open up.

A moment later there was a murmured exchange coming through from the hallway, and then Quinn's voice unnecessarily loud:

'It's Mr Faversham to see you again, sir.'

21.

'How splendid', I said. 'Always happy to get a visit from Special Branch.'

The warning had its effect. Nina jumped up too, lifted the hem of her skirt, reached up under the folds and pulled out a knife. A distracting and alarming performance, and now Sara had one too, apparently from up her sleeve. 'Oh for God's sake!' I hissed. 'Stop killing policemen when I'm around!' I glared at Sara. 'Quinn'll never forgive you if you mess up the rug. In there!' I more or less shoved them towards my bedroom door; there's another door from the bedroom to the bathroom and kitchen, and I had to hope the police weren't doing a full search. 'Just coming!' I called towards the hallway. I had the girls away and the door shut and I was gathering up teacups and wishing the silly little spoons didn't rattle so and dropping them into a drawer and then I was into the hall. 'Faversham, you say? Come on in, my dear chap!'

Dear Faversham came on in, and there was another man with him. Shortish, round-rimmed specs, odd suit…

I'd seen him: talking to Faversham at the end of the grandees' meeting earlier that day. I'd seen him gazing at me.

'This is Mr Ilyin. From the Russian Embassy. Security, you

know.'

I knew. I didn't feel secure.

Mr Ilyin gave me his hand and a little bow. 'Ilya Ilyich Ilyin', he said, the voice rather high-pitch and very quiet.

From the way he waited, I got the impression that the name might be thought amusing. Especially if you were Russian. The little glasses gazed up at me. The way the light fell, they were blank white disks, and I couldn't get his expression at all. He seemed to be daring me to react.

'Henry Delamere', I said. I didn't bother with my middle name. It doesn't tell you anything about my father, and the old sod wouldn't deserve that anyway. I got them sat down, and Quinn got them drinks.

'Mr Ilyin was interested to see you', said Faversham. For the second time that day I had the sense that he was edgier than his normal self. As well he might be, escorting this little blank-eyed whispering Russian policeman around.

'Sort of tourist attraction, you mean? Stop off and see Delamere on your way to the Kensington museums?'

The spectacles flashed. 'I am informed that you are worthy of it, Sir Henry.' As Ilyin's head moved, the eyes were glimpsed and then gone. 'Remarkable stories of your exploits and your… character.' A smile: a thin, controlled performance of mirth. 'Besides the many… exotic stories, I learn that, uniquely, you were in both the audience of an operatic entertainment last evening during which a citizen of the Russian Empire was apparently shot by one or more other citizens of the Russian Empire, and the subsequent violent escape by some of those same people and their confederates.'

He paused. I said nothing.

'You don't answer, Sir Henry.'

'You didn't ask anything.'

Again the dead smile. 'You could, I am sure, describe these people.'

'Be delighted to. Any of a hundred witnesses, including a

few policemen, could describe the ones in the opera. I assume the police have their names anyway. We spent a short time together in a pitch dark box, so I can't give you any more detail. As for the attack on the police carriage, I only got a glimpse of one or more people in masks.'

Still the voice was quiet. 'I received the impression that you had escaped with them for some way.'

'Did you?' I said. 'Can't think how. I made clear to the police' - I nodded to Faversham, perched watchful - 'that I staggered away on my own and never saw them.'

He paused again. 'Indeed.' He didn't look to Faversham, or show any sign of recalculation. I was trying not to show it, but I own I was worried now. I had to assume this chap was part of the secret police mentioned the previous evening - Okhrana, was it? - and that made him responsible for the men who'd dressed up as British bobbies and murdered that doorman. And if he could do all that, it wouldn't be much of a surprise if he'd somehow learned more about my evening than the Metropolitan Police had done.

He sat straight and still, all of that alarming possibility concealed behind the empty eyes. 'As dear Faversham here has said, I am responsible for all matters of security for the Embassy of the Empire of Russia to this country. I concern myself with threats to the interests of the Russian Empire, but also I concern myself with regrettable' - he emphasized the word delicately, and now he did manage a polite glance to his companion - 'occasions when Russian elements present a possible threat to the British Empire. Your new acquaintances from last night, Sir Henry, have made themselves my concern on both counts. They are sworn enemies of peace and law in Russia, and they pose a terrible threat to your country too.'

'Handful of opera singers?' I said. 'Sounds a bit of a stretch.' Having met George the previous night, I had little doubt of the capacity for ruthlessness and violence. But Ilya Ilyich Ilyin was talking like an over-heated editorial and I didn't intend to fall for it easily.

'To you, Sir Henry, revolution is something you read about in the foreign news when there is no horse-racing, and anarchy is a distant echo of a language you were briefly and badly taught in your peculiar schools. But to Russia, revolution is chaos and blood in our streets and the murder of policemen and the assassination of government ministers; and anarchy is a real and ever-present threat to every aspect of our civilized society. I pray God you never experience, in these genteel surroundings, what we have experienced in St Petersburg, in Odessa. These people lack all morality, Sir Henry, and they lack all restraint. They are vermin, and vicious.'

'Gosh', I said. I fought the instinct to clap. I knew that a lot of what he said was true, and I fervently hoped that England never saw one tenth of what Russia had seen. But I wasn't having foreign policemen lecturing me in my own sitting room.

Very slowly, Ilyin leaned forwards and stretched his arm past Faversham's foot. Delicately, finger-and-thumb, he pulled a teaspoon up into the light. He considered it. He looked at our glasses. Still apparently watching me, he placed the spoon on the table beside him.

'Dear Faversham tells me you are assisting' - he hissed the word, serpent-like - 'the police with their work. We have, as you see, a shared interest. I can only urge you, Sir Henry, that you do not compromise in your efforts. You will be doing my country a great service, and yours.' The head moved, and the blank eyes flashed. 'It may be beneficial to have the Russian Embassy as your friend. It may be… better for you.'

That was when the door from the hall and kitchen opened, and I looked up to see Nina standing in front of us.

22.

I like to think I'm not often stupefied, but at the moment

it seemed to be happening every hour on the hour. I may actually have been gaping open-mouthed, interrupted in whatever I'd been about to reply. Vaguely, like a man in a blown-up police wagon, I was clutching at reality, at the desperate wrongness of what was happening.

'Beg pardon, sir.' She dropped her voice into a mumble, and it covered any trace of accent. 'Anything more for you and your guests?' She glanced at them. Head low, hands folded in front of her, meek like she hadn't just done the most insane thing in living memory.

It took another moment to gather myself.

'Er... No. No, that's fine. Thank you.'

A little curtsey, and she was gone.

Slowly, I turned to look at Ilyin and Faversham, the Russian policeman and the British policeman.

They were just waiting. They'd seen nothing - unless it was me turning purple and sweating like a Cairo cat-house in the summertime. One of their anarchist vermin had stood right in front of them, and been invisible.

That's what happens if you're too snooty to notice maids.

Faversham said they ought to be going and Ilyin agreed and I tried not to agree too obviously, and we were away into the hall and through the front door. Ilyin was starting down the stairs when Faversham turned back to me.

'You may know you're not involved with last night's anarchists', he murmured through his nose. 'I may choose to believe you're not involved. But if I tell him you are involved with them, no power or law or gentlemanly pose will save you.'

I said nothing.

'Now, best way to avoid that is to assist me. Use whatever acquaintance you have to worm your way in with those damned people. Get properly involved with them, and I won't have to tell him you're involved. Bit of a conundrum that, but I'm sure you'll work it out.' He smiled insincerely and put his hand on my shoulder. 'You will help us. Yes, old chap?'

His arrogance only increased the heat with which I stormed back into the flat and slammed the door and made for the kitchen. 'What the bloody hell was that about?'

She gazed at me: quiet, defiant, sure. This was a new Nina. I'd had some idea of her resilience; no doubt she had to be pretty tough to keep the company she did. But in our brief acquaintance there'd always been a fragility, too; a reserve.

Not now. Now she was strong and certain and she didn't care.

I glanced at Quinn, and Quinn was looking pretty uncomfortable. Rightly so. 'I tried, sir; but she was too quick. I thought a scuffle would be worse.'

Still she just looked at me.

'I wanted', she said, 'to make sure I would recognize the faces again. It will be useful.'

And I'd thought Ilya Ilyich Ilyin made me uneasy.

23.

The atmosphere had been pretty grumpy when I'd turfed them out shortly after - Quinn double checking that we kept hold of my coat and front door key - but they'd insisted that I mustn't forget the invitation to their excursion. Eventually I'd agreed, as apparently the only way to get rid of them before they stole, stabbed or set fire to something.

So the next morning we were on the train to Weybridge, Quinn and I. He always likes a day out of town, and has the practical man's curiosity about mechanical things.

I was more curious - damn' worried, let's say - about my predicament with the Special Branch, the Russian Secret Police and the forthcoming European revolution. They were clearly on a collision course, and the only certainty when they did finally smash into each other was that Harry Delamere would be found dead in the debris.

Faversham had me by the short hairs, with his nasty little paradox. If he felt I wasn't co-operating, he only had to say a word to the deeply unappealing Ilyin; and Ilyin would clearly have no hesitation about cutting my throat. I wondered if Faversham knew anything about Ilyin's men dressing up as British policemen to do their anti-revolutionary killing.

And the only way to show I was co-operating was to ferret around the Russian immigrants, Nina and George and their alarming friends, in precisely the way that would justify Ilyin cutting my throat. Whichever way I looked at it, my life depended on the whim of some deeply shifty individuals.

I slumped in the compartment, gazing out of the window at the winter sun over Surrey, and feeling pretty sour.

A most peculiar figure met us at Weybridge. Its bottom half had the most robust weather-proofing imaginable, stout boots and puttees and oil-cloth trousers. The top half had a jacket a little longer than the ordinary in what might have been velvet, a pretty lively waistcoat and a cravat to match; almost. If Oscar Wilde had been obliged to muck out the pigs, this is how he'd have togged up.

I was trying not to stare when I realized that the figure was trying to attract my attention.

It was the chap I'd met at the opera two nights before, the government liaison bod for the visiting performers. Humphrey something. Erskine, I remembered just in time; Humphrey Erskine. Earnest handshake for me, introduction and earnest handshake for Quinn. Only a mile or so but did we want a taxi-cab? No we didn't, and we set off walking.

It was a nice enough morning, and after thirty-six hours skulking in slums and hiding in my rooms the fresh air and big open sky were a tonic. Humphrey Erskine was saying how he and the team had felt I'd got caught in the mangle the other night and deserved a day out as much as anyone, and I wasn't disagreeing.

'What's the story with the Russians, then?' I said. 'Some are imports and some are local produce, that right?' I badly wanted to check the vague impressions I'd got from Nina.

'That's right', said Erskine. 'The manager and the maestro - the conductor - they've come over with a company of a dozen and a half professionals. Not a full *corps de ballet* - typical of a certain type of Englishman, Humphrey preferred saying the foreign words - 'but enough for a slimmed down version of some of the ballet standards.' I nodded my familiarity with the ballet standards. 'Then half a dozen professional singers, enough for the principal roles in most opera. Plus a couple of admin. staff.'

Still the earnest breathless voice, genteel English standard and very young sounding. Don't think I was sneering at him. I was at school - on and off - with plenty of Humphreys, and I was in the army with plenty of Humphreys, and most are decent enough. The Humphreys did more than their fair share of dying in the South African war.

'And the rest picked up here?'

'Not dancers, but singers for the opera chorus. British orchestras, or *émigrés*. And naturally stage hands and so forth.'

We were walking away from the residential bit of Weybridge and into open country. The train had been half-full, and there was quite a throng moving with us. After a bit we'd left the made road and now we were on open ground. Despite leg-wear more suitable to wading up the Amazon, young Humphrey was treading carefully around the muddy bits.

'And now it seems some of the London lot have a few more strings to their bow, eh?'

Erskine looked rather startled, and glanced quickly around. 'Well… yes,' he said, and there was awe in the voice. 'I mean to say, I don't think any of the people who are directly involved in the performing are - you know - bad sorts. But yes, some of the *émigrés* seem to have some rather dubious friends.'

'I had the police quizzing me', I said. 'Guess it's made me curious.' He looked appropriately impressed by my inconvenience. 'I gathered there's some big official visit at the same time. You running that too?'

'Oh gosh no. No, I'm really just - well, junior, you know.' His voice dropped. 'The Russian War Minister is visiting. Plus Assistant Minister and officials, of course.' I wasn't sure why his voice had dropped: pretty sure the visit had been on the front page of the paper. 'All terribly important given the, er, European context of course.'

I never know what to say when people start talking about the European context. Especially when they make it sound like it's some terribly complex mathematical problem. You can usually take it for granted that the Germans are up to no good, and obviously you don't trust a Frenchman farther than you can throw him and his bicycle, and that keeps you straight. The rest's just the diplomats trying to make their jobs sound more impressive.

'It's being presented as a friendship visit:' he went on; 'big cheese visiting and the Embassy throwing parties and the government and, er' - furtive glance - 'Buckingham Palace, and the cultural aspect all thrown in. Gala performances!'

'Real *entente cordiale* stuff, eh?' I said. 'Er, *entente cordiale…ski*. Russian cordiality.'

For a while I'd been aware of the buzzing of what sounded like an insect. Then out of nowhere the insect's buzz became the roar of a lion and from behind me it pounced. The sky went dark and a great growling thundered over my head.

24.

I'm proud to report that I didn't dive to the ground and cover my head. But that was less about suavity and more about being paralysed by surprise.

The lion was dwindling to an insect again, and then it was just a buzz, and then the sky was clear once more. All around me the crowd were pointing and chattering and staring after the phenomenon. More than a few looked as startled as I probably did.

I'd just been ambushed by the twentieth century.

To give you an idea of the speed of progress: when we'd been fighting the Boers in the Cape less than ten years before, our most advanced bit of kit - the thing that was really going to give us the edge, just like all the other daft things over the centuries that have been going to give us the edge - was the balloon. Yes indeed, put a chap in a balloon - and I grant you, you wouldn't have got me in one of the damn' things for all the gold in Africa - with a packet of sandwiches and a pair of binoculars, and float him up on a long rope, and he can see a bit farther than, say, a man in a tree or a man standing on a box of biscuits, and there's your strategic advantage. Remarkably, it wasn't that much of an advantage after all, so they reverted to the traditional fallback of getting lots of poor young men led by a number of stupid young men to run at the enemy rifles. Bit of a touchy subject; sorry to bang on.

Anyway, in under a decade we'd gone from a man in a balloon to these terrifying flying machines. Perhaps you'll think them old hat, these days everyone's got his own and a frilly one for the wife. But try to imagine just how much our sense of the world had been transformed in those few years. Throughout human existence, all the way back to the Egyptians and the chaps in caves, we'd been land animals. Sometimes we moved a bit faster on land, on a horse perhaps, or when lots of angry Dutchmen were shooting at us, sometimes a bit slower, especially after lunch; always land animals. If you really fancied variety you could jump up in the air for a fraction of a second and see how the birds lived; but then, and always, land animals again. Not any more. Now a whole new dimension had opened; the world available to us had been multiplied. I'd not had my perspective, my sense of the possibility of life, so utterly transformed since the moment I discovered that girls weren't just tiresome cousins with an unhealthy fondness for poetry and kittens.

Oh, and also bear in mind that it had only been another decade or two since the oil-powered motor engine had become a thing. All within my lifetime. We'd barely started to get used to the idea you could strap one to a cart and visit your cousins more quickly. Now these fellows were strapping them to kites and launching into the skies. Not sure who they expected to meet up there, but you have to admire the initiative.

Quinn was looking up in thoughtful wonder as he walked. Too well-behaved to comment on what I looked like. Then again, his lot still believe in pixies and won't get into a boat if they've seen a rabbit that morning, so he can't get too snooty.

The land was opening out now, a vast flat field, undivided by fences or hedges for half a mile in any direction. At a couple of points around the edge I could make out structures: brick or wood sheds, a few big army-style tents.

'And today is… something special?' I said.

Humphrey Erskine shrugged. 'Sort of a… gathering of enthusiasts. Chap buys one of these machines, or maybe it's an off-shoot of his engineering business - that's how my uncle got into it - and then they find the nearest obliging farmer with a big flat space and set up camp. Like a race meeting, what?'

'And naturally it attracts the crowds. Including our Russian friends.'

Erskine nodded. 'Rather my suggestion, actually.' He was clearly proud, and I expressed adequate admiration. 'I think there's some official interest - one of the visiting Ministers is supposed to be a bit of a lad for the new technology. And a jolly good day out, what?'

I assured him it was.

'To be honest,' he said, 'I think these new machines are a bit fantastical. Speculative, yes? And dangerous. But my uncle's by way of being a fanatic, and I'm obliged to play the dutiful nephew. Thought we might as well make a day of it.'

Outside the tea-tent, we caught up with Nina and Sara and the gang.

25.

Nina said hallo, friendly enough, and Sara deigned briefly to smile at me before throwing herself at Quinn. Apparently we were all politely forgetting that the previous day I'd cursed them out of my rooms as lunatics and liabilities.

There were a dozen of them from the musical troupe, huddling together against the side of the tent until they got comfortable with English crowds and English days out. I recognized most of the firing squad, as I still thought of them. And I was introduced to everyone: a series of earnest handshakes and unpronounceable names, each with an artistic label: *contralto*, principal *danseur*, chorus - English word at last, well done lad - or whatever.

One face was not there. I knew because I was looking for him. George the gunman had decided to stay home and catch up with the revolutionary paperwork. Or perhaps he only came out at night; like bats, and tarts.

'I'm curious', I said to Nina. Our group had broken into separate conversations, so we were effectively alone together. Her face was immediately guarded. No such thing as a casual question for Nina; she'd always feel hunted. 'There are the professional dancers and singers come from Russia, and then there are people from the Russian community in London, and within-'

'Stop saying Russian.'

'Pardon me?'

It was quiet, and hard. 'Stop calling us Russian. Please. We are Latvian.'

'L… Latvian? Very well.'

'Most of people you have met. Our land is occupied by Russia. Our people are victims of Russia.'

'And that's… everyone, er, here?'

'Empire of Russia is hundred different peoples. So-called Russian community is hundred different peoples. Most of our group Latvian.'

'Most. Righto. Sorry. Anyway, in the Latvian community here in London, there are some people living regular lives, nice and boring, and because they're music enthusiasts and fancy a few extra bob they're helping with the opera and the ballet. And there are some people who are… I don't know what you'd call them - active, radical, revolutionary types. Bolsheviks, is it? I mean to say: how different are these groups?'

'We are united. We all have same dream.'

From my tiny exposure to European radical politics, that seemed highly unlikely. 'All right, put it this way: I don't believe that all Latvians run around with pistols blowing up police wagons.'

'You met many Latvians?' She smiled. 'We all have same dream. Some are more conscious. Some are more… busy.'

'And you, Nina? How busy are you?'

She shrugged. 'I agree with George. I work with George. Sometimes I sleep with George.' She gazed at me. 'Does this offend you?'

'Not at all. Once one's started dynamiting policemen, it'd be daft to get all moralistic about bedtime. Lucky old George.'

She considered this. 'Yes. Lucky old George.'

I glanced around us. Still the chatter, the shifting figures, the sense of being alone in the crowd. 'And how many others who are helping with the opera are also..?'

'Sleeping with George?'

'Working with George.'

She thought about it. 'This I do not say to you. You guess. It does not make difference.'

'It might make a difference in who killed your brother.'

The struggle was clear on her face: bitterness and defiance.

'Well then!' Humphrey Erskine was trying to take charge.

'Shall we go and see a flying machine?'

26.

Erskine led us towards one of the shelters that I'd seen looming around the edge of the field. There was a little jungle of structures there: canvas, a couple in brick, other bits tacked on in other materials: the engineers' shanty-town. The crowd was thicker as we got closer. With weedy courtesy Erskine edged us through, and then down between two shelters, and then we were being ushered through a door. Not sure if this was the VIP entrance or the Tradesmen's. It took us into a brick-built workshop, and another door on the other side of that opened into a large tent extension.

'Ah, Humphrey!' The cry was high and creaking, and very Scottish. 'So these are our guests, eh? You're most welcome, my friends, most welcome.'

We stood in a huddle, waiting for our eyes to adjust to the relative gloom; and then as they did so we were gazing at the wild contraption looming in front of us.

'Come, come!' said the voice, but none of us was paying him much attention.

It's all about what you're used to, isn't it? I've been around, seen plenty of this and that. Couple of years among rifles and guns, and then an outdoor, travelling sort of life have shown me much of what the modern world offers. But when I'd tried to contemplate a flying machine, the only things I'd had to go on were motor cars and birds. The mechanical transport thing; the flying thing. Put 'em together, and what you certainly don't get is the thing I was now gazing at.

What made it so eerie was that it seemed vast, but barely there. It filled the tent, and it had us standing there with our mouths hanging open, but there was no substance to it at all.

As a small boy I'd had a toy which let you build things out

of sticks - like matchsticks, but a bit longer. You could build absolutely anything you dreamed of, so long as your dreams were confined to small box shapes in outline. Skeleton of a cube: easy. Double it up and there's the skeleton of a cuboid. Keep going, and bob's your uncle there's an even longer cuboid. For the month or two before it got lost in one of our incessant moves, I'd been utterly gripped by it. Happy times.

Anyway, that's all this flying machine was. A stretched box-shaped framework of sticks of wood, the whole business forty or fifty feet long and a dozen feet tall. Two canvas wings - bit of aeronautical terminology for you there - in the middle, one above the other. Forty feet across, say. A couple of mini-wings at the back, upper and lower again. At the front end there was another mini-wing, sticking out flat. Underneath there were a pair of wooden runners, like on a sled, each with a pair of pram wheels.

From the side, it seemed to have no form: all the way along it you could see right through the lattice of wood sticks. On the lower wing there was a seat; just a wooden bench which they might have borrowed from an omnibus, enough for one, perhaps two if they were friendly. Behind the seat was the motor engine, and stuck to the back of the engine was the propellor. The engine, an ugly grey box of pipes and protrusions, was the only solid thing about it, the only part of the flying machine that seemed to have any weight.

It was ridiculous.

Standing over us, pale and silent in the gloom of the tent, it was terrifying.

'… seven cylinder, producing fifty horsepower', the old Scot was saying.

'But how does it fly?' asked Sara.

I was glad she did, because the idea continued to fascinate me and I kept reading explanations in the papers and they never made any sense. The Scot beamed; he got asked this one a lot. He started talking with great enthusiasm about aerodynamic forms and air speed and lift. Every now and then he'd add in 'as with the simplest of the birds in the sky' as if it was supposed to help. But in fact, looking at the thing close to, looking at the slight curve of the wings and of the other canvas bits - don't know what they're called; sorry - it started to make a glimmer of sense.

'Propellor is at back of engine', Sara pointed out, as if the poor man had made an embarrassing error. 'Why not fly backwards?'

'Fair question, dear young lady; fair question. A matter of the orientation of the blades and the direction of rotation. But we have to make sure we don't fix it on backwards, eh?' The old man chuckled. 'After that, the thrust is just a matter of good old pressure differential again.' We all nodded wisely, glad to be back on the firmer ground of pressure differential.

I say old: he was fifty, perhaps, or sixty, and he seemed pretty spry. 'You going to introduce your friends, Humphrey?' A mischievous grin on the bare bony face; he was shrivelled like some past-it bit of fruit at the end of summer. 'Young Humphrey thinks the old man's a lunatic, ladies and gentlemen. But we'll win him round in the end, eh?'

Not a lot we could say to that. Humphrey vaguely blustered the kind of denial that only reinforced what the old man had said, and eventually mumbled 'Sir Malachai Erskine' to us; and to him: 'Uncle, these ladies and gentlemen are from the-'

His voice was swallowed by a vast murmuring from outside the tent, and the crowd there was shifting away from the opening where they'd been staring in at the machine, and then old Erskine said: 'Ah! Out we go, ladies and gentlemen!'

27.

From the gaggle of shelters and everywhere else besides, the crowd was gathering at one end of the field. The centre of attention was another flying machine. A dozen men were holding a couple of hundred feet of rope in a large circle around it, by way of an informal barrier. I'd seen a few policeman dotted about the place too: lend a bit of discipline, and everyone likes a jolly.

The machine looked similar to the one we'd just seen with old Erskine, although my experienced eye noticed only one of the mini-wing things at the back, and the mini-wing thing sticking out at the front seemed smaller and set at an angle.

A man in overalls was stationed at each end of the lower wing, and another was fiddling with the engine while a chap in thick walking tweeds was watching him closely and making suggestions. The crowd looked on, as we might have done had some macabre religious sacrifice been underway.

I remembered the teams in the Cape getting the balloon ready: the endless fiddling with unknowable technical details. I remembered the number of times I'd seen motor cars being prepared and started. I remembered the moments before my platoon charged forwards in the attack: the shrinking of the world to tiny things; how loud one's breathing sounds.

We'd managed to wriggle our way close to the front of the crowd. I was near one of the lads holding the rope; I remember his fists clenched around it, his eyes anxious at the thought that his fragile authority could in an instant be overwhelmed if the crowd grew too enthusiastic.

Like everyone else I was mostly watching the flying machine and the men fiddling round it. Then a flash of colour caught my eye in the crowd on the other side of it. The crowd was thinner there, and better-dressed. A party of dignitaries, perhaps; what passed for the Royal Enclosure in this Surrey field. Among them a woman with very blonde hair, escorted by a chap in a uniform and a couple of others. I don't say I looked at the uniform immediately, but I swear I looked at it a close second after the blonde. Old soldier's habit to notice a uniform: you need a quick decision on whether to salute it or shoot it.

This one left me unsure. It almost certainly wasn't any British uniform I'd ever seen. Nor was it a Cape Dutchman come to revisit our disagreement of ten years before. But a foreign something or other.

'Mr Harry', Nina said from beside me; 'I think you have been noticed.'

For a moment I thought she'd caught me staring at the blonde, and then I thought she was saying the blonde had caught me staring, and then she was gesturing a little to the left of the blonde.

She was gesturing at Lady Victoria Carteret.

I'd not seen Victoria since the night before last, when my attempt to escort her to the opera had ended in murder, arrest and an outbreak of revolutionary violence. Which was about average for us.

'Don't think so', I said to Nina, scanning the better-dressed bit of the crowd indifferently. 'Don't recognize anyone, anyway.'

Victoria could not become part of this world of anarchists and secret policemen.

I let my eyes drift. When I thought Nina was looking elsewhere, and Victoria looking in my direction again, I slowly shook my head.

A shout from the flying machine, and we all looked, and the tweed chap was patting the engine chap on the back and then clambering up onto the wing of the machine.

It was actually going to happen. It was ludicrous to contemplate: I could imagine the machine trundling forwards all right; but the idea that this ramshackle assembly of wood and fabric was going to hop into the sky was impossible.

The shriek of a whistle, and now the lads with the rope were shouting at us and pushing forwards into the crowd, expanding the perimeter around the machine. The perimeter grew and then opened, to let the machine out across the field. More marshals were busy now, yelling and gesturing the crowd back. The kind of effort that normally achieves little, but the crowd was quick to obey: no one wanted to obstruct the machine; everyone, I suspect, was a little afraid of it.

Silence. Nothing happened. Had I misunderstood? Had someone forgotten something?

Then a rattling buzzing noise from the machine: the engine had fired and the propellor had disappeared in a puff of smoke and the chap in the overalls was hurrying away from it, and well he might. The idea of getting hit by it - the smoke had cleared and the blades were invisible, spinning so terrifyingly fast - was ghastly.

Still no movement. Except the machine was straining, like a drunk man pushing against restraint, like an animal shifting ready to spring. The power of the engine was fighting some other force, and the wings and the bits at the back were shaking and heaving and the noise was louder and the whirl of air was faster, and the man sitting on his chair in the middle of it all seemed so small and so frail.

And then something gave way. The machine began to move forwards, an ungainly roll over the grass, the drunk slouching blearily home, the animal slinking sullen. But as it moved past us and away it began to gather speed, and the crowd was gasping its excitement and shouting and the machine was getting faster and still faster and smaller and smaller and the buzzing was fainter, and as the machine got smaller it must have grown lighter because now the air was clutching at it and it was bouncing and at last it lost its weight entirely and drifted up and away.

That tweed chap sitting on his bench on his improbable fabric-and-wood toy had propelled himself into the sky, and the impossible had become real.

28.

The crowd was milling around and still pointing at the sky and chattering and applauding, and in the excitement I drifted round to Victoria.

'Sorry to seem churlish', I murmured into her ear from behind, and she'd the sense not to look round.

'I always think of it as differently charming, Harry.' She was half-turned. 'Are you hunting or hunted?'

'For once, neither.' Or possibly both. 'Just in odd company.'

'When are you not, my dear?'

'And why your interest? Daddy going to buy you a flying machine?'

Now her eyes snapped round to mine. 'I might one day choose to buy a flying machine, Harry, and I'm confident you'll think it no one's business but mine.'

'Quite right.'

'But not today. Harry Vanstone's hoping to fly, and I keep promising to come and watch.'

I glanced up, to check that Nina and Co. were still out of the picture. 'Vanstone?'

'Old friend. Terribly serious about flying.' Everyone who's anyone is a friend of Victoria's. 'I'm hoping you'll grant me a proper conversation sometime, Harry. When you're not undercover or on the run or whatever it is. I heard a rumour that your musical evening only got more exciting after I left.'

'Impossible.'

Now she looked me full in the face, and the expression burned with old unmentionable glories. 'I think Harry Vanstone's got a tent here. Perhaps we might chat there. Or will I need a disguise and a password?'

I blew her a surreptitious kiss, and drifted away into the crowd.

My Russians - sorry, Latvians - were still sticking together, so it wasn't too hard to catch up with them again.

We watched another machine taking off, and this time I concentrated on the man sitting on the wing. I tried to recapture my own feelings in moments of danger - waiting for the whistle to send us out of the trench; waiting for the eye to flinch and the trigger finger to squeeze. I tried to imagine what it must be like sitting there - was he strapped in at all? - and waiting for the machine to lurch forwards and bounce up. How much control did he have over the machine? What must he feel as the ground dropped away? How long before it was too late to jump clear?

He rolled and jounced away down the field, buzzing and getting smaller, and then he too rose up into the clouds.

I managed to find myself walking beside Nina again.

'Surely', I began, 'you can make a guess about why Kyril was shot, can't you?'

She glanced at me; shrugged.

'There can only be so many reasons for someone to get shot, and in that macabre way. Perhaps there are... rival gangs, and Kyril was killed for being in the wrong gang.'

She shook her head. 'This does not happen among us. And he was part of no gang.'

'Would the Russian secret police - these, um, these Okhrana - want to make an example of him?'

Another shake. 'He was not... political. He was not prominent. He was not active like this.'

'Personal matter then. He'd rejected some girl. Or stolen someone else's girl?'

A little smile. 'Kyril was not... not so interested in girls. And I don't think he had affair at this time. Normally I know if he is happy or sad like this.'

'All right. Does he have money? Money that someone inherits?'

I knew the answer. 'He had nothing. We have nothing.'

'I'm running out of possibilities here, Nina. A secret of some kind? Kyril was shot because he heard something or was part of something, and someone thought he was about to betray this.' Another shrug. 'What's going on, Nina?'

She stopped still, and turned to face me. The eyes were wide, lost. 'I must have revenge for him', she whispered. 'But... it is better not to know things.'

The crowd roared in excitement, and we all looked to the sky.

29.

The landing of a flying machine turned out to be as heart-stopping as the taking off. Taking off, the risk was presumably that you couldn't build up enough oomph to get off the ground, and ended up looking a bit of a fraud or rolling into a bush. But as that frail contraption drifted down towards the earth, it seemed inevitable that it must be smashed to smithereens. It's a solid enough lump, the planet earth, and if you dive onto it from a great height with a motor engine increasing both weight and speed you're surely asking for trouble.

It glid down towards us, and it seemed just to brush the surface of the earth and it bounced up again and we all gasped, and down again and a smaller bounce and none of us could breathe any more and then it was down properly and rolling steadily across the field. As it got closer to the crowd the noise of the engine became audible and then angry, and that creation of impossible elegance and fragility was once again a solid and mechanical construction sitting squat on the ground.

I get ratty if I'm stuck in a crowd for too long, and I owed Victoria a more civilized conversation. I wandered towards the shelters around the edge of the field. Old man Erskine's HQ seemed temporarily closed for business: he and his lads must have got their flying machine onto the field ready for a launch, or were watching the competition.

I walked along the line of a dozen huts and tents. The few idling mechanics I passed couldn't tell me anything about Vanstone. I got to the end of the line and, with nothing better to do, rounded the last shelter and began to work my way along the backs.

Outside the third construction, a big battered old tent that looked like it was army surplus, and not from the winning side, I found a woman.

She was slouched with elegant abandon in a folding chair, her back to the tent, gazing into the sky and pulling heavily on a cigarette. Her long legs were crossed, which drew attention to the fact that she was wearing something like riding jodhpurs, tucked into knee boots.

She glanced round as I came closer, and considered me warily.

Working women in diverse trades had always worn leggings, but among the kind of people who had leisure to hang around flying displays it was still extremely rare: you had to be very unconventional, to really not give a damn. More common in America, of course, but isn't everything?

'Sorry to interrupt the meditation', I said. 'I'm looking for Harry Vanstone's digs.'

Still watchful, she jerked her thumb over her shoulder. It was a handsome face: strong straight features; full mouth; dark eyes and dark hair - with an unusual shock of white in it. She was probably about my age.

I nodded thanks, and stood there, feeling rather spare.

Movement, thirty or forty yards off. A man had appeared from somewhere and seemed to be finding his bearings, as I had been, along the back of the tents and sheds. By the looks of it he was outside the back of old Erskine's.

The woman spoke. 'You don't know Harry Vanstone, I take it.' Her voice was low, cultured, quietly sure.

I shook my head. 'Probably another ghastly over-bred under-brained swank.' I caught myself. 'He's not your husband, is he?'

She looked as though she might say yes just for amusement, but shook her head. She took another pull on the cigarette. That wasn't common either, not in public.

She seemed to be considering me. 'You're not impressed by people like Vanstone? Papers are full of how brave they are.'

I thought for a moment. 'Brave?' I said. 'Certainly, but… Well, back in the day, I did one or two things that some people - who weren't there - considered brave. And I saw other men do things that were truly brave. But… the more apparently brave the deed, the more stupid you had to be.' Another pull on the cigarette; still watchful. 'I am… in awe' - I could hear my own sincerity - 'of whatever it is that sends Vanstone into the sky. But I know it ain't brains.'

She thought about it. Nodded.

My attention wandered for a moment, from her handsome profile and poise. Some distance off, a door at the back of one of the more solid shelters was pulled shut. It turned out to have been blocking my view of the chap I'd seen loitering at the back of Erskine's place. Unaware that he was now being watched, he was working a tent peg loose, and then another. As I watched, he bent and slipped underneath the canvas and in.

30.

'Excuse me a jiffy', I said to my companion. She seemed happy to forget me immediately, and went back to her cigarette as I began to sneak along behind the tents and huts.

I reached the point where chummy had been fiddling with the tent pegs. The old Scot's premises, right enough.

It wasn't my business. If one chap wants a sneaky peek at another chap's flying machine, it's fine with the Delameres; carry on. But curiosity's a terrible thing. And by this point I was feeling every new uncertainty as an extension of the bizarre events of two nights before.

The one thing I wasn't going to do was wriggle under the canvas after him. Curious yes, but not daft. Inviting a kick in the head, or at least a tricky question. But I already knew that there was the side entrance, through the brick workshop bit. I snuck along towards it.

Now I hesitated. Ideally I didn't wanted to be spotted by chummy as I was spotting him. And I didn't want anyone else spotting me spotting him. And I didn't feel I had the right to be barging into Erskine property throwing my weight about, more or less on a whim. Needing a better feel for the land, I snuck farther along to where the gap between Erksine's shelter and its neighbour opened out onto the field. There was always a chance chummy had friends nearby keeping watch and ready to lend a hand.

There weren't many people tight around the tents and huts. The action was in the middle of the field and above it. But as I watched, a couple of figures moved away from the back of the crowd and towards me.

Lurking in the alley between the two shelters, I'd hoped to be inconspicuous. But now the two bods had seen me. And they'd recognized me: a smile, a wave.

Two of the Latvians from the opera. It was too late to pretend I hadn't noticed them. I strode out in the friendly style, Delamere always glad to see a couple of fellow music enthusiasts. I explained that I'd just been having a piss round the back. They didn't understand - doubt I'd know the Latvian, either - and so there was a certain amount of indelicate miming. Eventually we all confirmed that we all understood having a piss, and enjoyed the moment of hearty fellowship, tough being a man sometimes, and are we having a nice day with the flying machines? Another of their number had joined us now - a bony, hobbling fellow - and in their rough English they expressed sober wonder at what they were seeing. I'll bet their lives were wilder and more experienced than my own, but I got the impression that they didn't get much in the way of touristic days out, and today was a bit of a treat.

Eventually I contrived to drop away from them - hang on, isn't that old Bob? - and work my way back to the shelters.

The front of Erskine HQ, the big canvas flap, was still

closed. I was still assuming that the man who'd slipped under the back would only have done so if he knew the place was empty. I made another cautious circuit to the side entrance again.

I listened at the door for a moment, hoping I'd be able to get in unnoticed. But you can never guarantee that with a closed door, and I was counting on bluffing it out - could have sworn they said this was the refreshments tent, any chance of a lemonade? - if I bumped into anyone. That meant not hesitating too long before opening the door, so I didn't.

I did bump into the infiltrator. But the lemonade gambit was not needed.

It took a moment for my eyes to adjust to the relative gloom, and then I was taking in the workshop space again, and through it the larger tent with the flying machine filling it, and most of all I was reassuring myself that nothing was moving.

Someone was there. Just a couple of yards in front of me, lying sprawled on the ground in the doorway between the workshop and the tent. But he certainly wasn't moving.

31.

Curiosity battles alarm. Experience versus animal excitement. I double checked that there was no one else around. No one to do unto me whatever they'd already done to the chap on the ground.

Then I was bent over him. I was pretty sure it was the man I'd seen sneaking under the back flap. The clothes could have been the same. I'd not got a good look at the face, and now the face was obscured by blood. There was an ugly wound in the scalp, a dark crimson stain. Someone clouted him round the back of the head, with something hard. I checked for breathing; pulse.

He was dead, right enough.

I wondered, more seriously now, who he was. Who he'd been.

There was nothing from his clothes to tell. I was about to check his pockets, but caught myself. This wasn't the first time I'd tripped over an unexpected dead body, and the first man on the spot is always in a bit of a tricky position. Especially if he's got my unreasonably shabby reputation with the police. Everything I'd done had been with good intent, but I was trespassing, and I didn't know the Erskines well enough to get away with having trespassed to follow a trespasser. I needed to be away.

I was still crouching over the body. Had I seen the face somewhere? Another moment of pointless hesitation, and then I was up and making for the side door. Sorry, thought it was the refreshments tent; any idea where I can get a lemonade?

Because I am now and then involved in something odd, and because I am more often unfairly suspected of being involved in something odd, my instinct on these occasions is always to get away unnoticed. But then I remembered Faversham, the Special Branch man, and his devil's bargain with me. I had to be the upright citizen as much as I could. I set off to find a policeman.

I was moving towards the crowd - I assumed the policemen would be there; they're a sociable lot - when I saw a pair of figures moving out of it. Ten yards apart, we saw each other at the same moment. It was the blonde woman I'd seen across the field earlier, accompanied by one of her uniformed chaps.

Now we'd all made eye contact, I had to slow. Beautiful she certainly was; and also foreign. Something about the face, something about the expression. The brightness of the hair, the hardness of the beauty, the very cold blue eyes, the full lips... German, perhaps? Northern European for sure. And, when I eventually glanced at it, the uniform her escort was wearing could have been German.

She nodded coolly and kept on walking.

It took a few minutes to find a bobby, but I got his attention easily enough. There was just a moment where he looked at me a bit warily - check I wasn't doolally or hitting the champagne too freely before luncheon - and then we were striding off towards the shelters.

I pointed out the Erskine establishment as soon as it was close enough to make out. 'Right you are, sir', he said. 'Best leave this to me now.' This suited me fine: done my duty without getting my hand in the mangle. I wished him luck. 'Have your name before you go, sir? Just in case there's any questions?' I tried even harder to look innocent, and gave him my name and told him I'd be loitering around the Vanstone tent for a bit if he needed me.

The woman was still slumped in her chair round the back. She was still focused on the sky, and another cigarette.

I said hallo, and got a barely courteous nod of acknowledgement. I began to lurk uneasily again. 'Told Victoria Carteret I'd meet her here', I said to the cold face.

At which the cold face warmed. 'Oh, you know Vicky', she said with unprecedented pleasantness. The magic of the Carteret name as ever; I'm always irritated by the certainty that the Delamere name guarantees the opposite reaction. 'Right ho. Fancy a fag?'

I was about to accept, when we were both distracted by Victoria walking towards us, beauty and a smile in the sunlight, shining against the shabby huts and tents. 'Hallo, Harry!' she called from a little way off.

'Hallo', I replied. And at exactly the same moment, so did the woman next to me.

32.

Uncomfortably, sourly, I turned to look at her. For the first time there was a smile on the handsome face: strong and a little malicious.

'Harry…' I said, wearily. 'Short for - Harriet?'

She nodded.

'You might have told me.'

'Where's the fun in that? Anyway, being such a… a ghastly over-bred under-brained swank - that was the phrase, wasn't it? - perhaps my pride was hurt at not being recognized.'

'Yes. Sorry. About all that.'

She stood. 'Or perhaps' - her voice was even quieter, and more serious - 'I find the world of the over-bred and under-brained rather ghastly myself, and I prefer not to be known.'

The sincerity was clear - the intensity - and I looked into her face. Still the watchful, guarded smile. After a moment she stretched out a hand. 'Vanstone', she said. 'Harry.'

We shook hands. 'Delamere. Likewise.'

'You two been making friends?' Victoria said. She touched my arm, bent to kiss Harriet Vanstone on the cheek.

Vanstone and I glanced at each other. 'Absolutely,' I said. 'Made a slight fool of myself, but…'

'I took that for granted, dear. Though before you'd even been introduced must be something of a record.'

'So, if you're the legendary swank Vanstone,' I said, 'you're the pilot.' The faintest nod. I own I was impressed. 'Hence the…' - I gestured towards her outfit - 'the sporting get-up. And hence you wanting to be left alone while you watch the sky and enjoy a gasper.'

Again the slight, reflective smile.

'I saw you the other night, didn't I?' I said. 'With Victoria, at the opera excitement.'

'I didn't realize you'd seen me.' She glanced to Victoria. 'The honour…'

'Anyone beautiful enough to be visible beside Victoria deserves a bit of honour.' They were subtly different kinds of beauty, but beauty they both were.

'Elegantly done. My witch's brand too, no doubt.'

'Your what?'

She pointed to the shock of white hair among the dark. 'The curse. The witch. The outcast.'

'I assumed you'd been struck by lightning while showing off up there.'

'With your notorious disapproval of flyers, you must really worry about a woman flyer.'

'Sex doesn't come into it. Anyone who gets into one of those things - man, woman or labrador retriever - has my... my equal horror. No, I...' - I glanced at Victoria - 'I've always admired - let's call it independence - in a woman, above all else.'

'That's why it was never going to work out with dull little stay-at-home Victoria', said very un-dull, un-little, too-many-homes-to-count-let-alone-stay-in Victoria.

'And because you're so bloody awful at needlework.'

'That is true.'

'Do you two need a quiet corner to rekindle something,' said Vanstone, 'or d'you want a chair and a drink?'

'The latter,' said Victoria; 'definitely.'

'Aren't we interrupting?' I said. I was getting restless myself, and I guess I'd glanced back towards the Erskine HQ more than once. 'Don't you want to be cranking something up or saying a last prayer?'

Vanstone scowled. 'Probably won't get up. Engine's burst a blood vessel. Marie and the boys have gone off to borrow or steal a replacement bit, but I doubt we'll get her fixed today.' I was fogged about Marie, the boys, and indeed 'her', but got the gist. 'Delamere, grab that empty crate, would you?' I obeyed. 'Vicky can sit here, and I'm sure we can find-'

'Not for me', I said, setting the crate down. 'Sorry to seem churlish, but... Well, funny business.' I looked to Vanstone. 'You know Erskine, the old Scot?'

She nodded. 'Most of us think he's mad. A few of us think he's a genius.'

'Well, I was introduced to him earlier, and I was back there just now, and... I found a dead body.'

'Not again, Harry…'

Vanstone looked at Victoria: 'This happen a lot?'

'Oh, my dear… Well, on what proportion of the occasions when you've seen Harry has he found a dead body?'

'Gosh, yes.' They both gazed at me, rather disapproving.

'Anyway,' I said quickly, 'Feel I oughtn't to be loitering.'

'Nor would we wish to be loitered with.' Victoria, of course. 'Are you planning on helping, or hiding?'

'Don't know.' I turned to the other. 'A real and rare pleasure, Vanstone.'

She smiled, and there was more warmth in it. 'Likewise, Delamere.' She almost sounded surprised.

'Harry…' There was urgency in Victoria's voice. 'That decision about helping or hiding: make it smartish.'

I turned to see what she had seen.

My policeman was striding towards us. Even if I had wanted to avoid him, it was too late. He stopped a couple of yards off, looking very official. 'Been wondering if I'd bump into you again, sir.' He made it sound ominous. A glance to the ladies, a nod, finger to helmet brim: 'Beg pardon, ladies.' Back to me: 'Don't appreciate foolishness, sir.'

'Nor do I.'

He looked doubtful. 'I checked over every inch of the place. There's no body there.'

33.

I have my faults, but hallucination ain't one of them; that's my story, anyway. I'd definitely seen a body in the Erskine hide-out. The body had definitely been dead. Assuming the policeman hadn't suddenly veered off course and looked in the wrong place, then the body had been moved. The situation, rather than Harry Delamere, was getting more odd.

I glanced at the two women. Harriet Vanstone was barely interested; dead bodies come, dead bodies go. With each moment I was getting a stronger sense of how indifferent she was to the cares of the routine world.

Victoria flashed a brief glance at me, unruffled and undoubting, and then looked at the policeman like he was the under-footman trying to give her the wrong knife for the fish course.

There was no point trying to convince the policeman of my sanity, nor in wasting his time any more. I pretended embarrassment - gosh what a muddle, perhaps he was asleep, sorry to disturb your afternoon, greatest respect for the police and so forth. A little mollified, he strode off.

The two women were looking at me with different kinds of curiosity: Vanstone curious about the unending chaos that seemed to gather around the Delamere species; Victoria curious about what I was going to do next.

'Good luck getting the machine fixed', I said to Vanstone. 'I do hope you come down safe. And if you don't, I hope the going up is fun enough.'

She smiled, dark and deep, and for the first time I felt I'd said the right thing.

I couldn't resist another peek at the Erskine residence. The old Scot was back home now, calling instructions to a couple of mechanics who were fiddling with the engine on the flying machine. He himself was tinkering with another engine, standing in the workshop section.

I'd not expected anything else, but I couldn't help noticing the absence of the body. No one was behaving as if anything had been wrong. I glanced a couple of times too many at the fatal spot, trying to convince myself that I could see a scar of dried blood on the earth.

The old man beckoned me enthusiastically. He tapped the engine with a screwdriver and, rather wild-eyed, said: 'Future of British aviation, right here!' Then he introduced me to another chap watching the proceedings, smartly dressed in gentlemen's sporting regular: tweed jacket and plus fours, cravat, soft flat hat. This, apparently, was 'Grahame-White'.

Grahame-White, it transpired, was another pilot. This one looked the part, lean and polished and rather stupid - I didn't tell him so; learned my lesson from the Vanstone debacle. But as I looked closer, there was a strange... weariness in his eyes. I wondered at the mental strains of throwing yourself up into the infinite on one of these ludicrously flimsy craft.

'You'll pardon me, sir,' came old Erskine's Scotch squawk, 'but... you're a part of young Humphrey's group?' I hesitated. 'You don't look like the rest; don't quite fit.'

'Story of my life', I said. I gave an abridged version of how I'd fallen in with Humphrey and his musical friends.

'You interest yourself in our machines, eh?' He sounded very hopeful.

'Chaps like you tell me this is my future', I said. 'If that's so, I like to come and look the thing square in the whatnot.'

He smiled. 'Do excuse me if I sounded a bit suspicious just then.'

'You... have to worry about that sort of thing? Oddbods poking around?'

'Oh, it's not so bad. A shared interest among enthusiasts, with a generally healthy spirit of competition to keep us on our toes. But there's a bit of dirty work now and then. And it'll remain so as long as we let the French preserve their dominance in engine design.'

'Er... sorry; lost me there.'

'There are a dozen different flying machines on this field. Most of them have British aviators, but they're sitting on French engines. Gnome and the other French companies, they're ahead of the game in engine design: both efficiency and reliability.' A pained smile cracked across the old walnut of a face. 'Patriotism's all well and good, but if you're asking a young fellow to take to the sky and risk his life, he prefers a better than even chance that the engine lasts the journey.'

The idea was terrifying. 'That sort of thing... goes wrong, does it?'

He glanced to where Graham-White was watching the

mechanics, and looked grave. 'Man is capable of astonishing vision and inventiveness, Mr Delamere. And I am determined to do my part in that. But in the end, for all our brilliance we're still in thrall to old Sir Isaac Newton.' He waited, in vain, for me to understand. 'What goes up, Mr Delamere, must come down. Only question is how fast and how hard.'

I nodded uncomfortably.

He patted the machine. 'You seem a sporting sort of chap. Adventurous type, or I miss my guess.'

'Just the one war, and then a bit of this and that. Nothing out of the ordinary.'

He gazed into me. 'Sort of restless young gentleman who'd like an outing in a flying machine, I'd say. See if you've a taste for it.' He was actually grinning, but the expression was intent.

I gazed right back, into the dark eyes. 'Sir Malachai,' I said, as firm as I could without actually grabbing him by the collar, 'you have to be absolutely bloody joking.'

34.

Quinn and I got the train back to town with Humphrey Erskine, Nina and the rest of the crew. General sense of a jolly day out, seeing flying machines for the first time. Some of us, of course, got to see a dead body as well as a flying machine; deluxe package only.

'Your uncle's quite a character', I said to Humphrey. I was, as I always seemed to be these days, squeezed in with the gang. By the carriage door, Quinn and one of the lads were comparing Atlantic and Baltic fishing.

Humphrey looked rather startled. 'Oh yes! Yes, he's a wonderful soul, isn't he?' He glanced around uneasily, and lowered his voice. 'Fraid he's a bit of a crank, really. The family business has always been bicycles, and-' He caught himself, looked even more uncomfortable. 'Sorry - that sounds a bit daft.'

'Not at all', I said. 'Delamere family business has always been ill-judged horses and out the back window; I'd have been glad of a bicycle or two.'

Still uncomfortable. 'Well - yes - gosh - I see. Anyway, bicycles, and the - the related machine parts. Of course, I don't really understand it all. Happier in the theatre than the factory, always have been. But it was a sort of family tradition, and now... Anyway, we're awfully fond of him.'

'You can steer clear of all that, I suppose? Foreign Office now, aren't you? He'll have sons or partners or whatever to carry the thing on.'

Now Humphrey Erskine looked positively alarmed. 'Well no. That - That's the snag. His wife died - desperately sad - and they'd no children - and it's all in the family, and I'm - I'm by way of being-'

'Gosh, you're in line to take over the bicycles?' He shuddered. He was an unlikely heir to old Erskine. Among other things, he'd managed to lose the accent. 'Bit of a change from the theatre, I can see that. He's not been able to rag you into a flight, then?' He shuddered some more. 'He tried it on me, and introduced me to one of the lads. Grahame-White?'

Now the face brightened. 'Claude G-W? Oh, he's a splendid fellow! School with me. Few years older. Oh yes, he's wonderful. If they hadn't invented the flying machine he'd have been a - oh, I don't know - Amazon explorer or something.' I smiled. Every generation of schoolboys has its heroes in the senior years. 'Not sure I'd take to the glamorous lifestyle,' he said rather wistfully, 'but... fine man.' Don't seem to recall any junior boys ever getting too devoted to me; then again, I'd have been a hell of a disappointment to someone like Humphrey.

He turned to face the rest of the compartment, happy to escape bicycles and flying machines. 'Now then - hallo? Can I just-?' The chatter subsided. 'I was thinking, as you've not got a performance tonight, I was thinking that we could go out for supper together. Wonderful club in Long Acre, always a couple of good singers.'

There was a bit of mumbling among the group, and translating for those who hadn't acclimatized to Humphrey's lingo. Then general nodding and murmuring of approval. 'Splendid!' Humphrey very chuffed that his idea had come off; after the success of the excursion to the flying machines, it was a real red-letter day for him.

Just one dissenter. A big lad leaned forwards, heavy smile - it was one of the lads who'd been in the Black Maria with me, the one who'd appointed me his brother after I'd lamped the policeman. 'Regret', he said heavily. 'I cannot. Other invitation.'

Humphrey never minded, other opportunities no doubt, we'll be thinking of you as the champagne flows, and everyone returned to their conversations.

I'd happened to catch Nina's expression, as chummy had put in his negative R.S.V.P. And at least one of the others had looked at him the same way. Instinctively sort of sober - almost alarmed. And then the expressions were gone. Big, steady chap: not someone you'd challenge lightly.

I wandered what it was about his likely evening activities that would prompt concern.

It was evening by the time we pulled into Waterloo Station, and dark. We all tumbled out of the carriage, and I was chatting with Quinn when Humphrey excused his way in. 'Sorry,' he said, 'just checking - just hoping - you'll be able to join us, Henry - Sir - er, Harry.'

Rather take a trip in a flying machine, was the real answer. 'Grand idea!' I said. 'Most kind. Delighted.' I tried to look delighted. I happened to catch Quinn's eye, and the suspicion of a smirk that lurked in it. Malicious sod. 'You're off now, aren't you?' I said to him.

'Fraid so, sir.' This to our jolly host. 'Sorry to miss it, Mr Humphrey. Thank you for the day.'

Sincere regret from Humphrey, who'd obviously not seen

Quinn in a nightclub. Then Quinn disappeared into the crowd.

The rest of us set off walking. It was only as the group was forced to adjust as we made our way onto Waterloo Bridge that I got another glimpse of the big lad - my brother, the one who'd got a better offer for this evening. He was now talking to someone I fancied hadn't been with us during the day. Someone somehow familiar.

Another moment, and he turned his head.

It was George.

35.

He caught my eye just for an instant, and the malevolent smile flashed across it.

No reason why he shouldn't catch up with the group, and no surprise that he should. Nor, indeed, could he complain that I'd popped up again. Free country, and I'd been invited hadn't I? Still, I felt uneasy. I knew him for a ruthless man, and I didn't know what he was really up to.

It also made me more curious about the bulky lad and his plans for the evening. Any friend of George's, etcetera.

Once we were across to the north side of the river - the lights from the theatres and restaurants more heartening in the cold darkness of the December night - I made my move. I'd intended this anyway, and George's unexpected appearance only reinforced the benefit.

'Tell you what, Humphrey,' I said from far enough away that I had to shout and be heard by most of them; 'I'll catch you up. Need to get changed if we're making an evening of it, and I've a couple of wires to send. Place on Long Acre, you say?'

'Right ho', he said. He'd looked startled at the idea of his plan going awry, then relieved that I'd be coming back. 'The Young Oyster. Not hard to find.'

I promised to be back soon as I could and offered a general wave to the company. I made sure to pass the big chap as I broke away from the group. 'Cheerio,' I said to him.

He offered his hand, and I shook it. He said something which sounded like a hiccough, and added: 'For English, "Jacob".'

'Jacob? Right you are. See you soon, Jacob.' I turned to the dapper dangerous figure next to him. 'Behave yourself, George.'

The smile, as ever. 'You too... Harry.'

I strode off along the Strand, leaving them to push on through Covent Garden. I didn't look back or double back or any of that sort of nonsense. If they'd wanted to watch me safely out of sight, they'd have been able to.

I did indeed go home, to my rooms on Piccadilly. I poured myself a drink. I changed, as I'd said I would: but into a darker, harder-wearing outfit than would have been normal for the Young Oyster. Then I waited.

I waited without anxiety, because... Quinn.

Sure enough, the telegramme arrived an hour and a half later, just as discipline was about to lose to temptation in the matter of a third whisky and soda.

In the East End of London again, somewhere behind Wilton's Music Hall, I tripped over a figure slumped on the pavement and gazing grimly at Cable Street.

I checked there was no one else within earshot.

'Some people'll do anything to get out of an evening of Latvian music.'

'Right disappointed I was', said Quinn. Having left the group so obviously there was no way that I could have seen or followed Jacob to whatever he was planning this evening; but Quinn, as arranged, had not buggered off at Waterloo and had instead been tracking them.

He nodded to Cable Street. 'The Blakeney's Head. They've been in there best part of an hour. The big lad and the natty gent from t'other night.'

'Jacob and George. Meeting someone?'

Quinn scowled. 'I've twice got a glimpse; doesn't look so.'

I passed half an hour on a doorstep opposite, comfortably enough apart from a couple of over-friendly and over-territorial street dogs.

Then Quinn whistled. I stood and rubbed the life back into my legs. 'George is out and heading east', Quinn murmured. 'Big lad's hanging back by the pub, watching him go.'

My hat and well-wrapped scarf and coat were natural for the time of year. George and Jacob would have to look very closely to recognize me. But having followed parallel to Cable Street for fifty yards before cutting up to it, I couldn't see George anywhere. Had he sprinted, or ducked into another building?

Then I saw Jacob. He was halfway from the Admiral Blakeney's Head to where I stood, walking steadily.

Amazing what you get up to in London of an evening, ain't it? All life is here, and so on. I wasn't technically doing anything illegal, surely, and even in the East End of London English Common Law just about applied.

It wouldn't help if George spotted me following.

Jacob passed in front of me, not even a glance in my direction. They were trying to avoid being noticed, certainly together. Another dozen yards and he ducked down a side street.

There was no one obviously following Jacob. I fancied I saw Quinn lurking at the entrance of his alley. He felt much more reassuring than English Common Law.

Half a minute later I was at Jacob's side street, and I just glimpsed the back of him before he was lost in darkness.

Tricky. Any more clever-clever tracking would lose the trail entirely. I had to rely on the hat and scarf. I followed down the side street.

The darkness turned out to be the shadow under a bridge, the railway line to the east coast passing overhead. Through the arch, further down the side street, I saw Jacob emerging into the lamplight.

He stopped at a door. I kept walking - odd otherwise - but slowly. I was starting under the railway arch myself now. I saw Jacob knock - three times, was it? - and take something from his pocket, and duck his head and disappear into the doorway.

Darkness all around me. Ahead the promise of light, and the doorway. From above, a sudden rumbling: a train, carrying normal sensible Londoners home to their suppers, free of Latvian anarchists and throats uncut.

The darkness was rather comforting. I was walking so slowly now, and silently.

A yard ahead of me the darkness flared into light, and a face. A man was standing there, right in front of me; he'd lit a match, a cigarette, and now he'd seen me.

36.

Call it lightning reflexes if you like; call it battle instinct, call it life experience. Or call it panic. I punched the chap in the face.

Perhaps something in me registered that he was surely a wrong'un, that he was out of place, that it was unnatural for him to be standing in the darkest spot he could, that he too must be biding his time for something screwy, that he was involved with whatever had brought George and Jacob to the door ahead.

It felt pretty smart in the moment. In the next moment it felt pretty uncomfortable. We're an odd and unattractive lot, the English, but in general we don't go around lamping total strangers unprovoked; that's what being civilized's all about, isn't it? I had just, very definitely, lamped a total stranger unprovoked.

He'd dropped like a stone and he wasn't moving. I bent to

him, lit a match over his face.

He was alive, anyway. Not a face I recognized, not in the tiny flame under that railway arch. Bloodshot skin, big moustache.

A voice murmured in my ear: 'Well done, sir. Doubt he'll remember you.'

'He'll surely remember me, Quinn', I murmured back. 'Just hope he doesn't recognize me.' Then I raised my voice to excited normal: 'Can you give me a hand? Not sure what's happened to the poor fellow.'

He was surely a wrong'un. He was surely lurking to follow George and Jacob. I lit another match, and rummaged as fast as I could one-handed through his pockets, Quinn shielding me from any helpful souls coming up behind.

Wallet. Papers, name of Peter something. Pipe, tobacco, matches. In his coat pocket, a bag - cloth or sackcloth, no bigger than a sandbag.

I dropped the bag, and took the papers.

Second thoughts. I put the papers back again - there were more uncomfortable circumstances in which to have them than useful ones. And why the bag? And why did the bag have a hole cut in it? Two holes.

I put the bag in my own coat pocket, and gave Quinn the wallet. 'Rent sorted', I muttered.

'Doubt I'll get past the pub.' We both knew he'd be stopping at the nearest church poor box.

'Get him away from here. Buy me time.'

'You're not - you're not going in, are you sir?'

'Having got stuck in this far, be a waste not to. Get going.'

Quinn got going, the chap's arm round his shoulders. I heard his voice as he staggered back towards Cable Street: 'Come along, lad, soon have you - Here mate, lend a shoulder would you? Bloke's been coshed or something.'

Lost in my darkness, I watched them away out of sight. Then I turned and made for the front door.

No sign. No number. Standard wooden front door, in

need of paint.

Deep breath.

Three knocks.

37.

The door opened immediately.

Hell, was there some kind of password?

I stepped in, not waiting for invitation or challenge. Always better to pretend you belong and know what you're doing: in daily life, and when busting into the occasional anarchist secret meeting.

The hallway was small, and little lighter than the street outside: a single candle on a table. A figure at my shoulder, behind the door. Another door a couple of yards ahead.

The gloom was good news. It suggested that this gathering, whatever it was, depended on anonymity rather than familiarity.

A murmur in my ear, a raised hand: 'Your face...'

Yours is nothing to write home about, I was thinking; then I understood. I took off my hat, and pulled the sackcloth bag over my head. After a bit of clumsy fiddling, I had its two eye holes in approximately the right direction. Fortunately Peter whatsisname took a large size in heads, so I'd a bit of room to breathe.

Another gesture, and I moved to the second door. As the front door closed behind me, this one opened.

Nerves screaming. Heart banging. What am I seeing? Where is the threat?

Another figure, a shadow in front of me, blocking my view.

I was way off course now. If I was unmasked, I had no explanation.

The figure loomed larger.

I took a step forwards. I belong here I belong here I

belong here.

What an idiot. The shadow held up a hand and spoke. 'Your name?'

The identity papers in the unconscious man's pocket. 'Peter', I said.

I waited. Volunteer the minimum necessary.

'You are welcome, Peter.'

It was hard not to stare at the figure blocking my way, the figure I had to convince, but I managed a glance beyond him. I got a sense of perhaps a half dozen people, some standing some sitting. Otherwise, there was a peculiar sense of clutter that I couldn't pin down.

The voice was deep and clear. He was speaking so that all could hear the introduction. 'What profession do you make, Peter?'

Odd, foreign phrasing. I was half aware of a picture frame behind the figure's head.

'Painter', I said. I guessed that 'gentleman idler' probably wasn't the form here.

I couldn't see any eyes in the shadowy figure. But I knew he was staring at me.

Behind him, a couple of the other shapes had shifted attention to me. All shadows, all looking at me.

Waiting for more. What was wrong? What else could I say?

'You profess no more?'

Hell.

'No man may dare demand more', I said.

This wasn't true, of course. Especially if there were half a dozen men, and they were all desperate radicals like George and they suspected me. They could demand whatever they damn' well liked.

The figure moved aside, allowing me into the room. I managed to give him a nod, quite right, no panic here. Then I stepped forwards and tried to take in whatever I could of the gloomy room.

The people, first and last the people. I looked slowly around at each of them. Not staring, but not scared. There were seven of them… eight. Most sitting now. And the damnedest thing was each one of them was wearing a sack over his head, and in each sack two dark holes were all that passed for eyes.

Gods, but it was sinister. I could tell myself that I looked just the same. I could tell myself that I had less reason to fear because I was a relatively law-abiding citizen in my own capital. I could, but I wouldn't be listening to myself, because those rough eyeless masks staring at me were about the darkest grimmest gang I've ever faced and I was sure those dead expressions could see through me and I was sure that if they found me out they'd kill me.

I sat. Make yourself at home.

Now I looked at our surroundings, and my heart only hammered more wildly. The walls were alive with faces, luridly-coloured, a hundred eyes staring back at me. Dolls' faces. Puppets' faces. The painted white of their eyes was the brightest thing in the gloom. Crimson mouths gaped, to scream at me or mock. Threat had turned into nightmare: the whole thing was macabre; insane. Among the dolls and puppets, above them and below them and behind them, endless shelves were crammed with mechanical devices and oddly-carved wooden forms.

I've earned more than my share of dangerous enemies, and I've wound up cornered in more than a few dangerous places: a Boer command conference, a Balkan bandit lair, the interrogation rooms of brutal policemen. For heart-stopping disquiet, I doubt I've ever felt worse than I did here, in the store-room of an East End toyshop.

I tried to focus on the people around me again. I was trying, as inconspicuously as possible and as best I could in the gloom, to get a look at their hands and their shoes. People can put on disguises and even cover their heads with sacks, but they much more rarely change their outdoor shoes, and hardly ever their hands.

The door had closed behind me, and now it opened again. I forced myself not to turn, even though I knew it was someone hurrying in to explain that good old Peter had turned up on the doorstep with a headache, and - oh hang on…

'Your name?' I heard the gatekeeper say.

'I am Max.'

'You are welcome, Max. What profession do you make, Max?'

'I profess the downfall of the rich man and the corrupt man, and the liberation of my people.'

Ah. No wonder Peter the Painter hadn't impressed. Max got let in rather more briskly than I had, and I heard the door shut again. Max took the seat next to me.

The table was a simple solid wooden business - in the daytime it might do service as a work-bench for the toy-maker. The seating was a mix of simple chairs and stools. The store-room wasn't large, and the table and seats were a squeeze.

Still the ghoulish faces, gaping at each other; at me.

Nothing on the table. No drinks. And in our sack-masks we'd have had trouble smoking.

Again the door opening, again the challenge. Max had spoken with a foreign accent of some kind; I couldn't get more than that, for it was muffled. Hector sounded English, and London English at that. Hector professed the equality of all men, and the true power of the worker. Perhaps it sounds melodramatic to you, but at the time it sounded ominous; and it's a damn' sight less daft than visiting cards and everyone caring what school you went to.

I should have mentioned that Peter had spoken with what you might - if you were charitable - recognize as a South African accent. I knew that if I used anything like my own voice, one or perhaps two of the men there might easily recognize it. I knew that if I tried anything European, one of my new chums might be a native speaker and spot my fake.

Likewise an English dialect; my cockney accent is pure music hall. But in my years fighting and recuperating in the Cape I'd spent enough time around Afrikaners and Afrikaans to pick up their accent, and I had a fair hope that there wouldn't be a big Johannesburg delegation here tonight to rumble me.

From his bulk, I thought I'd guessed which of the team was Jacob. And I fancied he'd been murmuring with one of the others for a bit, which might make that one old George.

Hector had sat, and now the lad on the door was sitting too, and he was the last, and we were all ready. The dolls and puppets leered at us expectantly.

38.

Another snag. What if Peter - and it wouldn't be too surprising - was a friend of someone here? How else might he have cadged an invite? If so, his mate was probably going to be wondering why Peter - who really came from Paris, perhaps, or South Norwood - had adopted a Cape Dutch accent for the evening.

'Welcome, brothers.' The last chap to sit was the chairman. The voice was deep, strong. I couldn't get any accent, not through the sacking. 'We pledge ourselves to the destruction of the oppressor and the overthrow of the established order.'

Everyone murmured a ritual agreement with this, and I joined in hastily.

Nothing like setting out your stall nice and clearly at the start.

The Chairman pulled a sheaf of papers from his coat pocket, and unfolded them in front of him. 'We have received a message from our brothers in St Petersburg', he said gravely. There was a pause, as he reached into another pocket and pulled out a little box, and opened it to retrieve a pair of pince-nez. Then he had to wriggle the pince-nez up under his sack-mask and squeeze them onto his nose, and then straighten the sack again without joggling the specs too much. The rest of us just sat very straight and tried not to look.

At last able to see what was going on, he read out the message from St Petersburg. St Petersburg, we learned, was in a rare old mess: prejudice and brutality by everyone from the chief of police to the local postman, and a revolutionary plot being heroically hatched in every attic and basement. Not top of the list for the holidays.

The recital was accompanied by occasional murmurs of concern or approval. Again I learned to join in.

The reading took a good ten minutes; bumper month in St Petersburg. We'd also received a message from our brothers in Lyons, and Lyons likewise sounded a pretty edgy place to be. Then it transpired we'd also received a message from our brothers in Cleveland, and Cleveland sounded downright dangerous.

My pals around the table listened closely to it all. Their attention never shifted from the Chairman, and their murmurs showing how emotionally engaged they were. I realized that if you were an exile from St Petersburg or wherever, this might be your only news of home - probably the only hint you got of life for your family, your community, during years of separation. Once again I thought of this peculiar network of affections and aspirations, reaching across Europe and the Atlantic and only coming alive in the darkness.

'We have a report', went on the Chairman, 'from the working group for the drafting of the Coal Mines Act.'

Dear Lord. I suppose it was a sign I was relaxing that my instinct at this point was to sigh. I don't claim to be a very dutiful anarchist, but in any case I couldn't see us getting much entertainment out of the working group for the drafting of the Coal Mines Act. Not when events in Cleveland were such good box office.

The Chairman began to read out the latest from the

drafting working group.

Now that the meeting was underway, I'd rather settled into it. And two things struck me. The first was that, as ever, London never runs out of surprises. Each time you think that there's nothing more to see, that you've reached the extreme of novelty or depravity or wildness, another ramshackle panel door opens and your mind has to get a bit broader.

The second was that, in all its essentials, this secret back-room gathering of ruthless anarchists was no different to the official Whitehall committee on public safety I'd crashed the other day. Men who sit in committee meetings are the same the world over, whether they're plotting to blow up humanity or designing a new bicycle.

I had only half an ear for the inside scoop from the drafting working group. Some well-meaning ideas to improve the lot of the average miner, stop him getting blown up quite so often. Even I'd heard of the ghastly explosion at a mine in France a few years before, which had killed more than a thousand men and boys.

What was more striking was the insight on the working group's discussions: so-and-so was taking a hard line, so-and-so was slacking a bit. The details didn't sound too interesting, but it was clear that this report was first-hand, from someone who'd been part of the conversation. That's the thing with secrets: what you know is often less interesting than how you know it. My sack-covered comrades obviously had a serious intelligence network.

The Chairman was reaching the end of the piece of paper, and so I started to pay more attention. The working group, we learned, had suspended its activities for the duration of the current general election campaign, and future progress would depend on the result of that. The Chairman folded up the sheaf of papers, and put them back in his pocket. Tidy and secure. 'We have previously discussed the proposed Coal Mines Act', he said, 'and so I propose we don't repeat that.'

Propose what you like, I thought, but anyone who's ever

been in a committee knows you've no chance. 'Window-dressing to keep the majority on the side of the owners', someone said. Murmurs of agreement.

'It's a plot to divide the labour movement.' Stronger murmurs and greater attention, the sack-masks turning towards the speaker. Any mention of plotting, apparently. 'The Liberals will expect Labour Party MPs to support the bill, and any true socialist who stands out against this obvious pantomime, who demands real change in capital relations and the conditions of labour, he'll be isolated.' Agreement, grumpiness.

'Only violence will make them understand-'

There was a knock at the door behind me, and Mr Violence clammed up. From the voice, I thought it had been my chum Jacob.

The chairman stood and went to the door. There was a murmured exchange through it, presumably with the lad manning the front door, and then the chairman opened up. Again the introductory challenge. The late-comer, we learned, was going by the name of Felix, and professing equality and something about borders. And presumably getting the buses to run to time. He found a seat, and the Chairman resumed his, and grabbed the chance to move the agenda on. 'What then of the election, brothers? I should say there have been no messages of encouragement or guidance from St Petersburg or Berlin. Clearly they expect no significant change whatever the result.'

'Why should they?' The voice might have been George.

'I hope there's no one will say the liberals should be supported to have a chance of reform?'

Murmurs of scorn. 'What of Hyndman then?'

'Hyndman's an old fool.'

'He's sincere.'

'He's a sincere old fool.'

'The others don't understand what he's talking about. That's good: he unsettles.'

'He himself does not understand what he talks of.' Yup, definitely sounding like George. 'His ideas are childish. A generation out of date.'

'He took a strong radical line on the war in southern Africa', the chairman put in. 'I fancy Brother Peter will have an opinion on his credibility.' And his sack face turned to me, and all the others followed.

Now, this was another snag, and unexpected. By the sound of it, this Hyndman was a political hot topic. Everyone who was anyone had to have a strong opinion on him. Unfortunately, I'd never heard of the chap. The name sounded foreign, but apparently he was involved with our general election. I learned later that he's as British as I am, and the head of something called the Social Democratic Federation, running his umpteenth campaign on behalf of the oppressed working man. Amazing what you can pick up in anarchist committees. Anyway, none of that was any use to me in the moment. The dead-eyed sacks gazed at me.

'What of him?' I said, trying to make it sound scornful rather than ignorant. 'In the Cape, the Boers and the English were fighting different wars and talking different languages. The English were fighting for political and economic control. The Boers were fighting for land and identity, for freedom from all control.' And freedom to continue to dwell in the eighteenth century and keep black men as slaves, but I skipped that bit. 'No Englishman has ever spoken sense about southern Africa, because no Englishman understands it.'

I've no idea where I was getting all this stuff from, but it sounded rather good, even if I do say so myself. I'd caught the tone right, anyway. The new chap, Felix, continued to watch me from behind his mask.

They didn't seem to have reached a conclusion pro or con Hyndman, whoever he might be, but George - I was sure it was George - had something else on his mind. 'Brother', he said, 'I have a warning.' His usual quiet strength in the words, and he got their attention. 'We have word that the Okhrana is suddenly more active in London. No doubt they show their strength because of the political visit. A loyal friend of ours was murdered by them two nights back.'

'The Okhrana' - it was Jacob now, his clumsy heavy English - 'he will try to break us. Disguise. Even there is Okhrana here I not surprise.'

At this, Felix of the broken watch jumped in. 'Brother Chairman, may I instead to ask a question?' Brother Chairman nodded, waited. The eerie sack face turned, and the empty eyes were staring at me. 'My question is: as you are not the Peter I know, not the Peter I invited to our gathering, who are you?'

39.

You may find this odd, but I've always had a thing about the Punch and Judy. Fun for the kiddies and all very jolly no doubt, but as a youngster I found that weirdly distorted dead-eyed hook-nosed face terrifying; and let's face it, the bizarre ritual and inevitable violence of Punch and Judy is pure paganism. Only a people who could think prep schools an appropriate formative experience for young men could force children to sit through that nightmarish display of viciousness and consider it light-hearted seaside amusement.

I mention it because Mr Punch was leering down at me now, from a shelf behind the chap opposite. The empty shark's eyes, the distended teeth, were pitiless and mocking. It seemed inevitable I'd be getting clouted round the head and sausages pulled out of my stomach.

The best form of defence is... Well, the absolute best form of defence is not to let yourself get into daft threatening situations in the first place, and I'd long blown that one. The next best form of defence is to run away, but I couldn't guarantee I'd get through the first door, let alone the second.

Then there's a strong argument in favour of drawing your Webley and shooting as many of the threats as possible. Tempting, that one, in my current state of funk; perhaps excessive.

In the absence of the really good options, the best form of defence might be attack.

'Hah!' I tried to make it scornful; it sounded more like someone choking. 'Of course I am not the Peter you know. I do not care to be known.' I put my two fists together on the table in front of me: poise; bravado. I gazed around the sack-faces. 'My origins are obvious. In my own land I am well enough known, and you may find my name if you want. While other people were debating and discussing and devising fantastical plots in cellars, my people fought a war against the bloody British Empire.' I gazed around the table again. My sack was slipping and I couldn't really see properly; I resisted the urge to adjust it. 'We are the only people in this generation to take up arms against this Empire. I come to London, to the belly of the beast, to seek men equally committed to the cause of blood. Still I seek.'

Still Mr Punch sneered.

All rot, of course, but it put them on the back foot. One of the many daft things about men: if you can make their argument against you unmanly, they instantly get distracted into toughing up rather than pressing their point successfully.

'Prettily spoke, Brother Peter', said the big cheese. 'But it does not explain how you come to be invited here.'

'Hah!' It came out a bit better this time. 'All that matters, Brother Chairman, is that I am here. I do not say the name of the man who invited me, because I grew up in a world of true struggle, of true fear, where every second ear was a spy's; Peter betrays no names to unknown ears.'

It was going rather well. Now I pulled out my pistol, held it up in front of me. They all recoiled: whatever I was, I was unpredictable, and no one likes an unpredictable man with a Webley. The Chairman's hands were raised, open, trying to placate. I always end up lowering the tone in committee meetings.

I set the pistol down in front of me on the table. I pushed it forwards, turned the barrel towards myself. 'I believe in the struggle', I said; 'more than my life. If any of you believes our cause will be served by my death, then take your shot.'

I sat back, put my hands together again.

Mr Punch still wasn't impressed. My heart was hammering. There was at least one man there - perhaps two - who I was pretty sure wouldn't mind shooting a stranger just to be on the safe side, and would be delighted to shoot me if they'd the faintest idea who I was. If one of them went for the Webley, was I going to try to stop them, lose the bluff?

'No blood today, eh brothers?' Casually, I leaned forwards and retrieved the pistol. My hand was sweating and I near dropped it. 'I give you good evening, gentlemen. Doubt I'll learn much more here.' I tucked the pistol away. I started to stand, then stopped. 'Unless any of you plans action rather than just words?'

'Of course we have plans for action!' Bloody Felix again, apparently annoyed now; again, good to have him distracted away from my identity. 'As our Brother Chairman may describe.'

At first glance Brother Chairman didn't seem all that keen. 'Of course', he said quickly. Then more cautiously: 'There is much we might speak of, and much we might not.' Good committee line, that, especially from the heavy voice and the sinister mask: sounded strong and meant nothing. They'd have loved him in Whitehall. Then an idea seemed to strike him. 'Indeed, I have recently learned of a new plan. Our familiarity with the places where a man may seek explosives, and the channels by which he might plan a scheme, all this tells us that London may soon be shaken.'

'I too have heard this story', put in George. 'I believe the specialist will be the watchman; and I have a hint of the target. But we do not yet know what exactly is planned. Better if we knew the details, and could decide if we agree.' It turned out that George had a touch of the British bureaucrat about him too: better no one doing anything than someone else getting credit.

'But what is it?' One of the others, foreign accent. 'It sound like fairytale.'

It was handy, this. They all seemed to have picked up my line and be using it to learn something new. 'It's a bit bloody thin, isn't it?' I agreed rudely. If you're trying to hang on to an accent it helps to have a word that's strong and distinctive in it, and no one says 'bloody' like a Boer. 'Someone else might be planning something, but you don't know what, and you're not planning anything yourselves.'

'Better we act than we plan.' It was big Jacob, sitting across from me and barking out his heavy crude English. 'Confusion good. Chaos better. We act now, no? Finish plan for them.'

'At the same time,' George put in, 'we build our strength.' The undercurrents of all this repartee were fascinating. All the resources of the Metropolitan Police, plus my own distinctive contribution, hadn't shaken this Mauser-waving bus-threatening wild-man one bit the other night. But now, in the company of these other lunatics, he was off-balance - jostling for position. 'We are ready for action at every moment. Also we are gathering resources, so that our fight may be sustained.' Another classic bit of committee work - sounding like you're agreeing while actually disagreeing totally. So George was turning out to be more careful than he'd claimed the other night, keeping the troops in training and on the defensive until the time was right, while Jacob was all for throwing them at the enemy front line and seeing what happened next.

'Good', growled Jacob through his sack. 'I not come to London to wait. We act.'

I was learning something about the relationship between George - here in London long-term - and Jacob the visitor.

Was this hierarchy or rivalry?

I was rather pleased with myself: I had diverted attention away from my iffy credentials, and more importantly I had started to learn about some forthcoming anarchist outrage.

I replayed the conversation. In effect, I had provoked it.

40.

The meeting broke up soon after. Brother Chairman didn't open the floor for Any Other Business, and after the mysterious Peter had upset the mood no one was wanting to hang around.

Without wanting to look too windy, I made sure to get out promptly. I didn't want anyone thinking I was trying to follow them, and I didn't want anyone able to see what I looked like without a bag on my head. I'd already made myself pretty damn' snooty, so it was natural to barge out first. I only started to lift the mask as I was coming out onto the street, and I immediately replaced it with hat and upturned collar and kept moving, a long stride that didn't look like unnatural haste but could only have been overtaken by it. Away from the lights of Cable Street, the first turn, and immediately up to a canter. I covered half a mile of brisk zig-zag inside five minutes, and then ambled home in good time to compare notes with Quinn over a couple of whiskies.

The next morning, two faintly disconcerting developments landed on the doormat.

The first was the newspaper. 'MYSTERIOUS DEATH OF FOREIGN GENTLEMAN AT WEYBRIDGE' was the headline at the bottom of page two. The half dozen paragraphs that followed didn't tell us much more: an unknown foreigner had been found the previous evening round the back of Weybridge Railway Station, his head stove in. The absence of wallet and watch suggested robbery with violence, and the poor chap was assumed to have been among the crowd observing the display of flying machines and on his way home fallen victim to one of the notorious thugs for which Weybridge was apparently renowned. I'd not realized things had got quite so bad in south-west Surrey, but after my own experience in old Erskine's tent it did seem that the heads of foreign gentlemen were remarkably vulnerable in that part of the world.

The second was an invitation. The programme of the visiting Russian troupe was going ahead, and tonight was ballet night. The one ingredient essential to the collective joy, it appeared, was the presence of Sir Henry Delamere, Bt.

In their defence, they obviously had no idea just how much damage I tend to do to collective joy, especially the cultural kind. Like the opera, I'm quite prepared to accept the artistic value of ballet, but incapable of appreciating it. I'm not one of those men who boasts of being barbaric and sneers at dancers; but it's just not how I choose to spend the evening.

As it happens I did once enjoy an evening with a Polish ballerina, one of ecstatic vigour and pleasant languor, but that's quite another story. I think she thought I was someone else, anyway.

The afternoon only brought one disconcerting message, but it was a belter.

A telegramme: URGENT REPEAT URGENT MUST MEET IMMEDIATELY STOP GRAVEST FEARS RE TONIGHT STOP REPLY THIS BOX URGENT STOP HE

Classic stuff. Can't get that kind of drama from a letter. The urgency-repeat-urgency of it. The anonymity. The total lack of useful info.

Quinn and I spent a good five minutes scratching our heads over the 'HE'. Given the telegramme's melodramatic style, it might even have been when the sender got cut off: sudden interruption; the wire cut by saboteurs; a knife plunged into the operator's back just as they were about to reveal what 'he' was going to do.

High Explosive. His Excellency.

H is my initial. Also of course Harriet Vanstone's, and I wasted a few moments recalling her remote beauty, her cool courage, her...

'E' though. We got there in the end. The style alone should have told us.

An hour later I was sitting on a bench in St James's Park. To my left the dull squat elegance of Buckingham Palace. To my right the great slab of the government offices on Whitehall, poor old Horseguards buried among them like a buttercup in a hedge. In front of me a mother duck leading the brood on a day-trip to the island in the middle of the lake; chilly for it.

London needs life, like the park needs flowers. In December they both seem stark and dead. Warmth and cheer are hiding elsewhere.

I readjusted my coat under me to stop my backside freezing up entirely. Wondered again if I'd misunderstood the instructions. South side, nearest the bridge; surely this was it.

'Psst.'

Oh for God's sake.

'Pssssst.'

There was no one else nearby. 'I ain't jumping into the shrubbery with you, Erskine. Stop fooling around and sit down. You ain't my type, anyway.'

A moment or two later young Humphrey was lowering himself tentatively onto the bench near me - uneasily, as if the paint might still be wet, or I a dangerous lunatic.

'Don't want to sound preachy,' I said, 'and I know you're seriously worried, but the best way to keep a secret is not to show that you've got it.' I glanced at him. He didn't look convinced. 'You and I have been seen together, in public, more than once. Nothing unnatural in us being seen together again. Here, have a gasper: warm you up.'

He was wearing what looked like three coats and a scarf

and an enormous fur hat. But his shoes were feeble fancy things that meant the rest of the insulation was wasted.

He took the cigarette, dropped it, lit it, coughed, and then settled down a bit.

'That's the spirit', I said. 'Looks like you're having a hard time of it.' His cold-reddened nose waggled up and down between hat and scarf. 'What's the trouble?'

I was trying to take him seriously, though from the moment we'd decoded the 'HE', I'd been wondering if the 'gravest fears' about tonight were because someone had lost a tutu or the second bassoon was playing flat.

He stared at me uneasily. He took a long pull on his cig. He coughed. 'Yes', he said at last. 'I'm - You'll think - I don't - Perhaps you-'

'Erskine,' I put into the inevitable gap, 'jump into it, there's a good chap. Much more of this and my arse'll be a permanent feature of St James's Park. You're an intelligent, reflective man. You're working on some serious and sensitive stuff. I'm here because I know you're worth listening to. Nothing you can say will shock me or upset me or bore me. Crack on.'

Mostly untrue, but when young officers start to fret you have to steady them before you get any sense. I'm lucky: over-thinking has never been much of a risk with me.

'Right you are', he said. 'Thanks, Delamere. Well, you know the Russians - and the Latvians, and so on.' I nodded; help him build up a bit of steam. 'Well, one or two of them - and some of their friends here in London certainly - they're more than a bit wild. In political terms. And, well...'

'And in terms of blowing up police wagons with people like me in them.'

'Oh yes! Gosh, yes, of course. Well, you understand then.'

'I understand.'

'So, anyway, this evening is the next public event in the Russian artistic tour - a ballet, yes?'

'Yes. Thanks for the invite.'

'Oh, you got it? Splendid. I do hope- Anyway- It's *Harlequinade*, by the way.'

'Well, that's good news at least.'

'Something a little jollier for English audiences, they thought.'

'Very wise.'

'From the classical repertoire, not the avant-garde pieces that Diaghilev is trying in Par-'

'Erskine…'

'Yes. Anyway, I was there this morning when they were getting settled in the theatre. Keep an eye, negotiate any little disagreements with the management. And two back-stage passes were taken.'

He paused for effect, his busy breath a cloud in front of the red nose.

'Sorry, lost me there.'

'Yes, sorry. Well, companies and theatres always try to keep a lid on the number of people wandering around the back of a theatre: try to stop pilfering, avoid confusion. Stage door guarded, only authorized people. This event is strictly ticketed for the public, too; no late-comers, no tickets on the door. And because this visit is big diplomatic business, special guest in the box and quite a few dignitaries in the audience, the front doors will be guarded too. Police presence.'

'And these passes…'

'So, a strictly limited number of back-stage passes have been printed. Red things, numbered, just a few dozen of them. And they're only being handed out to people who are known and who have a definite need to have free access to the theatre, front and back. Performers, obviously. Stage-hands. Few people like me helping to manage the visit. A pass gets you through the stage door into the back of the theatre. And it gets you past the policemen into the public areas. Free run of the place.'

'And some have… gone missing?'

The well-wrapped head shook. 'Not missing; taken. One

of the chaps who was with us at the flying display, one of the visiting chorus; a big chap-'

'Jacob.'

That impressed him. 'Yes - Yes, that's him. How-'

'Never mind.'

'It was quite deliberate. One of his companions created a distraction - an argument, a fall - when the passes were being handed out. And his body was blocking what he was doing. But there was a mirror, and I saw him take them. And - well, what with poor Kyril's death too - I'm awfully worried what he might be up to.'

I nodded. He had me worried now.

Big Jacob. Jacob of the firing squad. Jacob who I had provoked. Jacob who had not come to London to wait but to act.

'You told your Foreign Office people about this, or the police?'

'Of course, but... I don't know if they think it's that serious, and I just thought that - well, you know these people a bit now, and you seem to be...'

Two magic tickets for two of Jacob's friends.

Erskine's voice had trailed off. He could see I wasn't paying attention.

George. George with his Mauser and his explosives. George with free run of a theatre full of London high society.

'Erskine, any chance you could get me a couple of those red passes?'

41.

The Alhambra Theatre has one of the most spectacular frontages in London; but I went in the back way.

The main facade on Leicester Square is a great pyramid of domes and lights and fancy windows. Like a Chinaman's wedding cake, done in the grand style. It's been rebuilt three of four times in my life, and there's a fair chance they'll have changed it again before you read this. It's always been one of the best places in London for popular musical entertainment, its downstairs bar and endless passages a favourite spot for all other kinds of amusement besides. My Uncle Robert - who tended, once into the second bottle of port, to become spectacularly informative to my younger self about the more sordid side of London or any other city I could name - would get quite misty-eyed at the recollection of what - and who - one could get up to at the Alhambra in the 1870s. I remember family whispers to the effect that he'd been involved the night the whole place burned down in '82. But the Delamere family was always so prone to unmentionable truths and uncontrollable lies that it's never possible to know.

Anyway, Quinn and I used the magic passes that Humphrey Erskine had given us to get in through the Alhambra's Stage Door. There was an ancient sinewy midget on guard who looked at them pretty closely, but let us in smartly enough once he was satisfied.

'Anything in particular we're looking for, sir?'

'Villainous foreigners, Quinn. Barrels of gunpowder. Alarm clocks attached to mysterious boxes.' He stood waiting patiently. I shrugged. 'No idea. Hopefully we know it when we see it.' He nodded agreeably and we strode on down the corridor, exposed brickwork and crumbling plasterwork and an alarming mixture of old gas lighting and new roughly-installed electrics.

It wasn't long before the ballet was due to start, and the place was bustling. In the uneven glow from the lamps, ghostly figures hurried back and forth past us, girls in the standard tights and tutus, chaps in fancy Harlequin and Pierrot outfits, stage-hands in rough working gear. Quinn and I stood out, he in his smartest regular suit and I in my white tie and tails, and we attracted a few glances. But no one had time to stop and challenge us.

We came to a junction in the corridors. 'I think', I said,

'we just want the lie of the land for now. How does this side of the shop join up with the front? If someone wants to get at one of the bigwigs in the audience, that's what they'll have to manage.'

It was a hell of a warren, but we kept pushing in the right sort of direction and soon enough came through a door which divided the two worlds. We'd opened a plain, dusty, heavy thing, and found that its other side shone with lacquer and gilt. A step took us from bare floorboards to thick crimson carpet. The dancers and stage-hands who'd rustled past us in the back-stage dusk were replaced with a scrum of London's finest, starched shirts and fancy frocks and gold and jewels glittering under the lights. Every dozen yards there hung an enormous chandelier, blazing its glare over the luxury.

I fluttered my pass at a chap minding the door; he snatched and checked it. I don't say I felt at ease, but at least we blended in more naturally now. I didn't want to be noticed on this side of the door either. I kept an eye on the faces, though. I might get an idea who the intended target was. I might also have a chance of avoiding certain individuals.

I'd a perfect right to be there, of course: no law against spending an evening at the ballet, however dull it is. But more and more I was feeling that I didn't want any of the various parties in this mess getting too sure an idea of where I was and what I was up to.

With perfect timing, through the drifting forest of evening wear I glimpsed Ilya Ilyich Ilyin, the little whispering Russian villain who'd called on me with Faversham. We were following the curving corridor that ran around the grand tier of boxes, the fanciest of the fancy, and Ilyin was standing by the door to one box staring up at a couple of hefty lads and apparently giving them instructions.

A ballet enthusiast himself, perhaps. Russian, of course; why not? But Ilya Ilyich Ilyin didn't seem the kind of chap to take an evening off, and certainly not during an official visit to London. His amusements would always be deliberate, and usually unpleasant. The sort who'd started out torturing cats at the age of seven and never looked back. So, unsurprisingly, there was some official Russian presence in the audience for this Russian ballet performance.

We managed to pass by unseen, in the lee of a boisterous group of chortling 'what-ho'-ers.

There were uniformed policemen around; many more than would be normal. British bobbies, I mean; no doubt there were some un-uniformed Russian ones skulking in the crowd too, if they'd been able to find adequate suits.

A dozen yards farther on I managed to slip round the blind side of Inspector Ernest Bunce. He was eyeing the crowd grumpily, looking about as out of place as I felt.

'Delamere!'

Damn.

'Why, it's Faversham!' I said to Faversham; probably not news to him.

'Not sure I'd have pegged you for a ballet connoisseur', he said down his nose.

'Never miss it', I said. 'Like Rugby football, but with better tunes.' I leaned towards him. 'And, er, since you asked me to keep an eye on, er…' - a little pantomime of looking around myself - 'our foreign friends, I naturally wanted to be here.' And I gave him a huge wink, and walked on. No idea what he'd have made of that daft performance, but if I could give him the impression that I was vaguely co-operative as well as half-witted, it was all to the good.

I pressed on. Bustle and jostle, all well-dressed; a few faces I recognized but were too snooty to recognize me. In the distance, a glimpse of elegance that I was almost certain was Victoria. No surprise: this was probably the most fashionable ticket in town tonight. And yes, beside her was the handsome profile of Harriet Vanstone. I began to adjust my speed to the current of people so that I wouldn't be seen: my life's always been defined by having to keep my distance from that crowd, and tonight it was more important than usual. Victoria belonged in a brighter, safer world; I didn't like tempting her out of it and I hesitated to venture into it, not without wiping my feet.

Quinn and I were half way round the arc now, to the point where the grand staircase was delivering the top-priced punters up to their boxes. And there I got another jolt.

Another familiar face, this one coming up the stairs. Blonde, and coldly beautiful. The dress conservative - higher and fuller than some of the girls were risking this season - but all the key bits of the landscape emphasized right enough. I hesitated because I'm a simple sort of animal, and I hesitated because again I was trying to remember.

Her style matched her beauty: a touch haughty. She knew who she was and how she was and where she was going, and damn the rest of you for dull obstacles.

The field of the flying machines; the briefest exchange of courtesies. She'd been escorted by a chap in uniform then, and when I finally dragged my eyes in the direction of her consort tonight I saw a uniform again. Might have been the same chap. The uniform was fancier tonight: parade dress for a night at the Opera.

And before that, outside my rooms: the glimpse of a blonde head in a carriage window.

I pressed on. Behind us a bell clanged, the audience being chivvied to their seats. Almost immediately the kerfuffle in the curving corridor dropped away: a few hurrying feet; the soft thumping of the last well-lined box doors being shut on their inhabitants.

Each of the boxes had a number painted on the door, and under it a little brass frame to hold a name card, the owner or temporary resident of the box. Some of the cards were hand-written, some - presumably the permanents - were printed.

Dimly I heard a trumpet fanfare, and then applause: the evening's senior dignitaries being welcomed to their box somewhere behind me.

I was half-aware of the name-cards. Sure enough, near the end of the curved corridor, the printed 'AYSGARTH': Victoria and Harriet Vanstone were just the other side of the door, enjoying their pleasant world of music and no Bolshevik plots.

A great blast of sound came muffled through the walls: the orchestra launching into the overture.

The evening's entertainment had begun. The clock was ticking.

42.

Quinn and I completed our loop round the grand tier of boxes and found ourselves back at a door corresponding to the one we'd come through on the other side. Again there was a lad in theatre uniform guarding it.

Again we were only let through after a careful check. They were taking the business seriously. And big Jacob's stolen passes could be crucial.

In the back-stage gloom, we took a moment for our eyes to adjust. A stretch of bare corridor, a turn just ahead.

Then we took another moment while I tried to work out what the hell I was playing at. Longish moment.

One of Quinn's many virtues is silence. Now and then the urge comes upon him for what passes for Cornish wit - and after centuries surviving on tin mining and Atlantic fishing, hellish bleak trades both, they've a damn' peculiar sense of humour - and one has to grin and bear it. Otherwise he knows that I'm never the chatty sort, and he knows that if I'm trying to think about something it's best to give me a wide berth and plenty of time.

The turn in the corridor gave onto a straight stretch. Running along the wall, starting at the corner, was a thin table covered with the odds and sods of the stage and back-stage ready for quick use. Tools, pots and brushes, a tray of masks, a tambourine.

If it was a bomb and it was already in place, it was unlikely I'd be able to work out where it was or do anything about it. I'd have to hope it wasn't in place, and that I'd bump into the bomber setting up and be able to stop him or warn the police. If it was gun or knife, again I'd have to hope to spot the assassin *en route*, once he was drawing attention to himself but before he'd reached journey's end. All very chancy.

Quinn was still waiting patiently. 'I think', I said as I drifted past the table, 'this is where we split up.'

The police ought to be able to manage the basic body-guarding, whether or not they'd taken Erskine's warning seriously. Even old Bunce would raise an eyebrow if he saw a ferocious foreign anarchist hammering at the Royal Box with a hatchet. Faversham was an ass, but I assumed basic training and competence in the Special Branch. And I assumed a lot of competence in little Ilyin.

'We're keeping our eyes open for the chap who's out of place,', I murmured, 'the chap with too much on his mind. And ideally, we're not being spotted our–'

I'd reached the first junction in the mess of corridors and I guess I'd been aware of footsteps and murmurs from round the corner, but it was only when I glanced round it that I stopped and stepped back. That of course meant I bumped into Quinn. He was too smart to swear or make a noise, but he stumbled a step, and that was enough to knock into the table. His considerable bulk jolted it some, and its feet scratched loudly along the floor and beyond the corner, and everything on it was shifting and wobbling, and the sound hadn't been so bad but in that instant I saw a pot, precariously perched and now falling. I jumped forwards and caught it as it went, and then I was stumbling but Quinn had gripped my shoulder.

There we froze, Quinn holding me and me holding the pot of whatever it was. Paint or paste or something, pretty foul-smelling with a brush stuck in it. A glance at each other.

A breath.

Fortunately the man coming down the corridor had been looking at whoever was with him. He hadn't seen me; I was telling myself he hadn't seen me, my head appearing and then disappearing. But I'd seen him: it was big Jacob.

The door to the front-of-house was our only escape, but at that moment I heard it click open. I dumped my pot on top of whatever was on the corner of the table. Quinn was knocking at a door and opening it at the same time.

Nobody screamed or swore, which was an above-average result for us.

I shut the door, leaned against it. Approaching from the front-of-house door I could hear a voice calling quietly: 'Curtain well up; curtain well up', and walking onwards and repeating it intermittently.

Our room was spartan and lit by a single lamp. Some kind of stage and costume store. Rolls of fabric. Two enormous curtains slumped and abandoned in dust. A large mirror, dominating one wall, smeared and blotched. Bits of scenery: a tree; an oriental gateway; prison bars. I thought of Tosca, and poor Kyril coming out of his prison to get shot. Half a dozen trunks and crates lying open, with remnants of costume in them.

I kept my ear to the door a moment longer. No sound. The announcer lad had continued his round, and perhaps he'd made Jacob hesitate.

Quinn had done a quick survey of the room, as was his habit, and was now waiting patiently again.

'We're making ourselves a bit bloody useless at the moment, Quinn.'

The slightest nod.

'We split up, as I say. One takes front of house; patrol of the main lobby, the corridors leading to the auditorium. Nice and casual, just popped out for a piss or a ciggy, eyes peeled for bad men bent on mischief.' He nodded. 'The other takes this damn' maze behind the scenes. Same detail.'

'Aye sir.' He looked the question.

'Problem back here is that we stand out in our gents' evening wear, with everyone else in costume or stage overalls. Good chance big Jacob spots us, and he's bound to be suspicious. If he's as rum as he seems, suspicious means dangerous. And I don't know how many he's got with him, and I don't know the terrain; so I don't fancy a mill.'

'No sir.'

'So whoever's on back-stage duty needs a change of kit. In the gloom and the bustle, there's a chance we pass unnoticed.'

Quinn nodded.

We both turned, and looked at the open trunks and crates with their remnants of clothing.

We looked at the trunks and crates for quite a while.

It didn't change the fact that the only thing they contained were ballet costumes.

Eventually Quinn turned to me, dark and uncomfortable.

'Followed you alone into Jo'burg, sir. Follow you anywhere, you know that. But…'

There's no mistaking a Cornishman with his mind made up.

'I know, Quinn. Wouldn't ask you. Privilege of rank, etcetera.'

'Right you are, sir.' He was looking relieved and relaxed all of a sudden. '*Noblesse oblige*, all that.'

'Bugger off, Quinn.'

'Aye sir.'

'Oh, and you'd better take this.' I pulled my Webley out of my jacket and handed it over.

Quinn nodded, and put the revolver in an outside pocket, and turned to go.

'Quinn.' He turned back. 'Not a word. Ever.'

He nodding understanding. Manly sympathy. A quick check that the corridor was clear, then the door closed behind him and I was alone.

They're damned odd things to put on, dancers' tights.

Gave me additional respect for the more graceful half of the species, having to deal with stockings every morning; no wonder they take so long to dress. Even more challenging - in my now expert opinion - is the stage-standard all-in-one arrangement. I've never known a garment fight back so hard. I put my toe through the knee of one pair and had to chuck them and start again. You get halfway through and there's the strong sense you've got lost and then your balance goes and you're hopping clumsily about with one foot all squeezed and the other lashed up under your arse somewhere.

With a fair bit of swearing and bumping into things I got there in the end, both legs covered and the tights pulled more or less even, and bloody silly I looked too. The only top halves available were flimsy patchwork jerkins, a little bright and artistic for my taste and cut to a silly shortened length, as if all the Mrs Harlequins had made a mistake with the laundry. As for downstairs... I don't think my gentleman's accessories are the worst in the business - had one or two positive comments over the years - but I don't choose to draw attention to them. Like politics and privvies, you know they're there but you don't get a close look unless you really need to. Now it all felt very cramped and very exposed. How on earth the chappies dance like this I can't imagine.

I snuck out into the corridor, particularly cautious. My attempt at blending in had left me feeling the most ridiculously exposed man in London.

I moved onwards into the warren. I was trying to look confident. I felt absurd. More troubling than the idea of George or Jacob recognizing me and doing violence was the idea of them recognizing me and falling about laughing.

From far away, through all those floors and walls and doors, the distant sound of the orchestra. Act I of *Harlequinade* in full swing, back in a world of gentility and elegance.

I took a breath, and a more confident step towards the corner in the corridor.

Instantly there were footsteps and a voice from right round the corner. I funked it and turned away again, trying not to hurry. I knew that voice by now. I heard the steps and the murmuring men, big Jacob and his pal, just a few yards behind me. I walked past my changing room, no time to duck in, they'd see my face and know me immediately.

I had to keep going, except I was rounding the last turn and now I was trapped. In front of me a few yards of corridor, and the magic door to the world of carpets and gilt and high society, and I couldn't go through, I just couldn't, not like this. Behind me Jacob and friend, reaching the corner and about to see me and know me.

And then - it shattered me - a great clattering.

43.

For a moment I'd no idea what was going on.

Very well, for much of the year 1910 I'd no idea what was going on, but that moment was one of particular bewilderment.

My heart started to beat again. The clattering had been right in front of me, at the corner. Jacob and t'other chap had knocked into something and the clattering - hell, my tin of paint? - had been followed by a burst of hissing and presumably swearing. Take it from me, Latvian swearing sounds pretty fruity.

Then silence again. Again I waited to see them, to be seen.

But nothing.

Were they waiting for me?

Silence.

I slipped closer to the turn in the corridor, straining to hear the slightest breath, a shuffled foot.

Nothing. I stuck my head round. The corridor was empty.

Damn this. I tried another breath and started forwards. I am doing nothing wrong. I am doing nothing wrong. I look pretty damn' silly, but I am doing nothing wrong.

The door to the room where Quinn and I had hidden was slightly open. Through it, I heard murmuring. I continued a step or two, then risked stopping and looking back.

Handy: through the gap I could glimpse the big grimy mirror, and in the mirror I could see the two men in the room. I couldn't have sworn it was Jacob, but the figure was big enough, and where else could he be? Still the murmuring, and it seemed rather agitated. They'd obviously been up to no good, and been as startled as I by the blessed tin of paint, and had beat a tactical retreat to regroup.

I shifted a fraction, straining to see something more through the gap in the door.

I saw two things of particular interest.

Firstly, the chap who wasn't big enough to be Jacob was taking his trousers off.

Secondly, the chap who was big enough to be Jacob was holding a pistol for him.

44.

So there I am, loitering in the back-stage fug of the Alhambra, dressed in tights, watching conspiracy through a crack in a door. There were a couple of figures further on - stage hands, or dancers wearing coats over costumes to keep warm. It couldn't be many moments before Jacob or his chum happened to glance at the mirror and see me seeing them.

The discomfort got me moving, and the movement got me thinking.

The object of this present madness was to spot presumably Jacob or a confederate of his up to no good.

I had, surely, just done that.

The no good involved the pistol. Jacob had no cause to be holding it like that unless it was for the other chap once he'd changed his clothes. Presumably the change was to enable the no good.

I'd got a dozen yards farther down the corridor, and now I turned and retraced my steps, as fast as I could without being obvious.

The no good was going to happen among the dignitaries, presumably in one of the boxes. The action was about to move from back of stage to front of house. I was in the wrong place.

If I could get through the magic door first, I wouldn't be following or chasing any more; I'd have the advantage of time and position.

Why on earth was he changing his clothes? He surely wasn't going to do the deed disguised as a dancer.

The paint. Paint, or paste, or whatever: he'd spilled some on him, so much that it would attract attention, so he had to change. The damn' paint had bought me time, put me temporarily ahead of the game.

I was through the door into the shiny world and the chap guarding it didn't even glance at my pass. The benefit of my ballet costume. Obviously, no one in their right mind would wear such foolishness if he wasn't a dancer.

I felt horrible. There'd been no chance of changing back into my own clothes, and now I had to prowl the front of house looking like a plucked chicken in a fancy waistcoat. Fortunately we were still in Act I of the ballet, so the plush glittering corridors were deserted.

I made it to the grand tier, the long curve with the boxes for all the big cheeses. I began to follow it round to where the biggest cheeses would be. I wasn't sure what I was looking for: a vantage point from where I could see the gunman coming without being too obvious myself, perhaps, a point where I could intercept him, a point where him having the pistol would be proof enough he was a wrong'un.

I didn't find it. From just around the curve I heard a sudden explosion of voices. The distinctive sneer of

Faversham the Special Branch man was one. But this wasn't snooty Faversham; this was an alarmed Faversham. 'Gone?' he was saying loudly. 'How long ago? Why was no one with him?' There was another voice: quieter, less distinct. It might have been the sinister murmur of Ilya Ilyich Ilyin.

Whoever it was, they were coming towards me. I didn't know enough to be able to persuade them. Besides, there wasn't one chance in hell I was going to let myself be seen by Inspector Ernest Bunce looking like I was looking. I glanced around hastily. Nowhere: the corridor was fancily decorated but desperately short of hiding places. I couldn't run: worst thing for approaching policemen to see. I couldn't duck into one of the -

AYSGARTH. I was right by Victoria's box. I don't say I felt too cheerful doing it, but a breath and then I was inside, pushing the door to but not closing it.

Fortunately it was only Victoria Carteret and Harriet Vanstone in there. On a table next to me there was a silver tray: bottle of champagne and two glasses. The two women heard the door open, of course, and both turned.

I didn't have time for explanations and my eyes were still adjusting to the darkness and God knows what I'd have said anyway. I just sort of stood there a moment, until I was sure they weren't going to scream or summon the nearest policeman.

'Don't tell me:' Victoria said softly, not even looking at me any more; 'you left your ticket in your other trousers.'

She glanced at Vanstone, a shake of the head, the weary inevitability of me turning up in an opera box semi-naked. Then she turned back to what was happening on the stage.

Harriet Vanstone gazed at me a moment longer, her face illuminated in a way I'd not seen before. For once, that sober self-contained spirit was gloriously amused.

I had eye and ear to the crack in the door. Sure enough, there was Faversham. No sign of sinister whispering Ilyin. 'Ah, Bunce!' And there was Bunce. All present and correct.

'Hell of a business. Russian Minister of War has gone missing from his box.'

45.

No more than a grumble from Bunce. To his credit, he's never one to flap: if you gave foreign politicians boxes at the Alhambra, what could you expect anyway? 'Russian security are trying to keep it quiet, but we can't be having that. Not with the Home Secretary here as well.' Gods' sakes, Churchill had turned up here as well? 'If we lose him, it's a national humiliation.' Bunce nodded. He'd been getting that sort of line from Faversham quite a bit. 'Full search! The whole premises. Word to the men on each door.'

The lack of acknowledgement showed what Bunce thought of Faversham giving him orders, but he was away briskly enough to summon his troops.

I was trying to work it out. The Russian chappy disappearing was obviously the big worry now. But was his disappearance part of Jacob's plan? Or was it a complication? Could the Minister somehow be got back-stage, where the man with the gun would be able to knock him off unseen? Winston Churchill now, too…

I needed to be back-stage again. Handily, it was where my ridiculous outfit would give me the advantage.

'I say…' Vanstone's usual low murmur was further softened by the circumstances. I saw that she was still watching the ballet, but leaning towards Victoria. 'Delamere's got rather good legs, hasn't he?'

'Oh, my dear: Harry's legs are marvellous. I wanted him to let me keep one.'

'I'm standing right here', I whispered harsh.

Victoria turned. 'And with such poise.'

'Must dash, anyway', I went on. 'Thanks for the hospitality as ever. Save me a sandwich next time. Oh, hang on…'

I was still trying to stand back in the box, invisible to the adjacent boxes or anyone in the auditorium. I pointed across the theatre. 'There - t'other side, four... five boxes round from the end.' It was my acquaintance from the flying display - possibly my watcher in the street. 'You know everyone, Victoria: who's the blonde?'

'You chose life without me, Harry; it's not in the best taste to expect me to play matchmaker.'

'Quickly, woman!'

'Like a little boy at a sweetshop window...' She tutted, and lifted her opera glasses. 'Goodness,' she murmured, suddenly interested; 'Didn't know she was in England.'

'Who is it?'

'Good old Whipped Cream...' She turned back to us.

'Sorry,' I said, 'are you having some sort of fit? Hallucinations, or...'

'Gosh yes, I had the most extraordinary dream: Harry Delamere was dressed as a ballet dancer.'

'You're hilarious.'

She glanced at my legs again. 'We must naturally defer to you as the comic expert, Harry.' A heavy tut. 'Caterina von Falkenhayn. We had a term or two together: finishing school in Geneva.' She glanced across the Alhambra auditorium, and turned back to me. 'Damned arrogant. Ruthless. Bit of a swot. Had an uncle in the German Foreign Ministry and was going to travel with him or something. Unlike most of us, she always preferred the philosophy and the healthy excursions rather than the arts and socials. Splendid thighs.'

A little more detail than I'd bargained for; not for the first time, I was feeling what a disappointing education I'd had. Vanstone had turned away and was considering our blonde subject through her opera glasses.

'And the - the cream thing?'

'We used to call her Whipped Cream.'

'Of course. Because...'

'Cream because rich, in every way. Cream because elite

and elitist. Seem to remember she liked the stuff too. And Whipped because, well… we joked she probably liked that sort of stuff too.'

Blimey. And now tracking Harry Delamere around London.

'I said ruthless, Harry.' Her face was more serious now. 'Don't get in too deep.'

'As you say: having to plough on without you now.'

She wasn't smiling. 'I can assume that something's wrong?'

I nodded. 'Suspect a Bolshevik gunman's about to shoot the Russian Minister of War.'

'How tiresome.'

'Keep your heads down, yes?' They said nothing. They watched me go, expressions calm and comfortable. Two women less likely to keep their heads down I've never met.

I stuck my head back in. 'Victoria, what did they call you at finishing school?'

'Go away, Harry.'

46.

The corridor was temporarily clear of Favershams and Bunces and others who might laugh at my particulars. I moved quickly towards the dividing door. There were a couple of men in bad suits arguing with the doorman: thick accents and simple speech and trying to overawe the chap with their size, except he wasn't having it. A couple of Ilyin's thugs, on the hunt for their missing Minister. I slipped past them and through the door with barely a glance from the doorman; again the benefit of my pass and my costume.

On the other side of the door, back in the underworld, I felt oddly more comfortable. This was where my ghastly disguise worked, and everything was gloomier. I moved through the corridors with greater confidence. As before, I passed occasional fellow-ghosts: one or two in costume; stagehands in their ancient overalls. I brushed past a couple of uniformed policemen who were looking thoroughly lost; not sure they even noticed me.

My earlier reconnaissance with Quinn had given me an idea of the layout: I could cover the ground pretty efficiently. And I knew what I was looking for: either Jacob's gunman, or a lost Russian dignitary. Both ought to be clear enough.

Five minutes calculated wandering brought me back round to an area Quinn and I had kept clear of: the main changing rooms for the dancers. I still wasn't too breezy about being there: unlike the stage hands, the dancers would probably be able to recognize who was and wasn't one of their own. Most of the company were on stage, but I passed a few chatting in the corridor or lurking in doorways: understudies, would it be? or characters who didn't appear until later Acts? I looked purposeful and kept on walking, trying at the same time to spot anything out of the ordinary.

Fat chance I had of recognizing that, of course, with no sense of what ordinary looked like back-stage at the ballet. Then again, I guessed Jacob and friend wouldn't be active around this busier part of the shop either. Each of the doors I was passing now had a star on it.

Several yards ahead of me I saw a young woman in a maid's costume, leaning against the wall and smoking. She glanced at me, then went back to her cigarette.

Couldn't see how you'd have a maid character in the *Harlequinade*...

The old brain continued to stagger onwards: not a costume, of course. This one actually was a maid - presumably to one of the star ballerinas. Just as I was reaching that brilliant deduction, another figure appeared beyond her, walking towards us. Wearing a policeman's uniform, and surely that wasn't a dancer's costume either. Not with those boots.

The maid saw him more or less as I did, and she took a

quick couple of steps towards him and then pressed back out of his path in one of the doorways. He glared at her, and then he glared at me, and we went our separate ways. He was looking a bit uncomfortable. Inspector Bunce had told him to search, and so search he would, but he wasn't sure.

I was a few yards past her when I realized what an odd movement it had been by the maid. If she wanted to get out of the policeman's way, why had she first moved towards him? The corridor wasn't that narrow, and any instinctive movement should have taken her the other way.

I turned the next corner, and stopped. Her instinct hadn't been to avoid the policeman; it had been to block him. There was something through that doorway that she didn't want him seeing.

Just a ballerina with a fear of coppers? I peeked round the corner.

She'd drifted away from the door again, back to her cigarette and mind wandering. Only a few yards away from the door, but I had to make that enough. I started back along the corridor towards her, trusting to a steady pace and the good old costume not to alarm her. As long as she didn't move towards me, as long as she didn't look too close -

I veered suddenly to the door with the star on it and knocked and opened before she'd had a chance to react. 'Terribly sorry, thought this was Ludmilla's', I was saying before the door was even half open. Then it was fully open, just for a moment, and I'd seen all I needed to.

47.

Immediately I was backing away and closing the door and turning to the maid. She was clutching my arm now, alarmed and angry. I gave her my attempt at a roguish smile and pressed my finger to my lips, and then I was away.

In normal circumstances I couldn't have told you the

difference between the Russian Minister of War and my local bicycle repair man. But the chap I'd glimpsed in there had a bald head and an elegant chin-beard and looked pretty Russian, and draped over a chair there'd been a frock-coat with epaulettes like bloody great golden floor-mops and enough medals to satisfy a regiment. Unless the whole Russian General Staff was hiding in the Alhambra tonight, this surely was the missing Minister.

Missing, but apparently not lost. Unless you mean morally.

One hand up the ballerina's tutu, the other rummaging in her multi-coloured bodice, expression somewhere else entirely, the Minister was a ballet connoisseur after my own heart.

I left them to it. I was worrying again. I was in the wrong place again.

The Minister's disappearance had nothing to do with Jacob and his gunman. Not unless the ballerina was another Bolshevik and they were planning assassination by heart-attack. So what was Jacob up to, and where? That heavy-breathing Russian had had me wandering the back-stage corridors for another five wasted minutes. What had been happening out front?

I knew my way round now, and I was through into the front-of-house within thirty seconds. On the way there I'd seen two more uniformed policemen wandering the corridors, and one un-uniformed thug looking about as lost: presumably one of Ilyin's elite, who'd managed to bluff or threaten his way through back-stage.

In the grand tier of boxes, all was quiet. Just the gentle curve of corridor, luxuriant red carpet and gold, and the hanging forests of crystal chandeliers. Not a soul to be seen. In particular, not a policeman to be seen, which was all to the good.

Except it wasn't, was it? If the gunman chose this moment to try something, he'd have a clear run at Winston Churchill or any of London high society. By going absent without leave, that randy Russian had drawn away all of the protection.

Through the doors to the boxes I was passing I could hear the orchestra building up to some big moment. In my plush corridor, I felt very alone and very exposed. Just me, and my over-publicized legs, to try to get in the way of whatever was -

I was halfway round and now I saw movement. Someone coming up the grand staircase.

But it was a regular opera-goer: gentleman's standard tail-coat, white tie, the usual trimmings. I kept going, trying to avoid his eye, hoping he didn't know me. I was passing the centre boxes now, where the grandees were - all but one of them, anyway - and were the policemen were not. I was listening hard, but nothing out of the ordinary: just Act I building to its climax.

I pressed on. Still that damned endless corridor, its empty luxury, curving away into -

Odd time to duck out, surely? Either the chap was very late, or he'd picked an unlikely moment and a long route to get to the lav. I wondered if Quinn had seen him out there. I pressed on. Dressed as we were, I was the one out of place, not he. I pressed -

Surely not. I stopped, turned, just to be sure. I'd not seen clearly in the back-stage corridor, and I'd not wanted to look too closely at the figure coming up the stairs. Surely - He was outside one of the boxes, checking the name on the card. My stopping and turning had caught his attention though, and now he was looking at me.

Jacob's gunman.

Where the hell had he suddenly got himself a full suit of gent's evening wear?

Did he recognize me? His eyes went wider. He knew me for a threat, anyway. In an instant his hand was inside his jacket and out came the pistol and up towards me.

I started to stride towards him.

His pistol was level and firm, but he was backing away - away along the corridor, turning to and fro between me and where he was going.

He didn't want to shoot me; he'd want his first shot to be the one that counted. That's what I told myself as I charged after him. He was halfway to the next box as I reached the one he'd been checking. Still the pistol pointing at my head, still I had to hope, but if I got any closer he'd have to fire and after me he'd still be able to pot one of the dignitaries, long before any of the policemen could get back here. I couldn't stop him, not like this.

I wrenched open the door beside me and ducked into the box. Immediately, a barrage of new impressions: a roar of noise, the orchestra seconds away from the climax of Act I; I couldn't see; except gradually I could, as my eyes adjusted to the gloom of the box and then made out the light from the stage; the box was empty - the wandering Minister?

And then above all that: I suddenly worked out where the gunman must have got his evening suit.

Noise from the adjacent box. I had to move. The cheeky sod! I was clambering out of the box and swinging around over the stalls below and flinging my dancer's leg over into the next box and there were bewildered faces in front of me and all I could think of was that this blasted Bolshevik had pinched my trousers. I was running around the Alhambra dressed like Nellie bloody Navette in the Christmas panto, while he was using my suit to carry out his assassination. A man sitting in the box - another fancy uniform - but all I could see was the figure coming through the door behind him, the pistol up and picking his target. I mean, what the hell is the country coming to, when a chap can't have an evening's entertainment in Leicester Square without some anarchist stealing his gent's conventional to murder people?

Damn, but he was cool though. He'd seen me - he could hardly fail to - and I was stumbling towards him, but still he was looking past me. The Act I climax was roaring in my ears, I was staggering, I was too far away, one shot and he was sure he'd get his man, and then I'd snatched a tray and swung it up and as he fired it caught his pistol barrel. Another wild swing of my tray clattered him round the head, and with a final clash of cymbals Act I of *Harlequinade* was done and the Alhambra was applauding wildly.

48.

We went stumbling out into the corridor. I'd clouted chummy round the head with a drinks tray and he was still looking a bit surprised. But he still had his pistol, too, and all I had was my natural dancer's grace.

Up came the pistol again and I had no time and all I could do was lunge forwards, flailing at his barrel and he fired and another shot went wild and I heard screams, and past the barrel and I punched him as best I could. It wasn't bad and he went staggering back and I followed in, desperate not to give him the yard he needed. But as he fell, by luck or judgement he let go a great swipe with his pistol and the barrel slashed across the side of my head.

We were both falling, and stupefied, and my head was singing and I was trying to see and I tasted blood on my lips. Dimly I made out more figures, people coming out of the boxes for the interval. What I really needed was Quinn, or my own revolver, or preferably both. What I had was double-vision and a headache and a growing crowd of ballet enthusiasts presumably wondering why one of their number was wrestling with a dancer and blocking the way to the bar.

The assassin and I were clambering to our feet, lurching, grasping for vision and then for each other. Again the barrel was swinging towards me and I let my weight send me into him and again we went floundering. He had to try to keep hold of his pistol, which gave me a bit of an advantage in the scuffle and I had one hand round his throat and the other punching anything I could find, but then he caught me in the head again with a fist or the pistol-butt, and I went rolling away gasping.

Another spasm of confusion, a wave of nausea and delirium, and I was finding my feet and remembering which way was up and trying to stand. I needed Quinn, but Quinn was nowhere and he wouldn't be able to reach me in that scrum and he wouldn't have a clean shot.

One man who did have a clean shot was the assassin. Our clumsy dance brought us face to face again, approximately upright and two yards apart. His head was clearing faster than mine, and he knew he had the advantage now, and I saw the bastard smile, and his pistol barrel was level and steady and a yard from my face and he wasn't going to miss.

A shot, an explosion of sound, and the world was light and a shattering pain in my head.

49.

The Webley Mark IV revolver looks big and sounds big and makes a big impression, but it's not for fancy gun-play. Chambering .455 Webley cartridges, it ain't so much shooting out the Ace of Spades as blowing up the whole pack as well as the card table and any over-curious bystanders. For accuracy at any distance, the Webley requires a lot of luck or an especially good eye.

In that moment, I was lost. It was only later that I found out what had happened.

What had happened was Sergeant (retired) Quinn. He'd been patrolling the front of house as detailed, the main atrium and the area thereabouts. He'd been at the front door on Leicester Square when he heard the first shot. He'd have known it immediately for what it was, and he didn't need a second prompt. He came running. Like the Webley he was carrying, Quinn is built for impact rather than speed, but once he gets going he's not easily stopped. He was most of the way up the Alhambra's grand staircase, pistol out, when he met the first of the audience coming down.

Momentum and Cornish manners might have carried him over a dozen of them, but he was fighting a stronger tide and over the open balustrade he'd already seen the predicament I was in. He'd seen he'd never get to me through the crowd in time. He'd seen he wouldn't have a clean shot however close he came. So, standing where he was on the staircase, Quinn had glowered at the alarmed gentlefolk near him, raised the Webley's barrel, taken one long marksman's breath and from a range of two dozen yards blown the chandelier above us out of its mounting. The whole blazing crystal extravaganza crashed down on top of the assassin and me and took us both out of the running.

When I managed to get my eyes open again, my brain had given up its losing battle with reality. I was slumped on the floor and for some reason I was draped in glittering golden chains and my vision was flickering and flashing and I couldn't get my arms or legs to work. Beyond the sparkles in my eyes, there were shadows, figures, murmurs, a mob in evening wear and I think I saw Jacob, or perhaps he was another trick of my crazed head.

The thought of him triggered a faint memory of where I was, of what I was supposed to be doing. Close by me, slumped like me amid the ruins of the chandelier, was the assassin. From somewhere, there was blood. Or perhaps the crimson carpet was starting to soak up into us.

The murmuring sounded concerned, angry, a tide of cries and groans that sloshed around my head. Within it I heard one voice, faint but clearer, 'Harry, get up won't you?' A woman's voice, surely… I seemed to remember that I liked women. 'Harry darling, come along now.' Presumably this was an angel. Pleasant surprise to find myself on the upper deck for the last great voyage rather than in the hold, but perhaps I hadn't been such a bad chap after all.

Then another voice, again a woman's but deeper and firmer. 'Move your damned arse, Delamere, will you? No time to fanny around.' And somehow I was coming upright and stumbling and I had a stronger sense of the crowd around me but it was all shifting and the figures were appearing and disappearing and I was moving through them and then a door opened and then it closed behind me and all the people and the all the noise had gone.

I was in a tiny ante-room, decked out in the usual plush style of the Alhambra, couple of bench seats.

A slap across my face and my whole head rang. 'Harry dear. You need to wake up now.'

'Ow', I said. It was Victoria Carteret. But why had she slapped me? On the same spot where that chap had hit me with his pistol barrel, too. So unfair.

'You have to try to pretend to be normal now.'

'Assassins!' I said. 'Have to hit them with a tray. Dancing everywhere!'

Her face loomed larger and she kissed me. 'Get a grip, darling. And try not to speak.'

'Chandelier!' I called.

'Oh gosh.' She took me by the hand and pulled me through the next door. 'At last!' she said, unnaturally loud. 'My dearest Vladimir, now we can be alone!'

And she'd had the nerve to suggest I'd lost my grip, which hardly - But now two new realities crashed into my bewildered brain. One was that we were in the ladies lavatory, heavy porcelain sinks and gilt and big mirrors and lilac wallpaper everywhere. The other was a girl standing looking at us.

She was in a uniform, similar to others I'd seen around the theatre. Some kind of attendant, to help the ladies with their hats or hand-towels or whatnot. It turned out that the peculiar dialogue was for her benefit. 'Oh Vladimir, how your native tongue electrifies me', Victoria gushed on. Now she turned to the attendant girl. 'Well now, little sister.' Her usual commanding warmth, plus a coin to match the golden decor. 'Time for your cigarette break. This one's out of order for now.' I was just concentrating on trying to stay upright, and the girl didn't spare me a glance. Apparently no surprise to have top-end ladies bringing chaps in tights into the privy for a quick look at the old plumbing during the interval. She did spare the coin in her hand a glance, and offered Lady Victoria Carteret a polite smile and a curtsey and turned to go.

The door opened before she could get to it, and Harriet Vanstone stepped in. The girl was thrown: three's a crowd, and she wasn't sure if that coin had obliged her to be more helpful. She glanced between the two women.

Vanstone patted her cheek. 'I'm the choreographer', she said. 'Pop off now, sweetie.' And off the girl popped. Vanstone found a bolt at the top of the door and we were alone.

That's to say, three of us alone, in the ladies' facility at the Alhambra theatre, with an angry crowd outside no doubt asking why their ballet had included a gunfight and the roof falling in. Presumably the police had one or two questions too.

My head was just starting to clear, and I managed something like normal speech: 'Do ladies often drag ballet dancers into the lav. for a cuddle?'

Less of the warmth from Victoria. 'Do gentlemen ask questions like that?'

'Well, if they're dressed as ballet dancers I think they're entitled to.'

She ignored me and looked at Vanstone. 'I know the window opens because I use it for the occasional smoke, but we'll have to see if it leads anywhere.'

'It does.' Vanstone was already moving towards it. 'Fire escape. Bit of a jump, but easy enough.' She lifted the sash window, and turned back to us. 'I had to shimmy down once.' Victoria looked interested. 'Get away from Roddy Fortescue.'

'Naughty Forte? What on earth were you doing with him?'

'God knows. Keeping him away from the rest of womankind for an evening.'

'Talk about the fate worse than death.'

'I don't mind a bit of the fate worse than death. The clumsy repartee, though, and the feeble attempts to maul one, are a fate far worse than the fate worse than death.'

'Ghastly.' Victoria shuddered. 'Great flabby, clammy hands.'

'Fascinating though this is...' I began, rather terse.

'I'm sorry, Harry; do you suddenly feel competent enough to contribute?'

'Well...' I tried to sound more polite. 'I'm just losing track of all the fates. And getting a bit chilly.' I was also starting to feel the fact that my movements for the last half-hour had been essentially barefoot.

'No need to worry. You're not in Harriet's league, but you should be able to manage the fire escape. Then home as unobtrusive as possible, large whisky and go easy on the soda, then put some proper trousers on - if not before.'

Vanstone chipped in. 'I told your man you'd be coming down, so he should be waiting out there. I say, he's rather sound, isn't he? Cool shot that.'

They were all mad.

For Harriet Vanstone, though, madness was apparently normal. That poise, that handsome profile, were utterly untroubled. 'Incidentally, in the press I got him to give me your pistol. Easier for him to get past the police now.' She patted her handbag.

'Right', I said. 'Thanks. I can take it off you.' I offered my hand.

'I hardly' - Victoria hit the word sharply - 'think that's wise.'

'Besides,' Vanstone added, with a malicious glance at my legs, 'where exactly do you propose to hide it?'

50.

Having a chandelier fall on my head and escaping down the outside of the theatre while wearing dancer's tights was the last of that day's unpleasantnesses. Reckon that even old Uncle Robert probably never managed quite so lively a visit to the Alhambra, even when he burned the place to the ground. But he was always a sight more elegant in his adventures.

The next day's unpleasantnesses started promptly. I was half-way through my first cigarette and mulling the benefits of emigrating when Quinn passed me the *Daily Chronicle*. Mostly the continuing General Election campaign which had my radical pals so het up, plus the usual gushing excitement about aeronautical developments: various lunatics competing for some big prize. A last-minute piece on page 4 announced that the police were seeking Sir Henry Delamere in connection with a disturbance at the Alhambra the previous evening. I was scowling at that, and trying to brush the ash off the armchair without Quinn seeing, when he passed me the *Morning Post*. A headline at the bottom of page 7 announced that Sir Henry Delamere had been killed in a disturbance at the Alhambra the previous evening.

Beat that, Uncle Robert.

'Bit disappointing my death doesn't make the front page', I said.

'Sure the *Racing Post*'d give you your due, sir.'

Being declared dead by the *Morning Post* was only a warm-up unpleasantness. I was double-checking that neither paper had mentioned a mysterious stranger in tights, when there was a heavy knock at the front door. Quinn and I glanced at each other, weary certainty.

Thirty seconds later, Bunce and Faversham were in their usual places in my sitting room. 'You chaps ever think about taking turns?' I said, trying and failing to sound jovial. 'Must be costing the taxpayer a fortune in bus-fares, you tooling about together.' They ignored me. They were both looking rather forbidding. I focused on Faversham: 'You find your missing Minister?'

'Mm.' He wasn't paying attention. 'More interested' - it was drawn out in the usual Faversham nasal sneer - 'in what happened to the missing Delamere.'

I tried to looked confused; not so difficult. I tried to look innocent; trickier. 'What do you mean?' I said.

'Come on, Delamere…' Bunce's sour growl. 'Don't play dumb.'

'Wait - you don't mean that assassination story was true? Someone had a go at one of the dignitaries?'

They glanced at each other. 'Well,' Faversham whined at last, 'it's not entirely clear.'

'How can it not be clear?'

'It seems there was a disturbance in one of the boxes - two intruders got in, and there was a scuffle. But it wasn't the box of the Russian War Minister, nor of our Home Secretary. No apparent threat to either of them.' Might want to give the big Russian twenty four hours, I was thinking, see if he's picked up a dose of the Piccadilly Itch from his lady friend. 'The trouble was in the corridor. Witness statements all very muddled, but the result was a man lying dead; stabbed.'

Stabbed? And then I remembered: my foggy visions as I emerged from the wreckage of the chandelier; an uncertain glimpse of Jacob. Was that how he tidied up a loose end? His would-be assassin had failed, and couldn't be left to talk, and so the big Bolshevik had stabbed him in the middle of that scrummage? God, but the nerve of it…

'Most interesting thing of all' - as ever, Inspector Ernest Bunce was at his least attractive when triumphant - 'is that the laundry tag shows that the the dead man was wearing your coat, Delamere.' He'd put a clumsy note of fake wonder in his voice. 'For one happy moment I thought it was you lying there. We would be fascinated' - he thumped the word like a hesitant suspect - 'to hear how that came to be.'

'That's a very good question, Bunce', I said. 'And I'm glad you asked it.' He waited. 'A very good question indeed. In fact... I was going to be filing a report with the police this morning. Wouldn't normally trouble high-ups like you with this sort of thing, but-'

'You getting to the point anytime soon?'

'It was stolen.'

'Stolen?' from Faversham, surprised.

'Stolen...' from Bunce, scornful. 'Pickpocket sort of scenario, was it? All of sudden, dearie me, where can it have gone, had it just a moment ago? Getting bolder all the time, them. I know your sort are supposed to be daft, Delamere, but come off it.'

'Not like that, obviously.'

'Had it off you at gunpoint? Your suits that irresistible are they?'

'I wasn't wearing it at the moment.'

'Eh?'

'Look, this isn't the sort of thing I expect to have to talk about. Not in earshot of the staff.' I nodded towards the kitchen and Quinn. 'You two are men of the world, ain't you?' They continued to glare. I pretended - or amplified - my exasperation. 'God's sake... I was on the prowl. Bit of the old gallantry. Enjoying a private dance with one of the ballerinas. Can-Can, did-did. And while my back was turned some toerag pinched my kit.'

Faversham was looking rather shocked. Bunce was still sceptical. 'We'll need a name', he said grumpily. 'To get a witness statement.'

'Go to hell, Bunce; there's a statement. No ladies' names, not under my roof, not from me, not ever. Come off it: you've been policing London since forever; you know what it's like. Guarantee you half the Metropolitan Police high command and more than a few MPs have been back-stage at the ballet this week.'

'Do you mean to tell me' - Faversham seemed genuinely

shocked - 'that at a time like this - anarchists committing outrages in the public streets, our national reputation at stake, when you've been specifically asked for your assistance in a matter of the greatest sensitivity, right when the police are hunting for a missing foreign grandee - you're off philandering with a bloody dancer?'

'It's those tights they wear', I said. 'Can't resist them.'

51.

I'd hoped the police would bugger off and leave me alone. I'd given them a story that - while it wasn't what you'd call 'true' - was at least feasible enough to stop them arresting me for breach of the peace, aiding and abetting, treason, or public indecency. I needed time to myself and a bit of fresh air. Chance to think things over.

Fat chance. I was still trapped in the business enough for them to make trouble for me if they cared to. Bunce just wanted me where he could see me, and Faversham made a couple of nasty remarks about how pleased our Russian friends would be to know I was co-operating so actively. I was more or less ordered to join them at the day's committee meeting. I guess that they were feeling a bit edgy: meeting with the brass and they hadn't got much to show for another few days' investigating. Having me with them would show how active they were. Or I could just be presented as an early suspect; not sure what he's guilty of but he's something to be going on with.

As instructed, I sat at the back and kept mum. Fortunately none of big men at the conference table knew me well enough to wonder why I wasn't either arrested or dead. Off and on I paid attention to the discussion, but it seemed to be just the same as last time. Another mysterious foreigner had carelessly allowed his death to interrupt a British cultural event, and what were Special Branch doing about it?

Talking about it, was the strong impression from Faversham. But as ever he talked about it well: one got the impression of armies of efficient policemen, weeks of sleepless effort, triumph imminent, when in fact the only real action was one confused baronet in tights lamping someone with a tray.

Then there was a bit of chat about how the big visit was going, Russia's War Minister apparently enjoying himself - you don't know the half of it, I was thinking - and his Assistant doing all sorts of good things in the margins. All very satisfactory for British strategy and British business and not to be jeopardized by crackpot politics and protestors. Someone actually used the word 'tomfoolery', which I thought a bit flippant for those of us who'd been having chandeliers fall on our heads.

Again I was remembering my macabre gathering of anarchists, the impression of those ghouls with their sack-faces. The echo came more strongly when someone mentioned the proposed Coal Mines Act, still apparently a priority for the Home Secretary and all right-thinking people. At first it sounded tedious in the extreme, then I realized it sounded familiar, and then I remembered my radical friends discussing it. It transpired there'd been a bit of unpleasantness during the drafting and discussion process: anonymous threats and hints at possible unrest from the labour movement. I didn't really know what they were talking about, but I didn't get the strong impression they did either. Then someone else mentioned the name Hyndman, another name from the committee of shadows; apparently his conference this year had been the biggest ever.

I may have dozed off again at that point. The meeting wrapped up shortly afterwards, anyway, and I was eyeing a quick exit. But there was Faversham in front of me, and there was Bunce beside me, and I was being shepherded into a side room, and there was Ilya Ilyich Ilyin, the less charming face of Russian culture on tour. Another Russian was standing behind him: average sort of looking, smart but not showy.

Ilyin murmured a courtesy to me, its elaborateness in inverse proportion to its sincerity. 'I am delighted' - it was clear he got the same delight pulling the wings off flies - 'to have your continued co-operation. Indeed:' - he glanced at the two British policemen, and his little round glasses flashed white - 'I understand you were at the ballet with us last night.'

Faversham made a constipated noise from the back of his nose. 'Well… It's a bit unfortunate…'

'Depends on your point of view', I put in.

'Sir Henry was… entertaining a dancer.'

Ilyin's empty eyes gazed into me. 'What a very fortunate lady,' he murmured. The eyes gazed some more. 'That is… disappointing', he said at last. 'Such a conventional excuse, Sir Henry. I had expected - indeed I had heard - something… much more colourful.' He probably had, too. This lisping torturer was giving me the heebie-jeebies rather, and I wouldn't have put anything past his intelligence network. I knew his people were roaming London dressed as bobbies and knocking off inconvenient radicals, and I had to assume him capable of having any number of undercover bods in the theatre company.

Both of which ideas prompted a very stimulating chain of thought, but I had to park it for the moment.

He was still staring at me. 'But no matter', he said. 'Russia remains grateful for all British efforts against this… radical plague. And all of my resources remain at your service.'

Faversham said how grateful Britain was, and I wondered how much he really knew about what Ilyin and his resources were up to. 'Funny business, when you think about it', Faversham went on. The spectacles turned towards him, dared him to find something funny. 'We're concerned about the anarchist threat, right enough. But in practice all that's happened in the last few days is that two of them have turned up dead. Three, indeed: that chap with his throat cut in Whitechapel.'

I watched Ilyin's face. He was nodding thoughtfully. Not a flicker of a hint that he was responsible for that cut throat; shifty sod. Mind you, I suppose I was half responsible for the chap getting stabbed at the Alhambra, so I can't preach. 'It is a thought', he said, and then held up a finger, trying to summon inspiration. 'How is it, your English expression?'

'Never look a gift horse in the mouth,' Bunce said; 'specially if he's shitting sixpences.'

Ilyin considered him, and after a moment the little face broke into a genuine smile. He and Bunce considered each other, and I realized there was a mutual respect. Nobody likes an efficient policeman, except another efficient policeman.

The repartee wasn't really Faversham's style, and he tried to hurry us on. 'Mr Ilyin, you said you had some... some more information about anarchist planning.'

Ilyin nodded. I could see him calculating how much to share. 'I shall shortly', he hissed, 'be interviewing a man who has... not been as honest with me as he might.' That didn't sound like a wise career move. 'In the interim: there was a revolutionary meeting. Two nights ago. In east London. I believe I mentioned...'

'Indeed', Faversham said. 'Indeed. We were well aware. Touch unfortunate - These things happen, as you know - We had a man ready - undercover, you know - but he was assaulted on his way there. Probably unrelated.'

Well, bloody hell. I'd not felt exactly right, lamping that chap under the railway arch and borrowing his name.

I was trying to work out how I could have done any different, even if I'd known he was a copper in disguise.

Ilyin produced a great tut of sympathy, and he looked sadly at each of us. He seemed to look at me a little longer.

'No matter', he said. 'We have been able to learn something of what was said. I shall share a written report with you, naturally. Discussion of revolutionary activities in other countries. Discussion about your election campaign. Some unhappiness at the proposed regulation of your coal industry.'

Faversham and Bunce glanced at each other, remembering the meeting they'd just been in. Also' - he paused for dramatic effect - 'heated discussion of forthcoming acts of violence.'

He got his effect. Faversham and Bunce looked at each other again. 'Anything - Anything more specific?'

Without turning to the man behind him, Ilyin said sharply: 'Semyonov.'

Semyonov stepped forwards. 'Sir. More than one person in the meeting was reported to be aware of some specific act of violence. But no further detail was given.' The English was clipped but fluent. 'A general enthusiasm for violent acts was expressed. One person in the meeting is reported then to have stated his intention to organize some violent act.' That was Jacob's spat with George at the end. 'It was not clear if this was to be the same act.' He spoke crisply, looking through us, parade ground style. Disciplined outfit, this Okhrana of Ilyin's.

Faversham was looking worried. 'Were they talking about the ballet performance, d'you think?' I'd been wondering the same.

But Semyonov had nothing to say, and so Semyonov said nothing. Ilyin shrugged.

This Semyonov, though... This voice.

I'd heard it somewhere.

If he hadn't been talking about the meeting, perhaps I wouldn't have realized as quickly.

Felix. He'd been the one calling himself Felix; in the anarchists' meeting. I glanced at his hands and his shoes, but I couldn't recognize them from the toy-shop back-room.

And he'd been the chap who'd blown the whistle on me. The bloody cheek of it... Surely can't be the done thing, if you're infiltrating a radical gathering under false pretences, to start undermining other chaps infiltrating it under false pretences.

Smart, though. Just when big Jacob had started up about Okhrana spies. 'Felix', who was exactly that, had immediately shifted everyone's attention onto something else. Onto me.

And 'Felix' had been stoking the fire, hadn't he, provoking them to more outrage and revealing more?

My mind was all over the place now. Had blasted 'Felix' known who the British police bod was going to be, and so been telling the truth - if you can call it that - when he'd shopped me? Or was it just a lucky shot, a distraction that happened to hit the mark? And surely I deserved some credit, didn't I, for being more competent than the police bod and getting into the meeting and being in a position to add my own details? Show that the British weren't all useless; show that I was definitely on the right side.

At which point Felix asked permission from his chief to add something. 'Our information' - interesting the Russians didn't want to say they'd actually been in the room - 'is that there was a new person in the meeting. Perhaps he was in seat of British policeman. He was very extreme provocateur.'

'Provocateur?' said Faversham, alarmed.

'Yes, sir. A man known only as Peter; a painter. His every word, it was to provoke the other anarchists to more violence.'

I decided I wouldn't say anything after all. Turned out my performance at the revolutionary A.G.M. hadn't been quite as sophisticated as I'd thought.

On the way out past the committee room, another delay. Someone leapt up from a bench and grabbed my arm. I was startled, and startled enough to be about to thump him. Then I remembered I wasn't at the ballet now.

It was good old Humphrey Erskine, fretful and desperate for news. I unfastened him from my arm, managed a hallo, and together we walked down the grand staircase towards the open air and freedom.

Little Humphrey was chattering away, and I was trying to get a word in edgeways. Poor lad was terribly anxious about his beloved theatre visitors, and I had to sympathize. It must have seemed such a lark, to an artistic type like him, chaperoning the Russian visitors. He couldn't have known that his song-and-dance troupe would bring more mayhem than anyone since William the Conqueror.

I had to acknowledge that he'd been right, too. I'd thought his fears about big Jacob and the missing back-stage passes were fanciful. I now knew he was right. Unfortunately, I was the only person who knew. And for various reasons - some related to personal dignity, some related to not getting arrested for treason - I couldn't say. The police and the great men of the committee would continue to waffle about general threats and national interest. I was the one who kept bumping into very specific threats. I was the one getting hit round the head.

Standing in the doorway of the Home Office, I thanked Humphrey Erskine. And I meant it. Personally I'd probably have preferred to have given the whole evening a miss; saved myself no end of trouble. But Humphrey's anxiety, his alertness, had spotted the threat. He'd raised the alarm. And it was only because of that - and perhaps because the Russian Minister of War liked his ballet interactive - that the anarchists' plot had been thwarted.

Without going into the details of my involvement, I told him all this. I suggested he should keep his ears open, and continue to tell the police - anyone, frankly, rather than me - if he heard any more. I don't say he went away any less anxious, but at least someone was taking him seriously. And at least he went away.

I was alone, at long last, on the pavement. A chill winter morning, the sky a bracing frozen blue. The architecture of official London all around me, and happily enough I was heading away from it. I took a step towards the kerb, half-looking for a cab and half-wondering about a good walk.

I was vaguely aware of a carriage pulling up in front of me. I was more aware of someone bumping into me, and mumbling an apology. I was very aware of the pistol barrel he stuck into my side, before inviting me to get into the carriage.

52.

I got into the carriage.

'Ah…' I said as I sat. 'We meet at last.'

There she was. A cold beauty to match the winter morning: presumably the face watching me outside my rooms a couple of days before; the distinguished guest at the flying display; the spectator in the grand tier at the ballet. She had a pistol, held close and pointing at me.

'Caterina von Falkenhayn, I believe', I said. 'A face as beautiful as yours, you shouldn't need to force men into carriages.'

'A reputation as ugly as yours, you should not be surprised.'

It was a fair point.

'Any use my protesting, asking where we're going?'

The slightest shake of the head. 'Understand only this,' she said. 'I have a slight preference that you are alive to talk. I have a strong preference for your death over your escape.'

A professional-looking chap was next to her, pistol likewise. The chap from the pavement now squeezed in beside me, pistol into my side. Serious outfit.

I nodded. Sat back, adapted to the swaying of the carriage. Got my breathing regular. Worked out roughly what turns we were taking, as the carriage worked its way west from Whitehall. Watched, and waited.

Curtains covered both windows. Less to stop me looking out, I guessed, than to stop anyone else looking in.

Somewhere among the narrow streets of Mayfair, the carriage stopped. Just west of Berkeley Square, I reckoned. We weren't more than a couple of hundred yards from my sitting room, and I'd probably have known every tramp, doorman and pavement girl we passed. But it was no use.

We'd stopped, but as far as I could tell we hadn't turned in anywhere. My three guardians were silent, watchful.

I heard hooves and wheels on the cobbles. Another

carriage coming nearer. They'd be lucky to squeeze past, in this part of town. It was right beside us. And then it stopped.

A man's voice, muffled. A nod from the fair von Falkenhayn, and the man next to her pulled the window-curtain aside.

I saw the window of the other carriage, curtain also pulled aside. A man in it leaned forwards, and looked through into ours. A heavy man, with a heavy bald head on top of him.

Another nasty surprise.

'Von Hahn', I said. 'German Embassy running tourist excursions now, is it? Sixpence gets you a toffee-apple and a kidnapping?'

He ignored me. He snapped a curt question at Caterina von Falkenhayn; she made an equally curt reply; he nodded.

Otto Immanuel Von Hahn. No clear title or responsibility in the German Embassy. No clear limits to his authority or power. Distinguished guest at the highest dining tables in the land - even at Windsor, so I'd heard. Connoisseur of the arts, patron of the worthiest cultural causes.

I only know him because he keeps trying to have me killed.

'Surprised you weren't at the ballet last night', I said.

The faintest suggestion of a smile across the vast head. 'I care not for the *ballet comique*. A fit distraction for you and the rest of your *déclassé* society of tradesmen and parasites.'

'You'd have enjoyed last night', I said. 'Lots of drama and then someone tried to murder the Russian Minister of War. Classy as hell.'

He was looking at me - like I was a naughty music hall number that had cropped up in the middle of Wagner - but not listening. 'Sir Henry Delamere,' he said to the girl, 'is the epitome of the English gentleman class: degenerate, degraded - and yet defiantly surviving. You killed one of our men, Delamere.'

'I've no idea what you're talking about.' And I really didn't.

He still wasn't listening. 'I do not interest myself in mere revenge; it is inefficient. But…'

'I, on the other hand,' - la Falkenhayn - 'take a great interest in it.' Her voice was quiet, cold. 'The man died under my command. I have a duty.'

'Quite right', I said.

To von Hahn: 'With your permission, sir.'

'No repercussions, no interruptions? Then as you judge it best.' He gave me a heavy, humourless smile. 'One must encourage one's lieutenants, don't you think?'

'Oh, indeed', I said. 'And if by chance I am not responsible for your man's death?'

'I hardly think that is of any significance.'

53.

It surely wasn't a surprise, I supposed, that the Germans should be behind the events at the ballet. In my own limited experience, stirring up international radicalism as a cover for murderous espionage was an average day in the German Embassy in London. Presumably the Russian Minister of War was their number one enemy. And arranging an assassination in London and apparently the result of British carelessness about radicalism would be ideal. Two birds with one howitzer.

God, but London's a confusing place these days. This is why I prefer Istanbul. Or the Boer War.

We were away from the fun bits of the city now, and heading for the East End. I remembered my recent experiences there, with George and Co. Was it coincidence I was off that way again?

So, anyway, the Germans felt that not only had I interrupted their sneaky plan last night by beaming their assassin with a drinks tray, but also I was by extension responsible for the death of the assassin, by unexpected chandelier on head and then apparent stabbing. I could just about follow the logic. But surely I'd seen big Jacob lurking nearby when the chap was being stabbed. How did he fit in with the Germans?

We were well into Whitechapel. The carriage came to bouncing stop.

Without a word, one of the chaps stepped out. The other two pistols stayed steady. My options were narrowing. The slightest distraction, the slightest unexpected movement of the carriage… but nothing.

A word from outside, and the pistols were gesturing me out. A tiny East End back street. Steps leading down to a basement. One man halfway down watching me, another behind with his pistol in my spine, and down I went. I heard the carriage rattling away over the cobbles. I was disappearing from the world, and no one had seen me go.

Then we were in a basement flat, and almost as quickly we were through it and out of it again, via a connecting door into a basement in the next street. Even if by some chance someone had seen me going in there, I wasn't there anymore.

Too often in my life, I've seen what I'm about to get into and not liked the look of it. From the Boer defensive positions on the Modder River to a formal dinner with Victoria's father, too many prospects have made me want to stop the bus and hop off early.

I really didn't like the look of that cellar room. East End standard: bare, stone, damp, the light coming mainly from a thin window high in one wall and thick with greasy dust. This one had a single chair in the middle. One way in; no way out.

With their usual efficiency, the Germans had me in the chair with hands tied thirty seconds after I stepped in. Caterina von Falkenhayn and her two lads had been joined by another man now: tallish, thin, very pale, with a sorry-looking moustache hanging down in apparent sympathy with my situation. Fancy waistcoat and big gold watch.

He didn't look happy. That sort of moustache'll do that to

you. He started towards the woman. 'Fräulein, I am not comfortable with this. It is not-'

He didn't get far. One of her lads simply stuck out his arm and the newcomer walked into it. It caught him in the throat.

I couldn't place his accent. Foreign, but so was everyone this week. Familiar, even.

Miss von Falkenhayn hadn't even looked at him. 'Your comfort is the very least thing I care about.' They were speaking in English, so I guessed he wasn't German. Now she was looking right at me, from close up. 'The second least', she murmured.

'You pay me to spy for you, and I am good spy.' He had to cough a couple of times to get his voice right again. 'But these cellars are... have connection to me. You kill him here, people know.' A pickiness of manner to match his clothes.

Still she was gazing at me, still the voice was low. 'No one will ever know what happens here', she said.

I really didn't like the way this was going. And that voice. More than his accent... the particular voice, surely.

'I am useful spy with anarchists. You hurt my position here, I cannot be useful spy for you.'

Well, bloody oath. That voice.

She turned to him. 'We will not hurt your position. So cease your whining. You will continue to be useful spy for us, and you will stay rich, and you will stay alive. Now get out.' He got out. Not least because one of the henchmen had him by the scruff of the neck.

Max. Bloody Max. The chap had been in the anarchists' meeting with me. Another wrong'un. If I'd had a clearer look at their shoes or hands, I might have been able to spot him and the Russian stooge sooner.

And despite my very alarming predicament, I couldn't get over the madness of it all. There hadn't been so many people in that grim gathering of the sacks, plotting European revolution. Now it seemed that - what, nearly half of us? - were shamming. At what point does a meeting of anarchists have so few real anarchists in it that it ceases to count? I mean, you could hardly call that a quorum, could you, with one Russian policeman and one German spy and one confused British idler? Do the thing properly won't you?

Caterina von Falkenhayn was able to devote her attention to me again.

It ought to have meant less chance of the revolutionary meeting leading to serious violence. Except I had to wonder whether the Russians or the Germans were aiming at precisely that, with their undercover provocateurs.

She gestured to one of her henchmen. Immediately he had produced a chair from somewhere and placed it for her, so she could sit in front of me.

'Hallo again', I said. She considered me. 'Diplomatic career all you dreamed? Look, I'm sorry to be a bore, but what's going on? I do think there's a chance you're making a mistake. Shame to mess up a perfectly good cellar for no good reason.'

'What is going on is that we will kill you. I trust that is not too complicated.'

'All right; so far so good. And again, just to avoid misunderstanding: why?'

The slightest frown cracked the pure pale skin. 'Surely you do not play this game. Not now. The innocent Englishman, head filled with cricket and average wine, who has never had a moment of involvement with his police or his secret service?' She looked genuinely irritated.

'On the contrary: I loathe cricket, I can't afford even average wine, and I freely admit that the police special branch have involved me in some madness with foreign anarchists. What I don't know is what that has to do with you.'

The pale blue eyes had narrowed, little mountain pools. I've been in this sort of scenario a few times, and the vis-à-vis usually relishes their power a bit: you get sneering, you get tormenting, you even - damned uncomfortable - get a sort of flirting. Not this girl. She was all business.

170

'You are a loyal operative of your government. You investigate for them, not as paid agent but as patriot - so called "gentleman amateur". You fulfil tasks that regular personnel cannot.'

The way she put it, I sounded rather noble. I only wished Inspector bloody Bunce was there to hear. He wouldn't have stopped them killing me, but at least I'd be going out with a clean slate.

'You make it sound terribly heroic. I really have no idea what's going on, and am doing the bare minimum to keep the police off my back.' I'd the sense I was disappointing her. I wondered if I was her first. Unlikely: she'd been condemning peasants to death since she could talk. Still the cold, disapproving beauty gazing at me. 'And so, you're going to… to what? To torture me somehow? For information?'

'I don't need any information, thank you. I know far more than you do. No, Sir Henry Delamere, I am going to kill you. For revenge.'

'Didn't realize people did that any more. Must have been someone you cared about very much.'

'Not in the least. But the men who work for me, I want them all to know that we respect their loyalty; that I fight for them even after their death.' Gods, she was actually serious. 'And perhaps in the future your British secret service will think a second time before killing a German agent.'

'Right - yes - here we are again. Just to be clear - and I don't know if this helps - I really had no idea that the assassin chap last night was anything to do with you.'

I'd lost her again. 'Last night? What do you babble about?'

'And - just for the record; I know you won't take my word for it - I really didn't kill him.'

'This incoherence wastes my time.' She said something to the chap standing nearest, and he was immediately beside me. It was hard not to look at her fatal eyes, but then I saw a knife flash into his hand. 'You killed my officer at the flying display. I kill you. So.'

'What?' My shout was loud enough to startle them. 'The flying - What? Wait...' Now I really was babbling. 'You mean... the chap in the shed?' I was stupefied. With everything else, I'd almost forgotten the incident.

'He was a professional. He knew the risks. He would not complain. Nor should the British.'

I'd had everything upside-down. I'd been so caught up in the peculiar doings of London's anarchists I'd not given a thought to the dead body I'd found in Sir Malachai Erskine's flying machine shed. A German agent...

She saw that I was quieter now, and she took it for agreement. A glance to the chap lurking beside me with his blade.

I jumped in: 'Wait - So - It must have been you who moved the body! You didn't want him lying around - Awkward questions - So you dumped him at the station. Plays havoc with the timetable, that sort of thing.' The faintest nod from her. As the chap moved in closer, the knife flashed again in the single light.

And now I was quieter. I might have had a chance of talking my way out of whatever had happened at the ballet. But I'd no chance of proving that I'd not killed her chap at the flying display. Found the body, on my own; and she'd seen me leaving the place, still on my own, no doubt just before she'd gone in and found him herself.

I wasn't quite ready to turn my toes up, but I still couldn't see what I could do about it. I had to seem calm, slow things by even a moment, get them just a fraction more relaxed...

'I always wondered what my last sight on earth would be', I said, looking at this lethal handsome German girl. 'Don't think me impertinent, Miss von Falkenhayn, but... You'll do.'

Something flickered in her eyes. Arrogant, Victoria had said.

Victoria would be damn' cross with me, letting myself get stabbed by her old school chum. Knowing Victoria, she'd find out somehow. Probably get a mention in the

Headmistress's annual report: 'Miss C. von Falkenhayn was amused to discover that a chap she'd just offed in a cellar was the former lover of Lady V. Carteret; and it's also been a jolly year for the embroidery club…'. I wouldn't have put it past Victoria to have her own revenge. These old school grudges linger.

'You seem very confident my body won't be found', I said.

'I am.' Brisk; factual. 'Even if it is: from all that we know of your lifestyle and activities, Sir Henry, no one would be surprised if your body is found decomposing in a London cellar.'

I nodded. 'Quick as you can, then.'

The blade moving in. 'Ooh!' I said; he hesitated. 'Don't suppose you could get a message to my bookie?'

From somewhere above us: hammering at a door.

54.

Caterina von Falkenhayn moved fast. A word, a gesture, and I thought I'd had it. Instead the henchman was stuffing my handkerchief into my mouth.

The connecting door to the other cellar slammed open, we heard footsteps in the passage and the sad moustache barged in uninvited. The girl looked more irritated by him than anything else; her glance at me was almost apologetic.

'The police!' babbled moustache. 'They are at front door of other building. They are calling for me by name!'

She shrugged. 'So invite them in. You are honest citizen. Offer them a cup of tea.'

'But they could interrogate me! They have pistols with them; knives! They could search!'

This hit home. She glanced at me again. She'd be able to finish me off, not a problem. But the moustache could say inconvenient things about her and the Embassy. And she'd

173

prefer not to be found here herself, charming foreign diplomat skulking in a cellar with a slaughtered Delamere. Her discomfort didn't help me much, but... Every moment counts.

Sudden movement: the chap with the moustache bolting out of the room. Sounded like he wasn't going to answer the door. No doubt there was another way out, through this side of the building, and he was taking it.

Again von Falkenhayn's ruthless mind in operation. Commands snapped to her two German lads, and immediately one of them was out and, if I heard right, through into the other half of the premises. Answer the door, sorry to keep you officer, no, my moustachey friend is visiting a sick aunt. She looked down at me. 'A small delay, I'm afraid. Sadly I must miss the pleasure. Volker will see that all is concluded as soon as the interruption has passed. Farewell, Sir Henry Delamere.' I gave her a nod, courteous as I could, but she'd already gone and forgotten me. She'd be back in the West End in no time, the cool elegant diplomat as ever, and not a hint of the mayhem she was leaving behind.

So that left me and the chap with the knife. He checked my binding was tight, and went and stood in the doorway.

Something else nagging at me... After the first thrill had worn off, the noise at the door, the possibility that I might just live after all, good old Inspector Bunce here in the nick of time, I had to wonder: how in hell had they got here? The Germans were too competent to be followed, or for this place to be known, and Bunce and Faversham surely too incompetent otherwise. And there was no way Quinn could have tracked me here, not even him.

But the chap had seen police, he'd seen their... their weapons.

I heard new and louder hammering at the front door, and understanding came with it. These weren't regular policemen, were they? These were killers who found it convenient to dress as policemen. This wasn't Bunce and the British coming to rescue me; it was Ilya Ilyich Ilyin and his Russians, coming to do some more counter-revolutionary killing.

I remembered Ilyin's ominous statement that he would be 'interviewing' someone who had let him down.

I confess a certain irritation. I mean: what was the world coming to? The policemen weren't policemen anymore. Then again, the anarchists weren't anarchists either. What a bloody shambles. I seemed to be the only person doing the thing properly, being who I said I was. When I wasn't pretending to be a ballet dancer.

The newer noise had been different: different tone, different... location. More directly above us. Ilyin's boys trying to kick their way into this side of the shop too - or someone else? Whole thing was chaos.

The chap in the doorway was guessing too. The knife was still firm in his fist, but I could see the indecision on his face. Eventually - a last check that Delamere wasn't going anywhere - he began to move along the passage which would take him up to ground level and whoever was trying to get in this side of the building.

So there I was. Alone at last, gagged, and tied to a chair in a cellar in East London. It's the active life keeps you young, they say. Again the thumping from above. Just for the sake of clarity, that's to say that we had the Russian secret police dressed as British bobbies barging in from one direction, and now someone else barging in from the other. I didn't yet know what they were dressed as.

Then a smash, and that was the door dealt with, and then shouting and scrambling feet and a moment later someone - presumably my erstwhile guard - was back down and racing past my cellar and - slam - through the connecting door into the other basement. And jolly good luck, I thought: given what's coming through that side you'll be back and forth pretty briskly.

I was more worried about myself. When your least bad option is the Russian secret police, you know you're in trouble. Ilya Ilyich Ilyin was one of the most sinister and ruthless men I'd ever met. He'd be sure me winding up in that cellar meant I was suspect. If his throat-cutters didn't kill me in the first rush, there was a good chance he'd order them to do the job in the clear-up.

And that was the good option. More worrying was -

Stamping feet again, down the stairs and in the passage, and then a figure filled the doorway.

It was big Jacob.

55.

By this point I think I'd have preferred death to the madness continuing around me. Certainly a quick *adieu* at the hands of the lovely von Falkenhayn.

I couldn't begin to imagine what had brought Jacob and his Latvian revolutionary pals crashing through one front door just as the Russian oppressors were busting in the other and I was about to get knifed in the cellar. His boys sounded like they were conducting a fast search of the premises above. But with Team Ilyin and the two Germans hunting each other around the other half and making a hell of a noise about it, Jacob was looking wary. There'd been a pathetic moment when I'd thought he was rescuing me, but his reactions killed that thought.

They're a disciplined lot, anarchists. Noise of unknown threat through connecting door; nothing yet from the search upstairs; confused Englishman tied up in chair. A moment's calculation and then Jacob was dragging me up and out and bellowing to the rest of the crew and as he was shoving me out through the front door the others were with us. Into the back of a closed wagon - some borrowed commercial thing - and rattling away through the back streets.

Jacob had decided not to remove my gag or the rope binding my wrists.

Just a few minutes later I was being shoved across a pavement and into a house. It was dark now, the cold void of a winter evening. I heard the cart hurrying away again, the door slam, and then someone turned up the lamps in the hallway and we could catch our breath.

In the heart of old London, I had now doubly disappeared.

We seemed to be on home ground. Jacob, and the three or four men with him, relaxed as soon as the door was closed. Murmurs from the big man, and one chap settled on a chair by the front door and the others went off to smoke a pipe or peel the potatoes or whatever revolutionary stand-down looks like.

That left Jacob, considering me. The big hand settled on my shoulder. 'You - OK?' in the booming, simple voice. Well, no Jacob, obviously not. But I nodded. Arm round my shoulder, he escorted me into the parlour, and settled me in an armchair. And then he was gone.

He still hadn't removed the gag or the rope at my wrists.

A regular East End back-street terraced house; tall and thin. In better nick than that attic where they'd had me before. But all pretty shabby. The parlour had the minimum: two old armchairs, table, sideboard, one lamp only. From what I'd glimpsed in the hall, they seemed to have the run of the whole house.

A few minutes later, Jacob was back. And now George was with him. The two of them stood discussing me in Latvian. Quite the pair: the impressive remorseless bulk of Jacob, who'd stabbed one of his own bods rather than risk him telling the police anything; and dapper moustachioed George, elegant pistoleer who blew up police wagons for fun.

There was something like amusement on George's face. I wasn't reassured: I wasn't sure he and I had the same sense of humour.

Then hurrying feet in the hall, and another figure in the doorway. It was Nina.

She didn't hesitate. A few words of foreign and, before the two men could stop her, she was hurrying over and pulling the handkerchief out of my mouth and fiddling with the rope behind me.

The ability to breathe properly, and then to move my hands and rub a bit of blood back into my wrists, was marvellous. I did so with a sigh of sincere pleasure.

I was careful not to look like I was about to do anything hasty. The two men had instinctively moved closer, ready to club me over the head if I proved difficult. I settled back in the armchair with deliberate satisfaction; one of its springs let out a great twang of alarm.

'That's very kind, Miss Nina', I said as she came round into view again. 'Thank you.' I looked gravely at the two men. 'Basically hospitality, chaps; come now.'

'No time to make cucumber sandwich', said George with his usual sour smile. 'And I don't let them drink cocktail when we are working.'

'I'm just grateful you got me out of that cellar, and happy to have my hands free enough for a smoke.' I lit up, and offered round. Only Nina accepted, taking the other chair. 'Er, not wanting to pry - up to you whose door you kick in - but how did you end up there?'

Jacob said: 'Visit friend.'

But apparently the friend was out, and that was probably good for the friend's health.

George added: 'Now you say how you were there. Gentlemanly.'

'Can't all be as naturally charming as you, George.' I'd thought about this. Unusually, the truth might serve me best. 'Bit of a mystery', I said. 'As you know, the British police are suspicious of me. Guess they know I'm - well - sympathetic to some... unfashionable causes.' I looked sympathetically at each of them; more so Nina. I know, I know; I was building up to the truth, anyway. 'I was grabbed off the street at gunpoint and taken to that cellar. They said they were going to kill me. I don't know who they were. Foreign, certainly. German, maybe, or could even have been Russian.' The two men looked gravely at each other, and chattered away a bit. As I'd intended, they were now assuming it had been Ilyin and his Okhrana thugs. Who had, of course, also been there, albeit not in the way I'd said. Well, can you blame me?

They looked at me a bit more, and then they chattered a bit more.

'It is not convenient you leave', said George at last, and again the ironic smile. 'Nor is convenient you make noise.' I assume he meant noise when dying. 'Tonight you are guest here. You make trouble, we kill you silently. Do not try leaving, do not make trouble, do not ask question, ok?' I nodded brightly, trouble the last thing on my mind. 'Welcome. Please to enjoy your stay.'

The two men left. An anarchist's work is never done.

That left me and Nina. She sat smoking in silence a moment, looking at me pitifully. As ever, the sight of her brought back that first night: the melodrama of *Tosca*, the firing squad, her brother lying dead in the middle of that eerie garden.

'I think is interesting week', she said at last. 'Never you know anything about revolutionists in London. Now you know more than you want.'

It was so spot on, so perfectly put, that I actually laughed.

'Still we cannot know you, Mr Harry. Still we cannot trust you. Still it make no sense you are here. But also I do not think you are truly bad.'

I shrugged. 'I'm clumsy', I said, 'and that may be more dangerous for you.' I hesitated, and we both smoked a breath or two more.

Her sympathy and sharpness deserved a bit of the truth. 'If I say I'm sympathetic to your cause, Nina, I'm lying. I don't begin to understand it, so I can't sympathize. Freedom and whatnot, all that stuff, jolly good. The man Ilyin, the Okhrana chap in my rooms that day: I wouldn't wish him on any country. But throwing bombs and blowing up policemen and so on? Lost me there, I'm afraid. I'm naive about the world, perhaps, but I've seen too much violence to believe it's ever good for anything.'

I watched her. A pleasant enough experience, aesthetically-speaking: the handsome poise, the big dark eyes. But also the impression of tension as well as strength, contained with difficulty. Hers had never been an easy life; never would be.

'Not to be rude', I went on, 'but I'd have been happier if I'd never met any of you. Not George and the crew, not the ghastly Ilyin, and not the British police either. But I'm stuck in this business, because for different reasons none of you wants to let me out of your sight, and none of you is yet ready to kill me.' She didn't disagree. 'Matter of time, I realize. Also, I don't like the idea that your poor brother got shot under my nose.'

Her face darkened. 'Good someone remembers him.' She shook her head. 'Always I think of that night. Even I helped to give rifles to firing squad; even I helped to kill my own brother.'

She didn't seem horrified, as much as furious. Another shake of the head, and the eyes were hard. 'We say: evil comes quickly; good comes slow-slow. No hurry: at last I will make revenge.'

'I'd like to sort that out, at least, before someone drops me into the Thames.'

She considered that thought.

'You need sandwich', she said at last.

So there I was, alone again, relaxing in the anarchists' lounge.

I guessed the terms would be as before. Not convenient to murder me right off, but they'd get round to it soon as.

I didn't move. Through the doorway to the hall, I could see the chap sitting on guard; and he could see me. Short of a running leap through the front window I'd no obvious way out, and even then I'd only do myself a mischief on the railings. So better, for now, to reinforce the impression that I was relaxed in their company.

Nina returned with a very satisfactory sandwich. Whatever criticisms you may have about those striving for world revolution, they know how to do a snack. Nothing fancy, everything cut thick, and plenty of mustard. I tried not to think what the meat might be.

'Nina,' I said between mouthfuls, 'do I want to know what's happening here tonight?'

She smiled. 'No.' Emphatic shake of head.

'Right ho.'

'No policemen involved. OK?'

'Right ho.' Another mouthful. 'Just that I've had the impression recently that something big is being planned, some… some big act of violence.' I was feeling my way through the memories of the meeting of the sacks, guessing, trying to prompt. She showed no sign of being prompted. Also the memory of the previous evening's madness at the ballet. 'Maybe… maybe it's already happened. Maybe it's still going to happen.'

At any moment she could summon George, and announce that I'd spoken out of turn and wouldn't it be better to finish me off?

Eventually she shrugged. 'About that, I don't know so much. Tonight: something else. Don't worry.'

Easy for her to say.

Curious that Jacob should pop out for his mission of breaking-and-revenging just when there was something big on here. Perhaps tonight was George's more steady, longer-term business, while last night at the ballet had been Jacob's impromptu spree.

After a while Nina wandered out. I stayed put a few minutes longer, pretending to be comfortable. Then I sauntered out into the hall. The chap on guard at the front door was immediately watchful. I smiled. 'Lavatory?' I said.

'Hard day's anarchy, chap needs a piss, yes?' Apparently they hadn't covered this in Latvian elementary school English, so it was another outing for Delamere's famous mime.

It didn't impress. He looked very sceptical. He glanced uneasily towards the back of the house. 'Out the back, is it?' I said, and started to move when he grabbed my arm. He motioned me not to move; miming on a par with mine. He took a step along the corridor towards the back himself, but then stopped. He didn't want to leave me alone by the front door. Stalemate.

The hall, now I had the chance to look, was in a bit of a state. There'd been a rug, but that had been taken up - the shadow of relatively less dusty boards was clear. There were a couple of long scratches - gouges, really - in the long-faded floral wallpaper. And a door halfway along had been taken off its hinges.

With his pistol, chummy motioned me upstairs. In a tiny bedroom - not much more than a partitioned-off bit of a regular room, not even its own window - we found a battered chamber-pot, and he left me to my own devices.

As you may have realized, I hadn't needed the lav. But I now felt obliged to back up the story, and you know how it is when you're trying to force yourself and someone's waiting. Long story short, I eventually managed enough to prove the point, and ambled out again. It'd taken a bit longer because I also had to dismantle a dusty picture frame - Madonna and Child, not looking their best - and borrow the backing paper.

My escort was waiting in the main bedroom, and right away I stretched out on the bed. I lit up - filthy habit, which Quinn would never tolerate at home, but that's what anarchy does to you - and offered one. He was suspicious, but he couldn't see what I was up to, and he accepted. We smoked for a bit, in silence, me lying back trying to look relaxed while he lurked and watched. Eventually he wandered off and returned with a chair. I mimed opening the window, terribly stuffy ain't it, just a crack? Very suspicious, but I moved slowly and kept pretending to check and only opened the upper half of the sash. If I hadn't tried to do a flit through the ground floor window, I was unlikely from the upstairs, and he'd have all the time in the world to shoot me in the back if I went doolally and started clambering up to try it.

Top half of window successfully open, I returned to my pose of relaxation, and waited.

From somewhere, I could hear whistling. Not a tune I could name, yet somehow familiar.

56.

Not one of the most thrilling evenings. My frustration was only increased by my near-certainty that something fairly spectacular was happening just a couple a yards away from me, and I couldn't even be sure what it was.

There didn't seem much I could do about it, either. What I could do, I did.

It was Vanstone gave me the idea. That's to say, my mind having temporarily and not unhappily wandered in her direction, it happened across the solution. My guard was toing and froing a fair bit, trying to watch the front door as well as me. One absence of a few minutes was more than enough for me to scrawl a message to Quinn: short, urgent, and vague enough that only he would make sense of it. And then a couple of seconds, and the sight of a young lad ambling along the street outside long after bedtime, was all I needed.

I don't know if you found school as tedious as I did. One of the milder diversions, back in the day, was the paper dart: they'd hand out a sheet of paper covered in Latin or some such, and the only sense I could ever make of it was to fold it into as sharp a dart as I could devise and float it across the schoolroom towards the ear of a confederate while the authorities were looking the other way; fine sport. The paper I'd liberated from behind the Madonna was a little stiffer than the average, and it made for a good robust dart. It didn't take more than a step and half a second to send it on a nicely-judged trajectory up through the top half of the sash and out into the night.

Whatever was happening in the house was occupying some of the biggest names in London anarchy, it was taking a night to achieve, and it was happening somewhere round the back. The damage they'd done to the hall suggested some reasonably serious kit.

My first thought had been a bomb, of course. You can blame the sort of newspapers I read. But that didn't explain the apparent scale of the activity. And surely as few people as possible would want to be hanging around; whereas tonight seemed to be quite the hot ticket for the radical community.

My second thought, accordingly, was that it might be a really big bomb. I had visions of barrels of explosive under parliament, chaps with feathered hats and buckles on their shoes. As I say, it was a long evening. But again, unless they really were hefting barrels around I couldn't see why you'd need such a crew. Preparing something to transport elsewhere wouldn't explain why tonight was both so long and so hush-hush. And if they let off a big explosion right here, in the East End, what would it achieve? Over in Westminster they wouldn't even notice.

I got closer in the end. The sort of location; the time; the crew; the need to mess up the hall. And the difference of opinion I'd heard between George and Jacob, in the meeting of the sacks.

I was on these lines, also wondering if some blighter was about to detonate a barrel of gunpowder in the kitchen while I was stretched our more or less right above - and increasingly convinced that the lad in the street had not seen the paper dart dropping out of the night sky or had just taken it home to use in the privy - probably hadn't even learned to read properly; don't children pay attention in school anymore? - when all hell broke loose.

57.

All hell broke loose rather discreetly at first. But it gained momentum awfully fast, and the grim events of that night followed on.

It started with a knock at the front door. My watchdog and I were on the landing having a smoke together when we heard it.

Now, my message to Quinn had made two points clear.

The first was my belief that tonight was about robbery, not violence. The numbers, the timing, the heavy equipment, the importance of this location all suggested they were breaking into a building very close by; at this point I didn't know that the house backed onto a jeweller's, but my guess turned out pretty close.

The second point - and I'd underlined it - was that he was at all costs to avoid the police turning up at the front door. I knew George well enough to know that he'd cheerfully choose a shoot-out in a London street over a quiet sneak, and any fool could see that a frontal assault would create umpteen casualties. I hadn't allowed for the fact that the higher ranks of London's police contain some very particular fools. Or perhaps what happened was plain bad luck: I know now that Quinn got my message and got it immediately to Bunce with the underlining underlined, but I've never found out whether what transpired was Faversham going for glory or just evil coincidence.

Anyway, knock at the front door. Very wary, pistol in hand, my smoking chum crept downstairs and opened the door a crack. I didn't hear what the figure outside said. But I saw his sleeve and shoulder clear enough: unmistakably a police uniform jacket.

It was precisely the thing I'd wanted to avoid. At the top of the stairs I was frantic with possibilities: should I yell for help? tell him to get clear? make a leap for the sentry's gun hand? It didn't matter, because the chap at the door had said something to the policeman, and apparently the policeman was satisfied because the door was being shut without drama.

Not as bad as it could have been, I was thinking, but below me the sentry was hurrying along the passage towards the rear of the building. Moments after that he was back, George and Jacob hurrying in with him. As ever, George didn't hang around. First he was into the front room, presumably scouting the street. Then he was in the hall again and he and Jacob had a council of war.

It didn't take long. We'd already established that Jacob would grab any chance of shooting someone. And although George had wanted to get on with his big robbery without his pal blowing the world up first, now that there were actually policemen knocking at his front door he was more than happy to revert to Plan A. With his usual vision and efficiency, he'd organized the defence in under ten seconds. Couple of men I couldn't see in the sitting room with Nina. Another - chap I didn't recognize; presumably on burglary detail this evening - coming up the stairs. Jacob lurking down the hall. Again it would be in their interests to shoot me out of hand, so I hung back on the landing. George saw me, and gestured me away; no time to finish me quite yet. Then he got himself ready at the front door.

George's dispositions suggested he was aiming to break out, rather than withstand a siege. For the latter, he'd have had more men shooting from upstairs. But he'd seen that the police meant his robbery plan was a bust; he'd immediately abandoned it and moved on. Better shoot some folk and get away than shoot some folk and not.

As the chap coming up reached the top of the stairs and saw me lurking, he gave a little nod. 'I think you are the one known as Peter,' he said quietly.

'Eh?'

'From the meeting. You call yourself Peter. The painter, yes?' He pointed. 'I recognize boots; also mark on that hand.'

Told you it was a good system. I tried not to let my

surprise and alarm show too badly.

And like that we waited.

I was still roaming the upstairs, trying to find a new way to get a message out into the street, when the madness of that infamous night began in earnest.

58.

I didn't hear the knock at the door, and I didn't hear the few words between Sergeant Robert Bentley and George. Did the police still not know? Were they that unco-ordinated or unfortunate? They were unarmed, anyway.

All I saw from along the upstairs passage was chummy at the top of the stairs reaching to pull the pistol from the back of his waistband. I came running.

I was far too late. Halfway there and the shooting had started, more than one pistol firing, shot after shot but steady. From the top of the stairs: chaos. The front hall was a mess of figures and smoke. Chummy was moving steadily down the stairs, pistol up and firing. George was grappling with a policeman and then he got his gun hand free and let off a shot. Another policeman was collapsed on the floor, broken and done for. And now another uniform was in the front doorway and then he flinched as someone's bullet caught him in the leg and he was down and immobilized, and the man on the stairs was aiming and the policeman was doomed.

I didn't even see what I snatched up - it turned out to be a vase - but I hurled it down with all my outrage at this atrocity and the gunman never knew what hit him. In the smoke and the bedlam I don't think anyone did. The vase smashed around his ears and he went tumbling to the foot of the stairs, and the policeman would live a while longer yet.

The immediate threat was done, all three policemen lying wounded or dead in the hall, and after one quick glance through the door George was grabbing his people and shoving them out. Jacob went first, of course, gun up. Then Nina and the two men who'd been with her. George had the chap I'd flattened up on his feet and out he went too. From outside I heard more shots. Dear God, this was a London street, not a cowboy town in America or a South African battlefield. Lunatics letting off pistols did not belong here. And now there was one lunatic left; two, if you reckon for how maddened I was. George ducked out after his team, last rat leaving the sinking ship, and for a moment I was standing there, halfway down the stairs, gazing at the bodies on the floor. Not my first slaughter, but the shock never lessens.

Outside the chaos was worse because it was mostly darkness. Jacob had led the crew off down the street, firing as he went to clear the way. Sergeant Charles Tucker bought it then. Just as George crossed the pavement and made to follow, a new policeman hurried up from the other direction. Constable Walter Choate couldn't have known what was going on and he wasn't armed, but he heard shooting and he knew fellow police officers were in it and he didn't hesitate.

Nor did George. As the policeman hurried towards him, the devious bastard stopped still, raised his pistol, and took a careful aim and at a range of a couple of yards he couldn't miss.

That was when, leaping down the rest of the stairs and out into the street at a sprint and now wholly out of control, I launched myself at him.

59.

I couldn't save poor Choate. I sent George flying into next week just as he was about to fire, and knocked myself half senseless in the process. There'd been a shot, and a scream. The policeman lunged at George, but now the rest of the gang were back, blood-crazy and firing wild. That was the end of Walter Choate, and in the chaos and the darkness George had taken a bad wound too.

As I pulled myself up off the pavement, watching from just a yard away, I realized that the madness was not done. Not for London, and not for me. It turned out that my duty had bound me even closer to this wretched gang.

I lurched in and helped them wrestle the wounded George to his feet and, clumsy and staggering, we set off down the street.

I've never thought Londoners anything above the rest of mankind, but they put up one hell of a performance that night. As the bunch of cut-throats, obviously armed and angry, came rampaging down that back-street any sane person would have hidden. Instead one chap marched up out of the darkness, actually waving his finger in condemnation and cursing us for the outrage. Jacob's pistol came round, but even he seemed to have calmed down a touch: the man stared, and then backed away.

Our trek through those back streets was something out of hell itself, darkness and yelling and lurching and wondering what was out there, and I was stuck in the group because someone had to keep tabs on them, and terribly aware that they'd now abandoned all restraint and would murder me to tidy up a loose end or just to work off some surplus energy. Besides Jacob and Nina and the semi-conscious George, there were other jostling figures I couldn't make out. I heard someone addressed as Fritz, and in a snatch of lamplight I wondered if I remembered him from the firing squad and the Black Maria break-out: the man who'd gone over the wall.

We were taking turns to have George slung between us, all stumbling and staring crazed and wondering where the next threat was. One lurch had me bumping into Nina, and for a moment we were gazing at each other as the ambulance party lumbered on.

'Get clear!' I hissed. I can't think why: she was as complicit as any of them; but I somehow still felt her as much victim as culprit. 'This lot are finished. Get out now!'

She looked shocked, and wild - so did I, I guess - and it wasn't clear she'd heard me right. But at some point in the next few hundred yards she wasn't with us any more. The chap who'd been on the stairs and recognized me as Peter the painter had got separated too, he and another chap. That left Jacob and me and just one other, with our patient.

In one of our bits of grappling to keep George upright and moving, I managed to sneak his Mauser pistol and get it into my inside pocket.

It couldn't have been ten minutes later and we were in yet another shoddy boarding house. This parallel society of theirs seemed to have a network of hide-outs: their various lodgings, and reliable or threatenable acquaintances. A street somewhere off Commercial Road. The heart of the East End, between the endless clattering of the railway and the stink of the river, the echoes of the victims of the Tower of London and the victims of Jack the Ripper.

We dumped George on a bed, and he looked pretty grim. I've watched too many men dying of bullet wounds: couldn't tell you what was going on medically-speaking, but it looked to me like he'd a few hours left at best. Two women joined us. One I didn't recognize; the other was Sara, who'd hid in my bedroom in Piccadilly and taken a shine to Quinn. They took over the nursing, shooing the men aside. They were upset but looked pretty competent.

We others took a step or two backwards, leaving them to it. Catching my breath and trying to straighten myself out after hoicking George up the stairs, I turned to find Jacob with his pistol out again.

It was pointing at me.

60.

The great brute actually smiled at me. 'I thank for help. Now finish, OK? Good night.'

190

'Quite right', I said. 'Once you've started murdering policemen, what's another death between friends?'

'Sure', he said. 'Tidy. Sorry.'

I nodded. 'Hadn't you better check with old George first?'

I turned to look at old George, and Jacob naturally did the same. George was pale and breathing shallow and barely conscious, so didn't offer any comment. When Jacob turned back, he found that I had the Mauser out and pointing at him.

So there we were. Couple of yards apart, pistols fixed on each other. I had no doubts whatsoever about the big man's ruthlessness. 'Maybe we kill one another', I said. 'Even tidier.' Again the smile. I've rarely met a man so indifferent to life and death, even his own. 'Or maybe neither of us dies.'

Personally I wasn't quite so indifferent about my life and death. When you have to go, you have to go, and I don't intend lingering; but I had unfinished business.

Jacob was thinking it over. He, surely, had unfinished business. The death of one trivial and rather scruffy Englishman couldn't be enough of an achievement to justify his own. That's what I was hoping he would think, anyway.

'Perhaps you'll let me walk out of here', I said. I knew he wouldn't. 'Or…'

Mind like his, he'd seen immediately that if he let me out he'd be surrounded by policemen in no time. But if I let him out, he'd reckon to disappear into this terrifying unknown London of theirs.

He nodded. 'See you again', he said.

'I intend it.'

Keeping an eye on my pistol, he and his chum backed out of the room and away. A moment later I heard a door close, and the brute was loose again in London.

Sara had followed, presumably to lock up, and now the other woman hurried out on some nursing errand. So that left me alone, with the pale figure on the bed. And what a cold bleak grim scene it was; you couldn't want for a better image of wretched mortality than this chap slipping away in the small hours, in this shabby back-street boarding house.

His eyes flickered.

I saw them trying to focus. I moved closer.

The eyes adjusted. Saw me. Opened a fraction wider.

'You shot me', he whispered. 'When you jump on me. My own pistol.'

I leaned very close to his ear. 'Good', I said. 'Serves you right, you bastard.'

I lifted my head again. He seemed to be considering my words.

He nodded slightly.

'Mauser pistol', he murmured. 'Adequate for task.' His eyes were open, but I don't think he could see me. 'I am dying, yes?'

'Yes, George.'

The eyes flickered. 'Better like this... Quick. Action. And... And my work live after me. Pity... I don't see... the excitement.'

It's never jolly to watch someone checking out, however much I felt it couldn't happen to a nicer chap and was small return for those poor policemen. Now I forgot all that. I'd thought that the chaos of the last days was building up to more than the ballet. Tonight was surely all the mayhem anyone could want. But not old George: he was expecting more. And there might yet be a chance to get something useful from him, if I could handle him right.

His eyes had closed again.

'Yes indeed', I said. 'Must be good to know you'll achieve something big for the cause.' The white waxy face was still. 'From all I've heard, it's going to be spectacular.' Nothing. 'Explosion, of course; big one, right?'

The faintest - surely I wasn't imagining - the faintest nod.

'Clever old George. And of course you've picked something special, some... particular event.' Anything - any hint. 'How many d'you reckon you'll kill?'

Silence.

The eyes struggled open. They seemed wider now, clearer. Insanely, the face twisted up into a smile.

Damn.

From deep in his throat he coughed out a chuckle.

Clever revolutionaries are the worst.

The words came hoarse and faint, and I had to lean in again. 'I... tell you... secret.'

I leaned closer, ears straining, heart thumping. His breath was hardly there any more, but I could feel it against my ear.

'I... don't... know.'

He tried to chuckle again, but it came out more as a gasp.

I forced out a chuckle of my own; not much better. 'You've got one over me again, George. But how can you not know?'

'Watchman make bomb. So Fritz made arrangement.' To me this was just rambling. 'Said ballet would be same target. Please Jacob. But for ballet I don't know.'

'The same - You don't know about the ballet?' Nothing. 'Jacob, then - Jacob knows about the bomb?'

The head flickered left and right; the hint of a smile.

It was maddening. But it fitted with what they'd all been saying in the meeting of the sacks. Their networks were telling them something was going to happen, but it was somehow unofficial; off the books.

That's the trouble with anarchists: big ideas, shoddy staff work.

I suddenly felt the cold. All the energy of the night had ebbed. Now it was just me and this frail ghost, and even he'd lost the strength to tease me.

I heard breath struggling in his throat, and leaned closer again to listen. 'Just you now?'

'Jacob couldn't stay: busy man, things to kill. Couple of the girls are still here do the real work.'

The suggestion of a nod. 'We don't... escape each other.'

'Seems not.'

He was fading.

'On bus… together. Thanks… for company.'

'See you in hell, George.'

'I keep your seat warm.'

61.

The police found him later that morning, a cold twist of flesh wrapped in greasy sheets, hidden in the heart of the old city he had determined to upend. In the next room one of the women was burning papers.

The killings in Houndsditch sparked one of the largest police operations in the city's history. The police were set on retribution, and among them were some steady skillful men who'd worked hard to know the twilight world of the East End, and they had huge public support. Nina was picked up and questioned within a day. I confess I wondered what she was like in that moment. Scared, surely, as the big uniform jackets and shabby plain-clothes coats closed in. And defiant, and calculating: I'd seen her myself in greater despair and greater danger, and she spent her life waiting for the police of one country or another. One of the chaps from that chaotic Houndsditch hallway was arrested soon after, a smashed door and a police pistol in his face before he'd had time to think.

Having slipped out through a skylight and over the roof-tops, aware that Jacob might well be lurking behind the first corner to finish me off, I had given the police all I could.

I tried to tell them there was worse to come, but they weren't having it. I told Bunce, wary and doubting. I told Faversham, sneering and distracted. I told everyone from the Commissioner to the cleaner, and none was interested. The best I got was an invitation to make even more of a fool of myself at a grand committee meeting, with the big chief this time, the Home Secretary himself, Winston bloody Churchill.

Pending that, and having run out of people to annoy, I retired to my sitting room and settled into a routine of having a large drink, gazing out of the window to see who was spying on me from passing carriages, and being grumpy at Quinn. That circuit three times in the hour, good steady rhythm.

Perhaps understandably, the entertainment value of this began to wane for Quinn. Sometime in the second hour he plonked himself in my line of vision and, in the quiet growl, asked if we were still dug in at Maggers.

Don't ask: Boer War reference, particularly incompetent battle, entrapment, heat, imminent death; you had to be there. It was his way of asking if his employer was in a royal funk and going off his onion.

I was grumpy at him some more, listed the people who had been and/or might still be trying to kill me, and described the experience of the previous afternoon and evening with a growing intensity that turned into a series of single and not entirely coherent words until I ran out of breath.

I think he interpreted this as a yes.

He disappeared, which I celebrated with another drink. Ten minutes later he asked if he could borrow me a moment, and when I stepped out of the sitting room he had a coat on me before I could speak and then more or less pushed me down the back stairs, he following more sedately with a bag. Five furtive minutes had us clear away from Piccadilly, thirty had us in a train heading out of central London. He fixed me a mixture of entertainments likely to distract and soothe, and then let me drink myself unconscious. When I woke next morning, in what had turned out to be a very comfortable bed in the discreet hotel wherever it was, Quinn was the first thing I saw. He had spent the night on guard, slouched in an armchair at the foot of my bed with the Webley in his lap.

62.

People tend to assume I dislike Winston Churchill.

It's true enough that he's an unstoppably public kind of

person, and I'm resolutely private. I suppose they think that the noise he made over his exploits in South Africa - his escape from the Boers and so forth - might get up the noses of others who fought there. But it's never much bothered me. He was genuinely brave, and spoke out boldly and sensibly against mistreatment of the Boers, and deserved his renown. There was the slight impression that the whole British Empire was presumed to be waiting for news of Winston and the Army were lost without him, when in fact we were muddling through all right and hadn't really noticed he'd gone. But he had newspaper columns to fill, and I can't begrudge a man trying to pay his way. He can be hellish full of himself, but with his extraordinary family he's probably had every reason to be. I get the sense he's spent his life trying to get out from under the name: when your father's the most notoriously brilliant politician in the country, and your mother's the most beautiful woman in the English-speaking world, and your least significant relatives are dukes, it must be a bit hard to find your niche. I can never work out his politics or what Ministry he's running this week, but then nor apparently can he, so. On the rare occasions we've met, he's quickly found that I'm no threat to his image or his command of the conversation, and I've been happy to leave him to it and wander off for a quiet smoke.

Churchill strode into the committee room a calculated minute late, a posse of secretaries hurrying after him, and immediately everyone was leaping to their feet. He moved automatically to the empty chair at the head of the conference table, and for a moment just stood there, gazing at his audience. He's not the tallest, Winston, and the effect was of Queen Victoria about to say grace before letting everyone sit down to dinner.

A nod, a murmur of courteous command, and he sat and they all sat and got down to it. Churchill's a businesslike sort of chap, when he wants to be, but I still don't think Whitehall can touch the anarchists' alliance for efficient committee work. The meeting was an ill-informed re-hash of what had been going on, and an impressive if inconclusive summary of what the police were up to.

Only one thing made me sit up. This very morning, apparently, they had arrested Peters-comma-Jacob and one other.

On the surface that was good news for Delamere-comma-Harry. One fewer lunatic roaming London waiting for a chance to murder me was a step in the right direction. Still plenty of them out there, of diverse nationalities probably including my own, but Jacob had been the most alarming. It didn't settle me. With so much chaos, so much I didn't understand, it was hard to know what was important and what was real. From what George had hinted, Jacob's arrest wouldn't stop the greater crime that was planned.

Otherwise I wasn't paying a lot of attention. Faversham had been parked down at the lower end of the table, far from the Home Secretary, and behind Faversham Bunce and I were squeezed into the cheap seats. A short way off I saw Humphrey Erskine, anxious as ever. The room was stifling and the voices were monotonous and even when I wasn't dozing I didn't hear anything sensible or practical.

They got on to a summary of results of interrogations - negligible - and prospects for the legal process against Jacob *et al.* - questionable. And apparently that was that and time for biscuits.

I kicked Faversham. Actually had to kick him; serve him right for trying to shirk an agreement. He jumped satisfactorily, and babbled: 'Home Secretary - with your pardon, sir - there is...' Faversham was a high-flying sort of chap, moving up fast through the ranks, but in this room there were generations of men more senior to him and they were all glaring. You never saw such a forbidding collection of moustaches. 'There is another... There may be a complication...'

I stood up. 'Morning, Churchill.'

'Ye Gods', said Winston Churchill, 'Harry Delamere… It must be worse than we feared.'

'Sorry to butt in. Trust Mrs Winston is well.'

He has one of those faces that looks either eight or eighty and never anything in between. A heavy half-smile appeared on one jowl, and he spoke with the usual ponderous strength.

'Good to see you, old comrade. Should we expect a Boer commando raid in the vestibule? Are you hunted by the Turkish police again?'

'Only the British. No, just heard you might have a new potboiler out and wanted to be first in the queue at the bookstall.'

Oh, one other thing. Surprisingly for a man who can be so witty, Winston Churchill never has been able to spot the joke. 'Alas', he boomed gravely, 'I fear you will be disappointed. The story of these trying days may not be told for many years yet. If I do shed some glimmer of light, it will only be seen by future generations, when the remorseless machine of time has ground us here to dust.'

It being Churchill, that couple of sentences took the best part of a quarter hour to unfold. The grand moustaches watched on bewildered. It was the Home Secretary, so they couldn't interrupt. But they were grumpy at what had happened to their meeting. They kept turning to glare at Faversham. They didn't like the interruption to the agenda, and they certainly didn't like me. I had the impression poor Faversham would be in for a tough time round the back of the bike-sheds after.

'What have you for us, old horse?' he said at last. I'd got distracted by wondering whether one of the secretaries was responsible for jotting down the Churchill wisdom ready for the memoirs, or whether it was such good stuff he'd remember it all himself.

So I told him. Crisp and compact, military briefing-style, I gave him a potted version of my accidental involvement in the more hair-raising moments of the previous couple of weeks: the opera, the flying display, the ballet, the shootings in Houndsditch. I mentioned that the German Embassy was actively engaged - that got his attention. And I emphasized the radicals: their competence, their commitment, and above all the fact that something big was still due to come.

'Bigger than the pitiless murder of three brave policemen?' Churchill asked, and I nodded. 'In the arena of human struggle, it is ever the lot of the few, to suffer for the good of the many. Incidentally, I hear that at least one man owes his life to your intervention, Harry. You have lost none of your old dash, it seems.'

'I did what any man here would have done. The point is that that business was... unintended; a side-show. Those poor lads just got in the way. I know there was an assassin on the loose at the ballet, and he almost got through.' I wasn't going to mention chandeliers and dancers' tights, not in this company. 'Very close to the Russian Minister of War. And to you, Churchill.'

The faces at the table were very stern and very cautious. Unintentionally, I'd put them on the spot a bit. They didn't appreciate or believe me, but they couldn't be seen to take a threat to the Home Secretary less than seriously. Not with him sitting there, anyway.

A couple of them started in on the forthcoming Coal Act again. It would have seemed daft, except that I knew that the anarchists were hot about the Coal Act too. What I'd not gathered was just how involved Churchill was in trying to push it through. Nor how much criticism he was attracting: protests, anonymous threats of violence against him, all sorts. Apparently he was seen as very anti-worker. It didn't seem enough to make some rogue revolutionary commit a spectacular outrage, but the Home Office had to take it all seriously.

And for the kind of people I'd been mixing with, blowing up a senior politician would be just the ticket regardless.

There were a few empty words about the possibility of

Bolsheviks attacking the Russian Minister of War and his delegation while they were on British soil, and much harumphing at the possible embarrassment to Britain.

Then someone mentioned another recent attack on Churchill. I vaguely remembered it in the newspapers. Month or so back, someone had gone at him with a whip, on the train. At the time I'd not thought much of it - Winston had probably pinched the chap's seat, or got bogged down in an hour-long sentence about the history of the railways. It turned out the attacker had been an activist for votes for women; he certainly didn't sound like an advert for votes for men. Anyway, here was another source of threat.

I really couldn't see big Jacob marching round Hyde Park on Sunday afternoons prodding policemen with an umbrella. And Nina and Sara, with their toughness and their daring and their knives hidden up every sleeve and whatnot, didn't look like they needed anyone's help in securing their rights. But it was another insight on how lively things were in an average day *chez* Churchill. And any part of it could be cover or pretext for some more serious outrage.

Winston began to sum up, and I began to switch off again as we were clearly in for a long stay. We were going to go forward together, apparently, great respect and gratitude for the endeavours of the police, but it was his duty to maintain his public profile, what had he to offer but sweat and blood and so forth. Not too much of either, one hoped.

As I slumped down further in my seat, my attention was caught by a frantic performance of staring eyes and waggling eyebrows a short distance off.

Little Humphrey Erskine, it seemed, was signalling to me in his most secretive manner.

63.

Humphrey Erskine did not, for once, have anything new

to add to the melodrama. From his questions, I gather he assumed there was some deeper behind-the-scenes knowledge that hadn't been shared in the meeting. He further assumed that I would know it. I tried reassuring him that there was no great mystery, just a great bureaucracy. Then I had to admit that there might be a great mystery, but I'd be the last man in London to know it, the police being more comfortable collaborating with a foreign murderer like Ilyin than a patriotic but confused Englishman like self.

Humphrey was attempting a suit today, but the style was unorthodox and the material a bit plusher than Whitehall was used to. Poor lad seemed forever to be trying to cut a dash he couldn't quite carry off, but I rather admired him for ploughing his own furrow in this especially dull straight field.

My answer had done nothing for his perpetual anxiety. I tried to be sympathetic. 'Guess all of these excitements must have shaken up the tour rather.' He looked even more gloomy. 'Sorry to hear it. Good initiative, and you were doing the thing well.' He accepted this with the empty politeness it had been given in. 'No way you could have known what was going on.' He took this more eagerly. He'd probably hoped for a bit of boost from escorting the visitors; doubt the Foreign Office would be feeling so positive now.

He shook his head. 'I mean, it was clear that, well - with some of the people they met - some of the London people that were brought in as extra hands - there were a few rogues and rascals. But I think that's normal in temporary work around the stage. I never dreamed...' He looked a bit shaken. 'Even when things seemed a bit colourful, I just thought...'

'Part of the fun, eh? Bit of bandit melodrama off-stage as well as on?' I smiled, sympathetic; I think he was grateful to be understood. 'Listen,' I went on, 'I'm still trying to get my head around all these Latvians. Some, I know, were nothing to do with the troupe.' A nod. 'That mad evening - the shooting of that chap Kyril - that's mixed up with the rest of it somehow; must be. D'you think there's some way of getting the names of the men who were onstage for the shooting, the others in the firing squad? Might be able to check them against the names the police are picking up or looking for.'

'Yes, of course! Good thinking. Sure that's possible.'

'And have you come across a Fritz? First name presumably. Among the troupe, or the hangers-on?'

He was thinking hard. 'Rings a bell, yes. Dashed if I know right off. So many of the unfamiliar names... I'll check that too, of course.' I was glad to have a track to follow, and he was glad to seem useful. 'Oh, Delamere - just an idea - my wretched uncle is insisting I go and watch another flying display today. Fellow setting off across the Channel; big prize at stake. I ought to go - family loyalty, all that rot. If you fancy...'

Actually, I did fancy. Escaping Whitehall, escaping London, sticking my head up in the clouds: sounded just the ticket.

So I was on the Kent coast later that day, to watch Cecil Grace bumping and skimming across the turf in his little machine and then drifting up into the infinite. No circuit this time, no display for the crowds. He was aiming at France, and he had miles of open water to cross alone.

Some men are like that. No one's saying they have to do it. But they somehow feel they do. Test their limits; find out what's beyond them. Myself, I've done a rum thing or two in my time, but only when I really had to. Chaps like Grace - and indeed women like Vanstone - make me uncomfortable. The sense that I don't fully understand humans; that perhaps there's supposed to be more.

I got a glimpse of the pilot, shortly before he climbed into his machine. A large, open face, suddenly very young, not seeing any of us and staring somewhere else. The same unsettling combination of worlds as before: the ludicrous flimsy machine of wood and canvas with a chap sitting in it dressed for an afternoon's walk down the lane; the motor engine at the heart of it, delicate advanced inventiveness and screaming power; and the wild idea that a man could escape the world and see us all differently.

I saw Sir Malachai Erskine again, the old Scot obsessed by the new technology, waving a bony figure towards the flying machine and haranguing a group of listeners, no doubt about the deficiencies of the older British engine designs relative to the French. I saw Humphrey Erskine watching his peculiar dwindling inheritance from the back of the group, frustrated, dutiful, weary. A couple of the listeners were in foreign uniforms, and the more prominent chap doing most of the listening might have been foreign too. My mind moved naturally to the dead man I'd found - and then lost - in Malachai Erskine's tent at the Weybridge flying display.

I saw Harriet Vanstone, first of all with her fellow-pilot, Grace. Even a short distance off I knew the tone of her conversation: brisk, earnest, practical, fraternal. Then I saw her close by the motor engine of Grace's flying machine. The regular crowd were being kept well back, so she obviously had some special status as another flier which allowed her privileged access. Another woman stood close beside her: shorter, with a darker harder beauty, wearing an odd working outfit closer to a countryman's riding clobber than anything womanly. I remembered Vanstone had mentioned a Marie, who helped her with the mechanical stuff. The two of them were absorbed in this machine: observing, pointing, exploring, analyzing. I felt a touch of envy for Marie, for the easy harmony with which she shared Vanstone's space and interest, the way their hands moved and worked together. Once again I admired Harriet Vanstone's total indifference to the usual expectations of woman's role, interests, posture, conversation, decorum. If she and her friend wished to root around in that infernal and oily machine they would do so, and tea and gossip and all the other stuff she despised could wait.

I saw the grandees greeting Cecil Grace and wishing him good luck: local gentry, some foreign uniforms again. And they made me think of Winston Churchill. His necessary public prominence; his insistence on being where the action was. I remembered how close Jacob and his assassin had got to Churchill at the ballet. I considered how many other public events he'd have to attend over the next few weeks. I wondered how many anarchists were still out there: where they'd be holed up, how they'd arrange it, who would know.

Back in London that evening, I contacted - and I don't know which of us was more surprised - Inspector Bunce.

64.

The new Tower Bridge had been up and working for more than a decade. Astonishing structure. Very London: all you really need for a bridge is a couple of lengths of steel, but we're going to build all these towers and spans and whatnot bigger than anything you've ever seen, just because we can; up yours, Paris.

These days the upper walkway is mainly used by good time girls - or so I gather - and frankly anyone who's got any energy left after climbing all those hundreds of steps deserves a few minutes of joy.

This night I wasn't heading for the upper walkway, alas. Inspector Bunce led me into the ground under the southern end of the bridge. Ahead of us some vast engine was pumping away, its noise getting louder as we tramped through the gloomy brick corridors.

Eventually Bunce stopped in front of a metal door.

His usual London grumble: 'You sure you know what you're doing, Delamere?'

'No.'

He nodded, suspicions confirmed. He knocked on the door.

After a theatrical moment of pause, the door opened. Immediately, the noise of thumping hissing machinery exploded.

Ilya Ilyich Ilyin, voted world's nastiest Russian three years running, stepped out. He closed the door, and the noise was muffled again.

He was expecting Bunce, and gave him a courteous nod.

Bunce nodded back, and then turned and walked away. I stepped forwards into the lamplight. I saw Ilyin's immediate unease.

'Ah…' A little sigh as he recognized me. Surprised, but not rattled. 'Unexpected to find you collaborating with the Metropolitan Police, Sir Henry.' The high-pitched, rolling accent.

'Even more unexpected to find me collaborating with you.'

'Indeed.'

'Old Bunce is all right. He hasn't the imagination to be corrupt, and even when he's stubbornly getting the wrongest end of the stick, he's still trying sincerely to do his job.' I saw him reflecting on this. 'Like you, Ilyin.'

I saw the eyes widen slightly behind the little spectacles. 'You honour me, Sir Henry.' The humour was flat. 'To what do I owe the pleasure of this… furtive appointment?'

'I need your help.'

Again the suggestion of movement around the eyes. And then of amusement on the lips.

Still he did not speak.

'I'm trapped in a world I don't understand, and a plot I don't understand. You warned me about your revolutionaries and anarchists, Ilyin; and you were right. They're causing mayhem in British back-streets, and British policemen are dying. Now, maybe you don't care so much about that.' He certainly wasn't looking like he cared. 'But there's worse to come. Something more dramatic is planned.'

Silent. Still. Eventually he nodded.

'I take it for granted, Sir Henry. Always something more dramatic is planned.'

'And it doesn't disturb you?'

'On the contrary, Sir Henry; it reassures me. And if such a thing happens, perhaps it will convince your complacent government that they should listen to my government.'

Still so steady, so sure. I was running out of argument. 'Perhaps you don't mind about your anarchists causing outrages around London. No harm to you, just proves your point. But do you really want to be responsible for the lapse in security that allows the death of a British government minister?'

There was silence.

'You've something I want, Ilyin. A piece of information.'

Eventually: 'Mmm.' It came out as a thin whine. The eyes were blank as he considered. 'I fear I still do not see what possible influence you have to bargain with me, Sir Henry.'

'Couple of weeks back, a group of half a dozen men in police uniforms busted into a house in the East End of London, and cut the throat of an old man. I'd just escaped out of the attic that they were trying to get into. I saw them, and I wasn't alone. If I was introduced to the staff of the Russian Embassy, and your associates, I wonder how many of them I'd recognize. Then it happened again: a raid by fake policemen, just a few hours before the shootings in Houndsditch. This time I was trapped in the cellar. Again your men.'

The eyes showed nothing. 'My goodness,' he said at last. 'How you do get about.'

'Now, perhaps I can't prove you were there. But can you prove you weren't? The Home Office are being terribly polite to the Russian Embassy because of your Minister of War being here, and the European situation. But I doubt they've any illusions about you and your secret police. They wouldn't find it hard to believe me. As for the newspapers…'

He produced a little shrug, the face complacent. 'The strategic friendship of Russia is too important for your government to question. Despite any… more exotic entertainments my men might possibly indulge in, I fear that my reputation is rather better than yours, Sir Henry, even with your own authorities.'

I nodded. 'Exactly. I've nothing to lose. But you? Even the idea that you might be impersonating British police, that you might be killing British subjects on British soil... Precisely because the relationship is so important, precisely because your Minister is here and the Government wants to deal, neither your politicians nor mine would want the slightest hint of a public scandal about your activities.'

The eyes had disappeared again.

'One piece of information, Ilyin. One name.'

65.

Quinn didn't like what he had to do next. He's done his share of fighting and killing and generally fooling around, but he gets snooty about eavesdropping and spying. Not manly. In Cornwall, if you don't like a chap you punch him in the face or at worst sabotage his lobster pots. Sneaking about they leave to the English, and other foreigners.

Especially he didn't like the spying I was asking him to do now. But he did it, because I couldn't: I couldn't risk being seen anywhere near the place. He spent two nights lurking and wandering around St James's, and by the end of it he told me what I needed to know - as well as his intention of joining the next group of revolutionaries we met. Too close a view of social life in the West End of London can be as distasteful as its opposite in the East End.

My turn came the next night. I tried explaining to Quinn that my shift was considerably riskier than his. He wasn't impressed. He was sure what I was doing was lunacy, and probably more worried about me getting shot or banged up for life just before pay-day.

Caterina von Falkenhayn had the use of a set of rooms on

the top floor of a house on King Street. Convenient for the Embassy and the shops. No doubt the average German diplomat is expected to maintain a certain lifestyle, and young Caterina was considerably more than average in every way. Tonight, her entertainment had been strictly official: a new year's reception at the Embassy for all the staff. What von Falkenhayn got up to in her off-duty hours was beyond my feeble male imagination. Anyway, she was back in her apartment before midnight. Immediately she was into a hot bath and she soaked in it a good half hour: a rare sense of abandon, of that cold poise thawing, the tight-strapped costume cast aside on the tiles. Then at last she walked through to her bedroom, wrapping a dressing gown around herself.

I know all this because when she stepped into her bedroom she found me sitting in the armchair, still trying to work out if the book titles at her bedside really meant what I thought they meant, and wondering why anyone would choose to sleep or do the other thing under a portrait of Bismarck.

Her reactions were clear and fast across the crystal features: alarm, calculation, curiosity. She'd recognized me. If I was half as ruthless as she thought, or one tenth as ruthless as she herself, I had to be counted a threat. Yet I did not seem threatening.

I stood. A chap does.

Unrestrained by formal clothes, she only seemed more poised, more naturally powerful. 'Do you come to sing English lullaby?' she said at last.

'I'll tell you a fairy story if you like.' I was standing relaxed, hands visible and open. 'First, sincere apologies for busting in like this. Very bad form.' I was watching her face: there was a chance she'd scream, which I didn't want, and there was rather more chance she'd drop me through a hidden trapdoor or stab me with a poisoned hairpin. The suggestion of a frown; she didn't trust me. 'Second, just in case you still think

I am what I'm not…' - I pulled my jacket open - 'Nothing in here to harm you.'

Cold smile. 'We are told this about English men, yes.'

I pointed to a curious multi-barrel pistol on a table between us, next to a parcel wrapped in tissue paper. 'I found your pepper-pot special - didn't want any surprises - and I've left it out for you there. Please take a moment to check that I haven't interfered with it. There's been too much fooling around with firearms in this business.' She gazed at me warily. 'I want you to know that you can finish what you started in that cellar, whenever you feel like it.'

I was taking a risk on her psychology. I was calculating that curiosity about why I'd stuck myself in the lion's den - or the lioness's bedroom - plus confidence about my lack of threat would relax her enough to give me time.

She walked to the table, and picked up the pistol.

Taking one hell of a risk.

She lifted the pistol, and pointed it at me.

I tried not to look like a man whose luck in calculating risk had just run out.

She tested the weight, and then with rapid deft movements dismantled the unusual mechanism and reassembled it.

Again it was pointing at me. Just a yard or two from my chest.

She laid it back down on the table. Barrel pointing in my direction.

'I should be hurt that you didn't take my word for it.'

'You English are too free with your words.'

'Remarkable little machine that.'

'Schüler Reform Pistolle. German manufacture. Six millimetre calibre. Automatic gas-ejection system for the spent cartridges.'

'And four barrels.'

'For when I have four unwanted men in my bedroom.'

'No doubt a frequent misfortune.'

'Or just one very unwanted. How did you get in here?'

Now, if you liked Victoria and Vanstone's tip about the Alhambra fire escape, there's another that might come in handy provided you can find an excuse to be in Christie's King Street auction rooms late in the day and contrive to lose yourself while they're locking up. But a good magician never tells. 'I came down the chimney', I said. 'Seasonal approach. I regret to say that this isn't a social call. Why don't you put on something a little warmer? I'll shut my eyes.'

She reached for the belt of her dressing gown and then the collar, adjusting them so that they were straighter and revealed more of the body underneath.

'It's a wonder why you bother with pistols and knives. Now, you're probably asking yourself why I'm...'

'Not at all.' With her hair down, and most of her clothes, she looked even younger. But still the utter confidence. Whatever they do in those finishing schools, it breeds authority and style. 'From after the incident at the opera we follow you, knowing that you will reveal something useful. I know that you are strange, even for an Englishman. I know that I will kill you. The rest is irrelevance.'

'About that: you think I killed your chap because he was having a sneaky peek at old Erskine's new-and-improved flying machine motor, yes? I continue to suggest that I did not. Partly because the British government and I aren't on those terms. Partly because I very much doubt the British government knows, let alone cares, about the tinkering of one mad Scotsman.'

'If that were true, they would be very foolish. More likely you think us foolish. We know that the Erskine machine is not only the most innovative but also the most promising currently in development in your country.'

'Then you know a damn sight more than I do.'

'Undoubtedly. Including how empty is your attempt to escape your guilt.'

'Damnit, girl, there's more going on! Something bigger. A

man was murdered in an opera performance, and it's linked to Russian anarchists in Britain. The other night, when you were at the ballet, Bolsheviks tried to assassinate Winston Churchill and maybe a few other high-priced guests too.' I'd started to get her attention. 'And they're not done. Somewhere out there tonight, there's a man with a gun or a bomb, and mayhem in mind.'

She was thinking hard. I had to hope that was good. I let her. After a couple of moments, she said: 'Even so.'

'You don't care? What if - likely enough - it's a bomb? What if - likely enough - it's a diplomatic event? What if the German Ambassador happens to be chatting to our Home Secretary at that moment? You going to be quite so cool when you're back in Berlin explaining how you missed a chance to save his life?' The expression had frozen. She was thinking even harder, and she didn't like it. 'You were up to no good somehow with Erskine's machine. You were up to no good with me. You were at the ballet that night, when that assassination attempt almost came off. Leaving aside the revolutionary madmen, who benefits most from the death of a senior British politician and a senior Russian politician? If an attempt succeeds, who will be blamed?' I gazed at her, and now I could see from the hostility in those electric eyes that I was getting through at last. 'It won't be me.'

She stared a moment longer. Then she stepped to her dressing table, and pulled out the chair. Still watching me, she sat, very upright, and crossed one long leg over the other. The dressing gown fell away from the upper leg. She pointed me to my armchair. 'Proceed', she said.

By the time I'd got sat again, she'd picked up a silver brush from the dressing table and was pulling it down through her hair with long, regular, remorseless strokes. And all the time her eyes stayed fixed on me.

'Right you are. Miss Caterina, I've no doubt you're overseeing a very impressive intelligence operation in London, and I've no doubt I and the British Government don't know about almost any of it. But we know some. And there are a couple of things you don't know.'

The brush hesitated a moment. I'd really got her attention now. Or perhaps she'd just hit a tangle.

'There is a man named Leon Beron. Moustache, fancy watch. You have him, let's say... on retainer. He's one of your sources in the London underworld. He does odd jobs for you, when you don't want to get your frock muddy. He rents a few properties, for his own activities and for you to use for bits of work you don't want to been seen doing in the West End: wrapping your Christmas presents, say, or cutting my throat.'

Beron was the name I'd got from Ilyin. The name of the anxious man who'd been in that cellar with us. Just a name, but it was my only chance of bluffing von Falkenhayn that I basically knew everything and was just filling in a couple of gaps, rather than being in the dark and making it all up as I went along.

'He's a good spy. He said so when we were chatting in his cellar, and I know it. He was a participant in a secret meeting of radicals a week or so back, which discussed this forthcoming act of violence. An active participant. No doubt he reported... some of this to you.'

Now that sharp mind of hers was replaying what Beron had told the Embassy, and she was wondering how much he'd left out. For all I knew he'd given it word-by-word, but she couldn't be certain. And that was my slender advantage.

I didn't mention he was also earning a bit on the side - or keeping himself alive a bit longer - by passing on tit-bits to the Russians as well. Hence Ilyin kicking his door in when he'd felt let down. This Beron chap seemed a bit of a sneak, but given what he was up against my sympathies were largely with him rather than the international diplomatic thugs.

Into the silence, I said: 'I was a participant in the radical meeting too.' Her eyes widened. I was only confirming her wholly false picture of what a man of intrigue I was. But again, that bluff had become necessary. 'Jolly interesting it was, too.' Still she watched. Probably fancying a bit of front-line sack-wearing herself; she had that kind of energy.

'So', I said, sitting up and trying to sound efficient, 'some significant radical action is planned. I calculate it is not a German Embassy plan. If I'm wrong, and you really are going to murder our Home Secretary, maybe a slack handful of passers-by into the bargain, then you won't wish to give me any information. Fair enough, quite understand.'

Watching her face - its liveliness, its brilliance - I wondered if I'd miscalculated, yet again. It was fifty-fifty she might decide this was rather a good wheeze; gold star from the Kaiser for potting a British Minister.

'I'm getting cold, Sir Henry', she said. 'What do you want?'

'The answer to one simple question. I've no doubt it's German Embassy money that pays for the properties that Beron uses. And I've no doubt - you're an efficient lot - that he has to specify details to get you to stump up. That's all I want, please: the addresses you are paying for.'

It wasn't what she'd expected. I could see her re-adjusting.

'Unless you've got a battalion of Prussian Guardsmen stored ready to seize London, this can't make any difference to your activities. Won't take you five minutes to arrange new properties, and you'll be molesting baronets to your heart's content.'

Her mind was working hard.

'You're a professional, Miss Caterina. Your work is a constant balancing of competition and co-operation. Today I think we both benefit from a bit of co-operation.'

Still thinking. 'And for this co-operation, I get..?'

'You get to continue your activities here uninterrupted. You get another day of peace from the revolutionaries of Europe. You get my gratitude.'

Again the hard smile. I always struggle to come up with a third.

'Such a price it is impossible to measure', she said acidly.

'But it is probably enough for some addresses. You will have them.'

I thanked her, and stood.

'You were the companion of Victoria Carteret', she said, back to brushing her hair again. I stopped. Waited. 'This is generally known.'

I said nothing.

'You do not deny it, or confirm it?'

'You say you know it, so there's no point in me discussing it. I certainly don't intend to.'

She stood. The dressing gown was tight on her athletic body. She smiled; sneered, almost. 'The most beautiful - the most elegant - of our cohort.' The smile hardened. 'Everything I know about the quality of the English - the virtues, yes, and the pride and the arrogance - I know from her.' I suspect she noticed that my expression wasn't encouraging. It only made her stronger. 'You want to know the epithet - the nick-name - she had?'

'I do not.' It came out harder than I'd planned, and she saw it. She hesitated. Smiled again.

Still smiling, she walked towards me.

Her lips explored mine; good old rummage. She ran her teeth along my jaw; raked them over my cheek. Then she bit softly on my lower lip, and pulled at it, and bit harder and I could hear her breath and feel its heat and at last she drew blood and released me a moment. Those cold eyes were anything but, now: there was a wildness in them, a hot hunger. With the tip of her tongue, she licked the taste of my blood off her teeth.

'You will stay till morning.' Half a command; half a statement of fact.

I tested the remains of my lip with a finger. 'I doubt I'd survive that long.'

'Better purposeful destruction in a beautiful fire than empty endurance in tepid mediocrity.'

'That a personal observation, or an official statement of

German foreign policy?'

'You're frightened of me, Sir Henry Delamere.'

I stepped in close. 'Yes', I said. 'But not for the reasons you imagine.' I kissed her again, like I meant it. For England, that one: just to show that even we know how to get the propellor turning when we feel like it, and no one has to bleed. 'You can pass on as much of that as you like to old Hahn', I said. I made for the window. 'I'll show myself out.'

'Delamere!'

One leg out of the window, I looked back.

'You have left your parcel here, on the table.'

'Unthinkable to call on a girl in this season without a little something.' I turned away into the darkness, trying to remember the footholds. 'Happy new year.'

66.

Caterina von Falkenhayn gave me two addresses which the German Embassy was funding for Beron.

The first was a basement flat in Limehouse.

The door was opened by a woman in her twenties, with big alarmed eyes and an exotic dressing gown under two coats. I shoved my way in, explaining that I was from the GLCC and trying to track a reported gas leak, risk of explosion, terribly frightening, won't take a moment. It didn't take much more than a moment to confirm that there were no revolutionaries hiding in the place. And the lady's charms seemed strictly traditional. Beron's mistress, I suspect, comfortably installed at German expense. A glimpse of the attempt to carve out a bit of a normal life among the madness.

The second address was a set of rooms upstairs at Number 100, Sidney Street. Whitechapel again, and barely a mile from the scene of the shoot-out.

After two previous unhappy experiences when I found

myself trapped in a shabby East End boarding house - well, three in fact - this time I'd taken a precaution. Hang on, wrong again: four previous unhappy experiences in shabby East End boarding houses. Four; what a month.

The precaution, as so often, was Quinn. Hanging back, fifty yards behind me. Ready, if I didn't come out within five minutes, to bust in after me with the Webley, the Metropolitan Police, the whole Brigade of Guards, whatever he felt like.

We were well into the evening now, but I was let in the front door of the building easily enough, cheery smile and just returning ten bob I borrowed off mumblemumble. I climbed two flights of narrow creaking wooden stairs, through gloom and damp and winter chill and the many stenches of an east London squat.

I'd probably be recognized; I didn't want to seem a threat. Avoiding any obvious caution, swaying and squeezing up those stairs, I was a sitting duck for anyone with a pistol or something they fancied dropping on my head.

In the silence, in my anxiety, I heard whistling.

And then I recognized the whistling. Not a tune I knew, but… I'd heard it.

As I reached the top floor - a dingy corridor, bare boards, ancient wallpaper with the grease and mould clear even in the shadows - the whistling was clearer. I'd heard it during that mad night of the gunfight in Houndsditch.

And now, I realized, I'd heard it first during the performance of *Tosca*.

A minute later I had rejoined Quinn. Thirty minutes later, Bunce and Faversham had joined us. Travelling separately, if you please; that's where your taxes are going. After that, things began to snowball. A couple of more senior officers turned up: grim grizzled warriors who clearly knew what they were about. In the early hours of January 3rd, hundreds of policemen began discreetly to move into Sidney Street and the streets around it. I watched it all from the all-night eel-

and-pie shop that the police had commandeered as their forward base - cosy, convenient, and you never know when you need a snack - and they weren't fooling around any. One by one, during the hours of darkness, all of the houses adjacent and opposite Number 100 were woken, and given five minutes to get up and out. By back doors and dark alleys, the whole street was evacuated.

Many of the policemen were armed.

The police had tried tackling these radicals regular-style, and three good brave men had died. Now they were back to finish the job, and they weren't going to make the same mistake. They were coming with unstoppable force, and they were clearing the ground so that they could use it without qualms.

Which was very impressive, but it left me with something of a problem. The Metropolitan Police were making every proper preparation for an imminent battalion-scale armed assault on that upstairs flat. I, meanwhile, needed to get into it for a chat with the inhabitants.

67.

By dawn on the 3rd of January, there were only two residents left in the whole of Sidney Street. Two men, asleep and entirely oblivious to what had gone on in the darkness.

They were woken by someone throwing stones at their windows. In evacuating the ground-floor tenants, the police had got a look at that twisting staircase, and they knew a death-trap when they saw one. Again, no chances. One of the men stuck his head out of a front window, understandably wary, and even if the half-glimpsed figures in the windows opposite, on the rooftops and bunched at the nearest corners didn't tell him immediately what was going on, a shouted command from the street below did the trick.

It had begun.

The stones and the shouts would have suggested to the two anarchists that the besiegers were keeping their distance, for now. To get a fuller idea of the lie of the land, a little while later one of them opened the door onto the staircase. He found Sir Henry Delamere, cramped and mouldy-arsed, sitting against the banister post.

'Collecting for the Police Benevolent Fund', I said; 'dead Latvians chapter.'

I clambered to my feet, there was a tortured creak and if I hadn't adjusted at the last minute the whole banister would have given way under me. Saved everyone the trouble of shooting me, anyway.

I got upright at last, and tried to look composed. 'To answer your question:' I went on, 'the house is empty. The police are playing it careful for now, but there's an awful lot of them and they're not going away.'

It was the chap from the firing squad, the one who'd gone over the wall. Remembering the mad escape through the night after the Houndsditch shooting, I took a punt. 'Why, it's... Fritz, isn't it?'

He nodded. His bewilderment kept the door open long enough for me to get a toe in it. 'Thought I'd stop by for a chat. I was with George at the end; couple of messages from him.' Slowly, deliberately, I pulled my coat open to show I was unarmed. 'A peaceful chat.'

I pushed past him into the flat. I thought I heard a shout from downstairs somewhere, and a reply; maybe there had been someone else left. Then he was in, and closing the door behind us. Locking it.

From the street there were a couple of shots, and in the next room a window shattered. Immediately I heard shots in reply, the second Bolshevik returning fire.

I'd had half an idea that, as well as finding answers about the planned outrage, I might be able to encourage these chaps to give it up quietly. That was looking less likely now.

Fritz was watching me warily, curiously. 'You with police?'

'No. And they don't know I'm here.'

It didn't make him any less wary or curious.

'I think you go by Peter, no? Called The Painter?'

'No. Er… yes. It'll do.'

Keeping a watchful distance, he walked around me and took the key out of the door and put it in his pocket.

I fought down the instinct to step to the window and have a peek round the grey net curtain that covered it. If these lunatics were already firing out into the street, the slightest twitch of the curtain would draw the shots of a dozen police pistols. Picking my path as carefully as I could, I took a wooden chair and set it against the wall beside but as far as possible from the window, and sat. To have any chance of getting sense out of Fritz, I had to maintain some unlikely calm, and that meant this ludicrous pretence.

He watched the performance. I don't think he believed it.

The window exploded. I crossed my legs, and lit up a cigarette. Trying to keep my hand steady, I offered one to my companion.

He'd ducked when the glass smashed, and now he shuffled low to the window and let off a couple of shots. The police fired back, and plaster and a few last shards of glass tumbled down over his shoulders. As he turned and edged away, he found my hand out still offering the cigarette.

He stared, as though I were mad - I couldn't disagree - and then he took the cigarette, and let me light it.

'Police pistols:' I said, 'accurate range of - what? - twenty yards? They'll only hit you by accident.'

He was too proud to crouch. Instead he walked quickly across the room, kicked another chair round against the opposite wall, and sat facing me. He kept his pistol in his hand, laid loose in his lap. Despite the chaos of the moment, and the fact he was only in his shirt-sleeves - the armed police raid had forestalled a full toilette - he cut rather an elegant figure. The clothes were reasonable quality; fancy, even. The moustache was full and well-groomed, with a rakish curl. He held himself with arrogant poise.

'Hoping for a bit of a chat, Fritz', I said. 'If you're not too busy.'

The door from the other room opened and a face stuck itself through, dark hair and wild eyes. It gaped in understandable surprise at the two of us sitting smoking.

Yet again I had the impression it was someone I'd seen before.

They had a rapid unhappy exchange in Latvian or whatever. Then another shot from outside, and the second chap disappeared to go and retaliate.

'For form's sake', I began, 'I should point out that you've a fair chance of handing yourself in. Police won't like the fact that you shot at them - bit old-fashioned that way - but unless they can prove you murdered one of their own the other week, you'll be out and about again in no time, revolutionizing to your heart's content. If you try to make a fight of it you'll be dead by lunchtime.' He just gazed at me. 'But then I suppose you're the sort of chap who wants to go out fighting, eh? Blaze of glory.'

He let out a long jet of smoke from under the moustache.

'All right then. Tell me about *Tosca*. Why did you shoot poor Kyril?' His expression changed immediately: more serious. 'I thought he was singing rather well, myself.'

'I do not shoot him.' The accent was heavy, the words firm and insistent.

'Yes, thought you'd say that.' I wasn't convinced it was him, but I needed to get the conversation moving. 'And yet you ran. Five chaps in the firing squad, five rifles, five shots; and only you ran.'

'I do not shoot him!'

His vehemence was striking. This was a chap who was cheerfully starting a fatal gun-battle with half the police in London, and yet he was truly offended by the suggestion of that one shooting.

'Kyril was one of your own... Bad form, surely. Why did

you do it?'

He lifted the pistol, now firm-gripped, until it was pointing at me. 'I - do - not.'

I managed to fake a smile, at the irony of his gesture. 'So who did?'

He lowered the pistol again. Shrugged. Happy to pot policemen all day; very unhappy at the idea he might shoot a fellow-countryman.

'If you didn't shoot him, Fritz, why did you run?'

Shrug. He realized I'd got him rattled, and I saw the shoulders shifting and straightening as he re-gathered his poise.

'Doesn't look good, you running. Only you.'

'I know police will blame me. So I must run.'

'The police would look at all five of the men in the firing squad. All five could say that. But only you ran.' He was glaring at me. 'One of your own...' I tutted theatrically. 'Why should they blame you? Just you?'

'I... Maybe I know police better than others. I am hunted by Russian police. In prison. Not again.'

I didn't believe it. A firing squad with big Jacob in it would only ever have one winner in the 'most ruthless revolutionary' category.

'Anyway: all rifles have blank. I saw preparations.' My face showed what I thought of this claim, and he spoke more strongly. 'I have handled guns. Men have died at my hand. I am trusted with rifles.' Doubtful logic, I thought, but if you say so. 'All blank.'

I didn't believe him about this either. And yet I couldn't see why he would lie. He'd cover up for someone else in the firing squad, perhaps. But then the assertion that all the rifles had blank charges was unnecessary; he could have said nothing, not mentioned his role at all.

In any case, it seemed I wasn't going to get anywhere with him.

We smoked in silence a while, each trying to pretend we

were calm amid that madness.

Twice Fritz stalked warily to the window, and crouched beneath the sill. The first time he quickly stuck his pistol out and fired two random shots. A few came back in reply, but there was no more glass to smash. On a January morning, it must have been getting pretty chilly in that windowless room, but I can't say I'd noticed. The second time he just waggled the curtain, and waited for the volley of pistol fire from outside. As it ripped through the shabby lace above his head, he turned to me and grinned.

The sound of shots was coming now and then from the next room, too. So his chum seemed to be doing the same thing.

We sat there.

The sparse shabby furniture of the average lodging room; the dust.

The faint sour stink of meals with too much cabbage, privies with too little cleaning.

The awful pregnancy of all that firepower outside: not coming in, but not letting us out.

Now I did start to notice the cold.

Mostly I just watched Fritz, waiting for him to feel the need to speak.

The cabbage-and-privy mix seemed to be getting stronger.

I sniffed a couple of times, looked more curiously at Fritz.

'You smell gas?' I said.

68.

I couldn't be sure what I'd smelled, and I couldn't be sure what damage had been done to the no doubt shoddy fixings by all the gunfire shredding the building. He shrugged. I sniffed a couple of times more.

'Tell me about the bomb', I said.

I'd been building up to this. I knew I'd have got nothing

by busting in and trying to hustle him into it.

But Fritz just shrugged again. 'For bomb I don't know.'

'I know there's a big event planned,' I went on. 'George's last words. It made him happy, knowing the cause would triumph even after his death.' I was over-stating it wildly, of course, but I couldn't show how feebly I was feeling my way. 'Everything ready now, I gather. I suppose you've got it here.'

He was looking unsure, uncomfortable. He repeated: 'For bomb I don't know.' The insistence was different from his usual easy poise.

Had I miscalculated entirely? Jumped into this madness for no reason?

Was it my imagination, or had his glance shifted towards the next room, just for an instant, and then been brought back under control again?

'Suppose this morning's excitement will force a postponement. Rain stopped play, eh?' Nothing. 'Bomb's in the next room, is it? Or down in the cellar?'

Unaccountably, his confusion and unease seemed genuine.

I wasn't getting anywhere, and at that moment the door opened from the next room. The dark head thrust itself in again, and this time it kept on coming. The figure squeezed through, keeping the crack in the door as narrow as possible, for all the good it would do. Even in that brief movement I could see there was something wrong with one of his legs: he moved askew, favouring one side.

He was a scrawny, angular sort of fellow. The face was gaunt, the bones prominent, and his anxiety made him seem even wilder. He stared at Fritz and me, and pressed himself back against the door, pistol in one hand, one leg hanging looser. He let himself slide down the door until he was sitting in a spiky heap against it.

'Hallo', I said. 'Hope we didn't disturb you with our chat. Don't think we've met. I'm, er, Peter.'

He was gazing at me with a strange wariness, and as I gazed back I was thinking: but we have met. My earlier impression that I'd seen his face was stronger now.

He nodded, uneasily. Then he babbled something in foreign to Fritz.

The flying display. I'd not seen him with the other radicals on any of our other outings, but he'd been with them that day in Weybridge. I'd seen that face, sure of it, round about when I was bumping into Caterina von Falkenhayn.

I'd no idea what he'd said: protesting that three's a crowd even in an anarchist shoot-out, perhaps, or complaining that Fritz hadn't done the washing up again. Fritz seemed indifferent. He was listless now, while his companion was manic. He waved a finger towards him: 'This Sokoloff. We call Josef-the-leg. Comrade. We respect as honourable craftsman. Jeweller. Watch-maker.'

'Oh, jolly good', I said. 'Always admired that sort of skill. Good with the old fingers, eh? But hard on the eyes. Accommodation adequate?'

He was an uncanny figure, this Sokoloff: his look, his manner. Now he launched himself forwards across the floor, spider-like on hands and feet, and then he was half-upright, and his manky leg was apparent again as he lurched to the window in a crouch. I saw the face close by me, saw him take a deep breath, saw the lips pulled back from wolves' teeth in a grimace of tension, and then he thrust his pistol past the curtain and fired.

An immediate barrage of shots in reply. He went tumbling backwards onto the floorboards and I thought they'd got him, but then I saw his expression: panting, wild, giggling even, at the foolishness of it all.

It had been a dramatically different volley, and I'd recognized the change right away. 'Rifles!' I said, hard and urgent. The distinction had meant nothing to my two companions. Rifles, and more than a few of them. I looked up and around. A section of ceiling had disintegrated into fragments of lath and plaster, and there was an ugly spread of holes in the wall. Well-aimed rifles, firing from the street and from opposite windows and rooves.

'Game's changed, chaps', I said, through a haze of plaster dust.

When I'd suggested that potential reinforcements for my situation might include the Webley, the Metropolitan Police and the Brigade of Guards, I'd been exaggerating. Now it turned out that I hadn't. The police had realized that their pistols, rarely-used bits of ironware which the government had probably picked up cheap sometime in the 1870s, were inadequate compared to the modern kit these Bolsheviks were sporting. So they'd summoned reinforcements. At some point during the morning of January 3rd, a detachment of Scots Guardsmen was deployed in Sidney Street - in the roadway, in the houses facing, and on the rooftops.

Funny thing about dust. Sometimes it seems to rise, rather than fall.

Sokoloff scrambled back to his door, and slumped against it. He stared at the two of us.

The rifles had sobered me up rather. I was more aware of how very vulnerable I was. So many barrels outside, so much shooting at shadows. Even when I finally decided it was time to do a flit, there was now a much greater chance I'd be killed in the cross-fire.

The dust was very peculiar. Definitely rising.

It was typical of that mad morning that two very significant revelations came to me at the same instant.

'Oh, that's a great help', I said. 'I think the house is on fire.'

But inside I was thinking: watch-maker...

69.

The Watchman. The specialist Beron had mentioned in the meeting of the sacks, and George. A watch-maker.

I'd found him. This limping insect of a man was the

radical bomb-maker. The man above all others I had feared. Now at last I had him under my eye, with an unbreakable police cordon outside.

Despite the less positive aspects of being in the middle of both a gunfight and a house-fire, I think I let out a sigh of satisfaction. The bomb, the unknown and terrible threat I had feared for so long, was effectively in my hands.

But where?

The smoke was rising clear through the floorboards now, wisps drifting upwards from every crack. I pressed my palm to the floor and wondered if I could feel the heat. Sometime during the morning a stray shot had caused a gas leak; and now another had caused a spark and the whole building had gone up.

'Tell you what:' I said; 'one way or another you're not getting away from the police this time. So why not do yourself a favour? You won't be using the bomb, so show it to me and we can make sure it's defused or whatever, and the flames won't set it off.' I'd no idea what I was talking about, bomb-wise, but I presumed it was possible to stop it detonating in the fire, even if it just meant chucking it out the window into the back yard.

I imagined he'd have it close by him. A moment of concern as I thought through the fact that I was not only in the middle of a gunfight and a house-fire but also sitting on top of a bomb.

Sokoloff was staring at me as though I were half-witted. Was my technical knowledge so poor? I pressed on: 'You're really not going to achieve anything by blowing yourself up.' Still the surprise and scorn on his face. 'Come on, man! This doesn't have to be the end for any of us. Show me the bomb!'

Eventually he said, statement of the obvious, with a smile somewhere between pity and malice: 'But the bomb is no longer here.'

70.

This, I admit, was a snag.

To get my hands on that bomb, I'd snuck into what was temporarily the most dangerous room in Britain. Apparently that had been a mistake. And now neither the two gunmen nor the police outside would let me out. I was trapped in the madness, only waiting to see who shot me first, and somewhere out there the bomb was still ready to go off.

The room, I now noticed, had got very hot. The smoke was beginning to collect under the ceiling.

'So where is it?' I said. 'Hardly matters now, does it?'

From outside there was a shout. I didn't catch the words, but I guessed it was a demand for surrender.

Sokoloff scuttled to the window again and fired. Again the volley in reply, and the poor net curtain was further shredded and the ceiling and walls burst out in dust and splinters. Feeling he wasn't doing his bit, Fritz scrambled across the room until he was crouching near his pal.

The curtain settled still again. Silence.

With the tension of the moment, and the heat, and the smoke, we were each breathing harder now, hoarser.

'Where's the bomb, Josef?' And those breaths hurt.

He turned to me. Considered me like I was deranged. Bit rich coming from him, but I guess he thought I'd got my priorities skewed, and fair enough. 'Come on Josef, make me believe that this is worth it. Even if we die, your work lives on. Where is it?'

'It is in other hands, who will use it.' The thought made him happy.

'Who? Which of your - er, our - comrades?'

His attention had wandered again. In a half crouch, he used the barrel of his pistol to tweak the edge of the curtain very slightly aside, to give him a view of the besiegers.

'Not comrade', he said, peering intently through the gap in the curtain. 'Customer.' Then he fired.

'Customer?' I called, more confused than ever.

At which point the back of his head exploded, and he spun to look at me for one last time, the bullet hole neat in the centre of his forehead, and dropped dead on the smoking floorboards.

Fritz and I both stared at the corpse of his friend. Then at each other. No more doubts how the morning was going to end.

My vision was blurred, eyes watering. I wiped them, and still it was blurred: despite the smashed window the smoke was thickening the air into a haze. The floor was definitely warm now.

'Situation's looking a bit dicey, Fritz old lad', I said.

An average East End house: crumbling lath and plaster, floorboards, old timber, moth-eaten fabric and mite-riddled furniture: the first suggestion of a flame and it would go up like a rocket. This one clearly had. Only minutes left now.

'Myself, I'll be popping off through the back window shortly. Guessing that's not your style.'

In the dim image of his face I could see my own: the dust and smoke begriming cheeks thick with sweat; the eyes red and weeping; the mouth straining for breath.

'I'd hate for you to get the blame for something you hadn't done. After today they're sure to pin Kyril's death on you. And anything else they've got left over.'

I admit I shan't quickly forget that expression. That mad defiance.

'Why don't you tell me what it was about?'

He raised the pistol again. Again the smile. 'Maybe you don't escape through window.'

'In which case you might as well tell me. I'll never pass it on, will I?'

He produced a chuckle, which quickly became an uncontrolled cough.

'Hang on, though', I said. Odd how the most desperate situations get one thinking clearer. 'Kyril didn't know any of you, did he? He'd come from Russia. While the rest of your lot were based here.' Each sentence was harder now; shorter. 'He... he only knew his sister, didn't he? He got her involved helping out with the opera. And so it was Nina, wasn't it, who brought in the rest of you? Now we're getting somewhere...' Insanely, I was actually feeling quite pleased with myself. 'Now: your friend Sokoloff here - with his head all over the floorboards - he wasn't part of the opera and ballet crew, was he? Too busy with cuckoo clocks and time bombs to spend his evenings in tights.'

I had to stop to cough. My throat wouldn't clear.

'He's not part of that lot. But he is the person you're holed up with for the end of the world.' Neither of us could stand properly; neither could breathe properly. 'The link between the bomb-maker and the musical mob. It's you, isn't it Fritz? But why should that worry..?'

He was gazing at me, stupefied with the smoke and the fumes and indifferent to my rambling.

'Kyril... Kyril must have got wind of the bomb. The idea - that some outrage was planned.' A billow of foul smoke thrust in from under the front door, and we both scuttled away from it. I hissed in a breath. 'And he didn't like it. And he knew - if something bad happened - investigation would lead from Sokoloff to you.' His eyes were dead. A killer's gaze. 'And he knew it would then lead from you to his beloved sister. That's it, isn't it?'

Now, at last, some sense of fatalism got to him. Still the empty eyes staring at me. And then he nodded.

'But the police would... link you all together anyway, so why..? No. No, God that's it, isn't it? Kyril was so unhappy about the violence... So unhappy about the risk to his sister... He was threatening to blow the whistle. Wasn't he?'

A crack: one of the door panels had been too tortured by the heat and given way. Then it was glowing, and then it was burning.

'That's why this all started. That's why Kyril had to die.

And why you had to run. Wasn't it?' Now the flames were flicking up from under the door too.

The handsome face, now grimed and teary. The dead red eyes. And, at last, another nod.

'So... back to you again, Fritz.' Nothing. Our faces sweating and gasping, reflecting the evil glow of the flames gathering round us. 'It really wasn't you who shot him?' Slight shake of head. A roaring from the stairwell, now a furnace, and I had to shout. 'Tell me, man! If it's not you, you can tell me. The bomb's out there. You won't be setting it off. That's for damn sure. Tell me!' Nothing. 'You're not the bomb-maker; you're not the bomb-setter; you're not the man paying the bills. The police can't touch you for this! You can save - I don't know - dozens of lives!'

Eyes screaming with smoke and heat, skin greasy and sickly, the handsome face gazed at me - and then smiled. It was the smile of a man who enjoyed the prospect of not saving dozens of lives.

'You don't know who'll die! Maybe friends of yours, countrymen, fellow-radicals. Tell me!'

He glanced around the chaos: the smoke, the occasional shot from outside. Still the smile, the words rasping through the teeth: 'You really think... you live through this...Englishman?'

'We both will! Who's got the bomb?'

But now he was chuckling at my foolish hope. He shook his head. 'OK,' he said, 'maybe I tell you.' The smile, mad in that furnace. 'Big surprise: you know this person.'

At which point the floor collapsed and I dropped through the inferno.

71.

If you've ever wondered what new torment could possibly follow after you've gone from the frying pan into the fire, you'll understand how I felt after I'd been trapped in a burning building with the British Army plus a couple of Bolsheviks all about to shoot me, and then had the whole place collapse round my head in a maelstrom of blazing timber, and then come to to find myself in the middle of an impromptu speech by Winston Churchill. My desperate moments in that furnace were as close to an idea of hell as I care to try. You can't get a better idea of purgatory than one of his sentences.

The floor gave way slowly and incompletely and the cascade of burning floorboards and Delameres was cushioned by the furniture in the room below. That was well ablaze too, of course, but the effect of the contents and inhabitants of the room above coming down in a rush was to briefly suppress the flames. Animal instinct had me scrambling upright and away from the hottest things around me and I came half-conscious - stupefied, bruised, scorched, mostly blinded by smoke, choking - in the midst of another burning sitting room. Some part of me knew it was hell and that I wasn't quite due there; some part of me knew that this floor would go any moment too. I looked around for Fritz - I swear I looked for him - but he was gone in the fury. I was lurching, staggering, crawling towards the side of the room, my simplest impulses seeking the more promising bits of floorboard, the faintly clearer bits of air, and then dimly I saw a window and I grabbed something that wasn't fully aflame and chucked it towards the glass and then I was tumbling forwards over the sill. I only fell as far as a privy roof below, and rolled and wriggled down and off it and dropped dead into the back yard.

A voice in my ear. 'Up you come, sir. Quick march.' It was Quinn, the old devil, skirmishing near the building to keep an eye out for me. His arm under my shoulder, I felt his strength hauling me upwards and forwards and out of the smoke and away from the heat.

By some foggy mystery of alleyways he had me out in the

street again, and there was a scrum of people and fortunately they were looking the other way. 'Let the unrighteous know', a voice was calling over them with relentless momentum and fruity grandeur, 'that the forces of British justice are remorseless and ever-vigilant, that though it be our finest human instinct to garland retribution with mercy, never shall we fail in the office of securing a precious peace for our people, nor in repaying the debt we owe to those noblest of men, who swear their duty to our ancient Crown and offer up their young lives in its honour, and dare to defy the most insidious of foe, nay, wheresoever...'

'Dear God, no...' I mumbled. 'Put me back.' Quinn dragged me away, through and out of the crowd. And then we were in a pub and he was pouring water down me and a bit of brandy, because military medicine is simple but strong. And then we were in a cab and then, insanely, London was around me and the sky was clear and the world was normal. And I came out of that inferno into Piccadilly, and a bath, and a late lunch with a bit more brandy.

So that was that, then. As far as the police were concerned, the last of the Latvian anarchists had met his end in the Sidney Street fire. They found both bodies, sure enough; the effort cost a poor fireman his life. The drama had had its climax, suitably tumultuous and with a free speech by the Home Secretary thrown in. All done.

Except that it wasn't. I - and I alone, it seemed - knew that the greater danger was still out there. I had been with George Gardstein in his last moments, with Josef Sokoloff and with Fritz, and from each of them I had learned the same ominous truth.

72.

I tried to tell the powers that be, and because they were polite enough to acknowledge that I'd led them to Sidney

Street they gave me a hearing. Bunce and Faversham, and Churchill himself. But they didn't want to believe it, for it was so inconvenient. And I had no clear evidence to offer. Churchill pointed out that he spent his whole life wondering who was going to attack him next - take a hint, I was thinking - and so my vague warning didn't really change much. I couldn't argue.

The next day he had yet another formal beano with the visiting Minister. The Russian was getting an honorary degree from Oxford - for the right sort of person they hand the things out like sixpences - and so the government had borrowed a big house near Abingdon for a slap-up celebratory luncheon. Another glimpse of the efforts Britain goes to when it really wants to get pally with a foreigner.

I cadged an invitation because I could think of nothing better to do than hang around the Home Secretary looking out for Latvian assassins. They let me, partly because they thought it might shut me up and partly because after my morning in the Sidney Street inferno I was looking pretty wild, even with a bath and a change of shirt.

The Russian War Minister seemed to be spinning out his visit rather, but I suppose London in January is a bit less bleak than St Petersburg. And having seen what he got up to just in Act One of a ballet I could hardly blame him for wanting to linger. I recognized some of the big-wigs from the Home Office meetings in London. Faversham lurking in the margins, trying to look busy and efficient. Evil Ilyin, forever on the edge of vision: perhaps the only man as attentive as I was to the possibilities of danger; or, knowing Russian politics, awaiting the chance to assassinate his chief himself.

By the strange mysteries of official protocol, it had been necessary to find some notional host for the occasion. Stranger still, they'd fixed on Victoria Carteret's father: the appalling Magnus, Lord Aysgarth. He's President or Patron of umpteen Committees and Commissions and what-not related to industry and international relations. Hilarious, given that the old ogre considers all foreigners to be thieves and still thinks the steam engine's a dangerous modern fancy, but the aristocracy have to give a lead on these things. On the upside for Britain's relations with the world, this meant that Victoria would be acting as hostess. Her father's a brute, but shrewd enough to defer to his daughter when it comes to civility and intelligent conversation. She'd shipped in a team of the family servants from their place at Shustoke, so things would run smooth. I'd also glimpsed Harriet Vanstone.

No Germans, which was one less thing to worry about. Otto Immanuel von Hahn is a regular fixture at these affairs, and Caterina von Falkenhayn would have been a substantial intellectual as well as aesthetic improvement to this crowd; but they probably couldn't trust her not to start garrotting guests behind the shrubbery, and if you're a top-level Russian guest of honour the last thing you want to see is Germans. I'd also given Special Branch my suspicions of unhealthy German interest in British flying machine motors.

It took me a moment to realize I was missing the opera and ballet contingent. That whole business was under a cloud now, of course. There'd been a couple of select performances to wind up the tour, but the authorities were pretty leery. Given that people had been getting killed at an average of one per performance you couldn't blame them. And I suppose it rather cramps an impresario's style when half his back-stage staff and chorus have been locked up for conspiracy to murder. No Humphrey Erskine with his innovative suits. No risk of big Jacob suddenly looming out of the crowd. No Nina, dark and ever watchful.

Not for the first time in those few days, I thought of her in a prison somewhere. Daft thing to say, perhaps, but she was probably putting up with it better than most. She never expected life to be anything other than struggle and threat, and being banged up by the British police probably proved several of her points. I was certain she would still be carrying that handkerchief, her brother's blood on it, unavenged. I could see her sitting in some grim cell, silent and contained and bleak, eyes lost in the distance of her eventual inevitable retribution.

While I faffed around, not much use to her or anyone. I was sure that her brother's death was directly linked to some planned outrage. The person responsible for killing him was still on the loose, waiting for their moment.

Churchill was making a speech. Well, when was he not? I was only vaguely aware of the words. Lots of diplomatic guff boosting our distinguished Russian guest. Ancient affinity of our two great peoples - crowd-pleasing stuff, ungentlemanly to mention that unfortunate Crimea business, least said soonest mended - now reinforced by the bonds of diplomatic alliance and practical collaboration in the most modern science. Typical Winston gag about how we didn't need political revolution when together we were advancing the technological revolution. For a moment I thought of wretched George, creature of an older London, now lost and forgotten in an unmarked pauper's grave somewhere. On rolled the speech. Indeed, he said, great developments were in hand even while he was speaking - let's face it, whole empires could rise and fall while Churchill was speaking - the Russian War Minister's esteemed Assistant Minister was finalizing an agreement with Malachai Erskine, most innovative of British aeronautical engineers, and we could all look forward to...

My eyes were roaming the room. Trying to recognize faces in the crowd, among the waiters. Looking for the unnatural movement, the person not paying attention. Realizing that I was accordingly the most suspicious of all.

Churchill had stopped talking now - no, really - and was re-joining his guest, clink of glasses and murmur of fraternal small-talk. I found myself with Faversham and Ilyin. They were both considering me warily - but the feeling was very much mutual, so fair enough. 'Truly you are indestructible, Sir Henry', the Russian was saying, the usual sinister whispering whine. Typically, he'd heard more of my adventures than anyone. 'If you will allow me to congratulate you on coming out of that house, perhaps you will allow me to enquire how you came to be in it...' I was about to tell him to go to hell, but I realized he was the only person with whom I could have a serious conversation about Bolshevik sympathizers who might still be on the loose. I was thinking up some reply - witty-yet-empty, diplomatic standard - and wondering how much I wanted to let on.

And then Victoria was in front of me.

No pleasantry, no diplomatic nicety. 'Harry:' she said, voice clear and low, 'now.'

73.

No hesitation.

Immediately I was following her away. Victoria is steadier than the Sphinx, and wiser, and I'd trust her judgement over anyone's - certainly over my own when it comes to social protocol. Victoria says now, it's now.

We were striding through the crowd. A footman went ahead of us, his presence clearing the way even if deference to the lady did not.

'There was another flying machine display just before Christmas', she said over her shoulder. 'A boy went up for a flight: a cross-channel challenge.'

'Grace', I said. 'I was there; I watched him go.' I remembered the big honest face; his youthfulness; his anxiety.

The footman was opening a door into the conservatory. Victoria turned and looked at me. 'Apparently he didn't make it back on the return leg. Everyone hoped he'd landed in the French countryside somewhere and was just having trouble re-establishing contact. Harry's been fretting; that's why she flew down here to join me for a few days.' A breath. 'We've just had a telegramme: some of his kit has washed up - definitely his. He must have crashed into the sea.'

She glanced into the conservatory. 'Harry is... I've never seen her like this.' She shook her head. 'I can't help her. It's... it's soldier's business.'

I just nodded. Held her gaze a moment longer - another unforgettable unmentionable intimacy between two people who know each other too well - and stepped into the conservatory. I was aware of the door closing behind me, and the footman's bulk filling its glass, and I knew we wouldn't be disturbed. The Aysgarth servants have a feudal loyalty to the Honourable Victoria that's essentially mediaeval: when she asks one to block a door, he will die doing so if that's what it takes.

I found Vanstone standing alone between two monstrous plants, gazing out into the garden. She had the doors open, and in a dreary January the chill was no joke, but she wasn't aware of it despite her flimsy dress. Her skin was paler than ever, the handsome profile turned to stone.

'It's ghastly', I said. I wasn't looking at her, but into the garden with her. She didn't turn. 'And you think: what's the bloody point? Each time I saw a friend die, I felt littler by their absence, and littler because I was still part of this wretched mediocre world and hadn't had the greatness to die.'

I was aware of her turning to me.

'And the hell of it is, you know that... however much you want to chuck it all in, there's life still to be lived. That you have to walk a while longer with those of us on this side of the line.'

Now I looked at her. She hadn't wept. There was emptiness. And there was something like fury.

'Dull prospect, I realize, but there are one or two who'll offer you an arm.'

And she collapsed into me.

'I am so deeply weary of it all', she hissed into my chest. Her hands were gripping my biceps fit to crush them.

I held her in as firmly as I could. She needed to lose herself. She needed to be part of a larger rock.

We stood there, an age or two. For much of the time, I imagine that Harriet Vanstone was in the sky over the English Channel.

Eventually she pulled herself away. She kept her fierce grip of my arms - considered my ravaged shirt-front - looked up and explored my face. Then she unlocked one of her hands, clenched it till the knuckles were white, and softly thumped it against my chest. At last she took in a great sniff, and released me.

Over her shoulder I saw a small metal table, where old Aysgarth could get himself a refresher when sitting in here of an evening plotting mischief against the neighbours. I poured her a substantial whisky, and didn't waste time with soda.

'Drink to dull the feelings?' she said sourly.

I nodded. 'Usually works for me.' She took it, shrugged, and knocked it back. So I poured her another, and one for myself; wasn't my whisky. This time she managed to look at me before starting on it. She held my gaze. We raised our glasses: no words - no attempt to speak of the brave man gone - but we knew.

I began again cautiously. 'Forgive me… He - Cecil Grace - was… special?'

'Yes. Oh - but not like that.' Looking into her drink, she said more quietly: 'I… I don't really go in for that sort of thing.'

'No', I said into my own drink. 'You, ah… you fly on the other side of the Channel.'

The eyes wary. The most independent of women, but she still had to survive in a dull conservative world. 'You'd heard?'

I shook my head. 'Certainly not. Wondered; vaguely. There's a kind of… of distance, about you; not on this earth.'

'Aghast I didn't leap into your bed?'

'One adventure I regret I shall never experience. But no, it's more that… Well, even Victoria, who despite occasional lapses is the most discerning of ladies, even she's still playing

238

the game.

The expression darkened slightly. 'Ah yes. The game.'

Another penny dropped. 'And Marie the engineer..?'

Defiance. Satisfaction. 'Has a heart more powerful than the finest motor engine in Europe. And she's good with her hands.' I smiled, but she wasn't sure. 'A certain horror is traditional, I gather.'

I scowled. 'Lots of things are traditional in British society, Vanstone. In war and beyond I've seen every kind of atrocity and corruption and depravity; how people get their jollies when they're off-duty is the most harmless thing of all and none of my business. The established order, all of those rules and expectations, they've only ever diminished or excluded the Delameres.' She nodded. Another thought struck me: 'And... flying, then?'

'You mean: did I catch it up in the clouds? Lack of oxygen shrivelled my womanly instincts?' I waited. Her face grew harder, more resolute. 'Yes, escape. Yes, liberation. Yes... being out of this damn' world.' Then she was unsure again, and I realized it was more openness than she was used to. She recovered. 'There's supposed to be a tradition among boys in the better schools, isn't there?'

'I wasn't at any of the better schools long enough to find out. Never fitted in financially, socially - or probably aesthetically.'

'Did you make contact with that glorious German creature you spotted at the ballet?'

'I did.'

'How were the famous thighs?'

'As advertised.'

'And I had to look at you in tights instead.' She topped up our glasses. 'Did you and the Falkenhayn indulge? I'm not interested in gossip, but observing men in social situations is cheaper than going to the zoo.' I didn't say anything, and she considered my face a moment. 'No... No, you wouldn't say, of course. And I don't think you did. According to your sweet mediaeval manners, to have succumbed… would have suggested to her that you don't respect Victoria.'

'As you say.'

'Good man.' Another exploration of my face. 'I can see why Vicky sometimes regrets you chucking her over.'

'But you understand why I had to.'

'Oh, God yes. You're a shambles.' I nodded. 'Branded or not' - a gesture towards the flash of white hair over her forehead - 'you're just as cursed. You're darkness and chaos, Delamere; always will be. We disreputable types will have to remain in the shadows of her brilliance, not the light.'

'To the shadows, then', I said. We raised our glasses again. 'Right ho. I ought to pop back. You going to be all right, Vanstone?' She nodded - sober again, but that hard resolution was there. 'Not too much thinking, eh? Go and talk to your engineer instead.'

That got the suggestion of warmth in the gloom. 'Vicky says you're nannying Churchill.'

I scowled. 'Seems pretty clear they were trying for him that night at the ballet, and seems pretty clear the threat's still out there.'

'Unlucky for him. He was only there that night by accident.'

74.

I'd been shifting to leave, but now I stopped. 'How's that?'

'We were chatting with someone in the entourage before we went in. Guest of honour at the ballet was supposed to be the Russian Assistant Minister. And an Assistant anything doesn't warrant any serious turn-out from the home team.' I remembered the the other foreign uniform, in the box when I was fighting the assassin. 'But then the War Minister himself suddenly announced an interest' - having seen who he was with back-stage, this I could understand - 'and so the British side had to stump up someone a bit more box office. Hour or two's notice, the best they could do was Churchill. Feeling seemed to be it was no bad thing to show a bit of fraternity on domestic security as well.'

I was gaping at her, mind racing and not gripping. 'But that... that doesn't make any sense!'

'Should I speak slower?'

I was fighting to remember what George had said. 'The target was supposed to be the same. But then... That can't...'

'Delamere, is this when that mighty valet of yours would be telling you to get a grip?' I suspect the look I gave her proved her point. 'Well then.'

I breathed out the irritation. 'Some particular attack has been planned for... weeks now, I guess. Then a different chap had the idea for the business at the ballet. This, I was told, would coincidentally have had the same outcome. But if Churchill wasn't supposed to be at the ballet, then he can't have been the intended target. Nor the Minister.' I was still struggling to absorb it. 'You say the official guest was the Assistant Minister. But why on earth should a bunch of serious anarchists care about him?'

I was gazing far away, as lost in the distance of the garden as Harriet Vanstone had been. She didn't say anything now. Just waited; watched.

The cloud began to clear. I turned to her. 'Oh hell.' Still she waited. 'It was in the speech: that old Scotch maniac, old Erskine, he's agreeing something with the Assistant Minister, right now. D'you-?'

'Erskine's improved engine. At Brooklands - Weybridge. Starting at noon.'

'Oh hell.' I was striding to the door already. I caught the footman by the shoulder. 'Lady Victoria. Now, please. And we'll need to make a telephone call.'

I was drifting again. 'Quinn. Quinn then Bunce. But Weybridge is miles from London...'

'Twenty or more', said Vanstone.

'It's pushing eleven o'clock now. However fast they jump, Quinn and Bunce surely can't get there. And from here, it must be…'

'Fifty miles.'

'Hell. There's no way on earth I'll ever make it.'

'No way on earth.' The hint of a tease in her voice made me look up. Harriet Vanstone's face was alive in a way I'd not seen before. 'But you'll make it.'

75.

I suspect the urgency kept me sane. A rushed exchange with Victoria. A telephone call with Quinn. By then Victoria had horses ready and we were up and thundering over the back lawn towards some distant flatter bit of the estate which had been commandeered for Harriet Vanstone's visit. Vanstone was already there, and she and her engineer friend and some assistants were bustling around.

Vanstone was once again as I'd first met her: the trousers, the country sporting style, the hair up - and already she seemed freer and farther from the world of convention.

And it was taking too long and I could concentrate on worrying about the distance and the dwindling time and the inevitable explosion and why someone wanted to murder Sir Malachai Erskine and the Assistant War Minister of the Russian Empire and what would happen to our international reputation and the European balance of power when we got a foreign politician killed.

But at last I could escape the truth no longer. Harriet Vanstone's flying machine was uncovered and in position at one side of the meadow and malicious arms were helping me into a heavy coat and offering me goggles and gloves and leading me forwards.

Standing in the trench, waiting for the whistle. The line of men to left and right. The certainty that someone was about to die and it was going to be my fault, and oh I was going to have to go first towards that death. The hollow gaping faces, the whispered swearing, the effort not to tremble or fart too obviously. The churning in the gut. All other consciousness falling away, and only the parapet of earth and the line of sky above. The ghastly silence, the insects fiendish, the heat.

The most complex devices I've ever operated are a Webley pistol and a box of matches. I walked towards the machine.

Close to, it was bigger than I'd gathered from previous glimpses. But before I'd only looked at a flying machine as a curiosity: gosh what a lark, a funny-looking kiddie's toy with a motor engine attached. Now I was offering up my life to it.

Vanstone looked up from whatever important bit of pre-briefing she was doing with the excellent Marie, and considered me. 'Not sure I didn't prefer you as a ballet dancer.'

'Damn sure I preferred me as a ballet dancer.'

She looked carefully at my face. It was not, I fear, all that heroic. 'Hell of a thing', she said. 'Best get on with it, eh?' She thrust a folded map at me. 'Perhaps better if I do the flying and you do the navigating, unless the male prerogative…'

'Shut up.'

She pointed out where on one of the exposed faces of the map we were starting and where, should the good Lord prove more of a sportsman than hitherto, we would land. 'For the first minute you'll be utterly thrown by how what you're seeing is an exact copy of the map. Then it's easy.'

'If you say so.' The map was on a lanyard, and I wrapped that round my wrist.

'Right ho. Mount up.'

At that point, whatever passes for higher brain function in the Delamere skull went Absent Without Leave, over the garden wall and away faster than any anarchist.

Because it was clearly ridiculous that this contraption - a

few bits of wood and some fabric struggling to support the dark mysterious machine at its heart - could lift up from the earth. And it was clearly insane that I would be sitting on top of it when it did so.

'Bit of a squeeze,' said Vanstone, 'but it's built for the occasional passenger. Hope you didn't overdo at the buffet.'

The horror could not be postponed. We were standing in front of the... the seat. That's all it was. Just a plain wooden bench in the middle of the lower wing. Vanstone hopped up like a colt taking an easy fence. I lumbered closer like an elephant approaching a unicycle. Marie had to help me up, eyeing me rather doubtfully. No doubt suspicious of what I was getting her friend into, and I couldn't blame her.

Then it was just the two of us, on our little bench. Perched up on the wing. No suggestion of restraint or support to the side or in front. Vanstone pulled her goggles down over her eyes, and so I did the same. Our feet were on a sliver of raised board, and I think it was that final bit of insubstantiality that near finished me. 'Bugger me...' I said, desperate, and angry at myself.

Her face turned to me. 'Buck up', she said, gentle, firm. 'You know there aren't so many people in the world who've flown? You're probably some sort of milestone.'

'First Boer War veteran to foul himself at an altitude greater than fifty feet? Longest death scream, minor gentry category?'

'That's the spirit.' And then the noise burst around me. A coughing, then a fitful growling, then a roaring from just behind us and I felt the chaos in the air and the ridiculous contraption was shuddering like a silly horse and sure to fling itself to bits. Vanstone looked around us - slowly, carefully, and the steadiness in that handsome face was the only reassurance I had - and made a couple of hand signals. A great jolt and heave and we were rolling forwards over the meadow. Faster, and faster, but surely not fast enough, and the grass was rushing beneath my boots and the flying machine was swaying and bouncing, and now the grass was a blur and with a sickening lurch in the machine and my stomach we hopped off the ground - and then a second later thumped clumsily down. 'Oh for God's sake!' I yelled, and heard a new deep strange sound beside me. Joyously, unrestrainedly, Harriet Vanstone was laughing, and then once again we jumped and the world fell away.

76.

Dear God, the beautiful terror.

It's possible that I died for a couple of minutes there. I suddenly found myself in the sickening position of being a few hundred feet up in the air, and all I could see was my boots and then the whole of ruddy England spread out beneath me. I have no recollection of how I got there. The air was roaring around my ears and I was dimly aware of some eerie wailing noise.

After several moments, I realized that the eerie wailing noise was coming from me. The cry you make to wake yourself from the nightmare, only it wasn't working. This nightmare was endless and inescapable. I could only hope the assault from the wind and the motor meant that Vanstone couldn't hear me.

Eventually I got my screaming under control. Restricted myself to vast desperate breaths. Thing about being on a flying machine is that you can't see the flying machine. It's all under you and behind you. Twist round and maybe you catch a glimpse of wing-strut; but the one time I tried that we happened to hit a bump and I found myself staring not sidewards but downwards and sure to fall and I gasped in horror some more and didn't do any more twisting round. Otherwise all you can see is... perhaps a bit of footboard; nothing.

It's just you, rushing through the sky.

My breathing came hoarse, hard, desperate. And at last steadier.

How to describe the beauty?

If you've ever stood on a hill and admired the scenery below, you'll know the power of the distance, and the light on the fields, and the gentleness of our landscape. You'll have thought about all the lives continuing down there, and all the lives of centuries past, bimbling along and doing their bit. Now imagine a perspective farther than you can possibly imagine. And it's all so soft, and so silent.

I've met too many English people to be truly patriotic about England; and we get up to worse when we're abroad. But distance does generally make me fonder of the old place; and distance up turns out to have an even more powerful effect. I have rarely felt such love for my native land, as when I saw its cool winter patchwork drifting beneath me on that mad morning.

I glanced to my left. There beside me: Harriet Vanstone. In her freer world now, in her own element. I could just make out her eyes through the goggles: unblinking, blending with the sky.

I felt the sudden desperate hope that she had some idea where we were going, because if she really was depending on me for the navigation we were probably halfway to Brazil. The map, it turned out, was clenched in a ball in my fist. I smoothed it out as best I could.

It's the damnedest thing. Normally with a map, you look at it and then you try to imagine what the reality might look like and how they might relate. From a flying machine, the map is real and unfolding beneath you, and you have to guess how they might have captured it on the map and you find yourself checking they got it right.

Vanstone thumped my leg with her gauntleted fist to get my attention, and then pointed down to the right: a church. Then to the left: a lake. After a moment I understood that she wasn't merely pointing out sites of touristic interest.

Assuming she'd aimed us in approximately the right direction, I was able to place us on the map. Then she wriggled, and from one of her coat pockets pulled out a compass, also tied on with a lanyard. She held it flat in front of me, and I adjusted the map and reckoned a bearing. I stuck my arm forward on the course we wanted. Obediently, she adjusted one of the levers and we drifted round. I only panicked a little bit, got my stomach under control again, and made another gesture once we were pointing the right way. Then I held up ten fingers: a bearing of one hundred degrees, and she nodded.

The compass seemed like an excessive precaution: with the world laid out so tidily beneath us, and the map adequate, we could find our way easily.

Then I realized that my vision was blurring, and I wiped my goggles, and it didn't help and I started to worry whether there might be something about lack of oxygen, or too much oxygen...

We were flying through a cloud.

Damn, but we were flying through a cloud... Oh, the madness of it all.

So: the compass not excessive but very sensible. It would keep us on the right course. It couldn't, though, do anything about the up-and-down. What, I wondered, was to stop Vanstone flying us into a hill or a church tower?

Deep breaths.

I don't think I wanted that wild silent journey to end.

Partly because I have never felt so free, so untroubled. Partly because I was dreading what I would find at the end of our journey.

I was sure there was going to be an explosion at old Malachai Erskine's flying machine shed. I was sure it was going to be arranged for when he was there with the Russian Assistant Minister of War. I was sure it was going to ruin Britain's relations with Russia, at a time when that meant the destabilization of all Europe - not to mention the lives destroyed, and indeed the shed. I was even sure who was going to be responsible; fairly sure now, anyway, given the things I'd been told by diverse anarchist murderers as well as the extraordinary woman beside me. The one thing I couldn't be sure of - quite the contrary - was getting there in time to do a damn thing about it.

We were flying over Wallingford, and then over Henley - assuming I hadn't got the map upside down after all. It was even more uncanny being above a settlement. Flying over open country you could sort of pretend was like looking down from a hilltop. Seeing the streets laid out below, the carts and even the individual people moving through them... well, it was damned peculiar.

I also had the vague idea that landing in an uncontrolled manner in a field might be survivable, but that coming down into someone's house surely wasn't.

Then Weybridge. I double checked it was Weybridge according to the features on the map: the road, the mess of waterways. I checked our bearing from my own reckoning and with the compass. I pointed our new course to Vanstone, and immediately the machine edged round accordingly. Most extraordinary business.

I checked my watch. Hell! - just a minute before twelve. Even if they were running a bit late, we couldn't get there. Twelve was the one certain moment in the programme, and surely the explosion would be arranged soon after.

Open country again, gliding away under my boots, but too slowly.

We'd see the explosion, of course. It would be visible for miles, and up here we'd have the best view of all. And all we could do was try to find the bodies in the wreckage.

Twelve. We were close now, surely. There was the railway - and St George's Hill. Gods, but it was going to be close... And there! There, surely, coming in on the London Road was their motor car. They'd still be a few hundred yards short of their destination. We would actually beat them to it.

What I'd entirely forgotten, of course, was the need to land. I'd been panicking about the danger of it, but not the necessary time and manoeuvring. Too late I recalled something about wind direction when you're going up and coming down. We were getting lower now, and lower, just a couple of tens of feet off the ground for God's sake, and Vanstone had us on a converging course with the motor car. She surely wasn't going to crash us into...

We swooped low over the car and I forgot all fear and sense and was leaning out and gesturing wildly at them as we went, yelling, desperate to confuse them, slow them.

Now we were making a long loop round towards the landing field. The machine was on a hard tilt, Vanstone squeezing me against the edge of our little bench, her eyes lost in the feel of the machine as the wind strained at its every joint. The car wasn't more than a hundred yards from the shed and we were much farther. Just for a moment I was distracted from the inevitable explosion by the movement of another car, half a mile behind the first but coming in at a hell of a speed. Quinn and Bunce: it had to be them, but they too would be too late. The explosion leaping into the sky, the deaths and the destruction, the international chaos...

I pressed my mouth to Harriet Vanstone's ear and shouted as distinctly as I could in the wind: 'Must - land - between - them - and - shed!'

And she just nodded, and the eyes were stone and beautiful, and we were gliding down on our fatal course. We were aimed straight at the shed, and again we were converging with the car, and surely it would get there first and we were still too far away. The grass leaping up at me and a thump in my gut and we were down, except we weren't: another long bounce, Vanstone's eyes, the grass racing past and towards us and another thump but gentler and now we were racing over the ground.

I had flown up into the sky, and come down again, and I hadn't died. We were rolling relentless towards the shed, and still it hadn't exploded. The car was drawing ever closer, slowing down now that we might be in the way. I could see the shed so clearly, I could see the car, the bewildered faces in it, and now we were all going to crash into the shed together.

The wing on my side of the machine smashed into the wall of the shed, and six foot of fabric and wood crumpled and at last we stopped. Away to our left, beyond the other wing, the car had slewed to a halt. We had won the insane race, by the width of a flying machine.

Then the sky exploded.

77.

I should, I suppose, have been getting used to it. I was after all being incinerated on a daily basis.

Again the stupefied return to consciousness. The deafness, the distant moaning and roaring in ears that had ceased to function normally. Fighting for sight, and then awaking to a blur: fumes, smoke, my bewildered mind.

All around me flames. The shed had exploded and, though something had shielded us from the immediate blast, the fabric and wood of the flying machine were instantaneously alight. And the machine had fuel of its own, and that must have spilled and was now burning fierce.

I was buried in the wreckage of the machine. Above me a crumpled tent of wooden struts and ragged canvas, and all of it flaming and the scalding heat was too close and all around me. I couldn't see properly, I couldn't breathe properly, eyes and throat failing with the smoke.

I kept looking. I couldn't find her.

Then something stirred under me. For some reason, I couldn't move. I twisted my head as best I could. I was lying across Vanstone, my shoulders over her legs.

Then movement, another puzzle for my vision. Some dark figure of the fire was moving through the wreckage, some...

Quinn.

Of course Quinn. Of course he had made it in time. And if he was coming into the wreckage then he'd already checked that Sir Malachai Erskine and the Russian had survived: I had been so clear on the importance.

I was trying to speak. There was something desperately important I had to say. Right now: I needed him to hear me right now. But my voice wouldn't come.

Fortunately, Quinn knows me well enough. He reached down, and I was vaguely aware of him lifting my shoulders and setting me straighter. He needed no telling. He picked up Harriet Vanstone and carried her out of the flames.

Good man.

So, a certain satisfaction. We had, in spite of it all, stopped the plot. And that remarkable woman was safe.

I was not, of course. On the negative side of the ledger, it turned out that I was after all going to be cooked in the wreckage of the ridiculous machine. Irony, or something.

I felt some strain in my leg. Numbness, or perhaps the opposite - the feeling of pain returning. It was as if someone were trying to yank my leg off.

Saint Peter calling me home, perhaps? Or the other fellow, confident of having me away for himself? I was being stretched now. Come on chaps, one way or t'other, make your minds up…

'Bloody 'ell…' said Saint Peter, in an outraged growl of pure Cockney. I was being dragged across the turf and out of the wreckage, my shoulders knocking through bits of flaming wood. 'Bugger me you're a shambles, Delamere.' Perhaps Saint Peter was working undercover in the Metropolitan Police. 'Who deliberately crashes a flying machine into an explosion? No wonder the bloody aristocracy's obsolete…'

78.

It ended where it had to end. In a theatre, behind a stage.

Dimly, through the walls, the final act was underway.

It would have taken more than a flying machine crash and an explosion to dent the extraordinary life-learned resilience of Harriet Vanstone; she'd have to walk among the mediocrities a little longer. Or fly: old Malachai Erskine was even more impressed by her flying ability than by her saving his life, and had offered her a replacement machine, a pioneering motor engine and the chance to test all of his latest wheezes. So maybe she wouldn't be stuck on earth for too long. He'd been kind enough to offer me much the same opportunity, now that I'd proved my secret affinity for flying. I fear my reply was not diplomatic.

I'd picked the theatre, and I'd looked out this empty room, as the right spot for my rendezvous. No one would attract too much attention slipping back here.

Quinn was at my side, of course. He seemed to feel I couldn't be trusted on my own for this sort of show, and I'm not saying he was wrong.

We were just stepping in when a figure appeared at the end of the corridor. Not the person I'd expected, but not perhaps a surprise. It was Inspector Faversham, prowling the theatre trying to look alert. The Russian Minister of War was in town again, and that meant another evening of theatrical diplomacy, and that meant the Special Branch responsible for security.

Trudging along behind him I saw Bunce, as cheerful as ever to be working late and doing what he didn't consider proper police work.

Faversham had spotted Quinn and I as suspicious prowlers and hurried forwards. When he recognized us he slowed, and distaste came into his face and voice. 'Oh…' he whined down his nose, 'it's just you, Delamere.'

'Disappointment as ever', I said. 'You lost, Faversham?'

'Why are you fooling around back here?'

'None of your damn' business.' He didn't like it, but for once he had to go easy on me. As of today, British justice had concluded its interest in the case of the Latvian anarchists, and I still had a bit of credit in the bank for having got myself blown up instead of a Russian guest. 'Rather a low-key end to things today, I suppose.'

The final verdict in the trials of Nina, big Jacob and the others had been delivered that day. All off the hook, for lack of evidence. Which seemed extraordinary, if you knew what I knew, but perhaps that's the difference between us and places like Russia. I'll never be fond of Bunce or Faversham, but we're a damn sight better off with them policing us than the likes of the ghastly Ilyin.

He scowled. 'The worst of them will be out of the country inside twenty-four hours. Those that aren't, we'll find something else to pin on them soon enough.' I nodded. 'And after all the kerfuffle in Houndsditch and Whitechapel' - he looked at me as though the kerfuffle had been my fault - 'I don't think anyone wanted any more noise.'

He was right. For the public, the story was weeks old now. George, who'd certainly been responsible for killing one and perhaps more of the dead policemen, was himself dead. Fritz and Sokoloff, who might well have been partly responsible, were dead. After that, there was no comparable finality in trying to prove who exactly shot whom in that chaotic hallway and that dark back-street. And besides the fact that they were obviously dangerous lunatics, bizarrely the police didn't have many specific charges to lay against Jacob and friends. Nina was free; they were all free.

'Let's hope they've read your script,' I said, 'and don't feel they've unfinished business with the Russians here, or with anyone else.'

He gave a nervy smile. 'That is why the Special Branch is still engaged. We have the right scrutiny and precautions in place, and I'm sure we'll muddle through, Delamere, if we don't keep tripping over you private enthusiasts and the more, ah, pedestrian bits of the police.' He made to stride off, no doubt wary of tripping over Bunce or me while we were all squeezed in this gloomy corridor.

He hadn't got a yard when he was stopped by a voice hurrying in from the other direction. 'Inspector Faversham sir!' It was one of his plain-clothes bods. 'Sir, just had it from re-questioning one of the back-stage staff who'd got it from one of the theatrical types: somebody with a Russian name - 'fraid we didn't get it clear, sir - Russian name, anyway, is lying in wait for the War Minister in one of the dressing rooms.'

Faversham's eyes went wide. 'Bolsheviks!' he hissed. 'Come along!' And he hared off into the darkness, with his man close behind. Bunce gazed after them grudgingly, and decided he ought to follow.

'Quick bit of background before you go, Bunce', I said. He stopped, and looked at me without enthusiasm. 'You having dragged me out of that fire. One good turn, and so on.'

'Yeah, still wondering why I did that', he grumbled.

'Your instinctive moral judgement, no doubt.'

'Don't count on it, Delamere.'

'Anyway, just thought you might be interested, you being a protocol enthusiast. I'm pretty sure that good old Faversham is not about to stop a Bolshevik assassination. He is, instead, going to bust in on our esteemed Russian visitor enjoying a private performance by his mistress.' Bunce's eyes widened. It was that kind of an evening. 'I imagine our esteemed Russian visitor will respond very badly to being bust in on. Like flying machines, you know? One prefers the smooth descent to the embarrassing premature crash. Now, if you ran very fast, I'm sure you could stop Faversham before he causes a diplomatic incident. Otherwise, though you might be able to warn your superiors and patch things up with the Russians, I fear you will not be able to save the Special Branch reputation.'

A bleak hungry smile spread over the face of Inspector Ernest Bunce, and off he strolled. Never did a policeman walk more cheerfully or slowly.

At our second attempt, Quinn and I made it into the room. Years of dust and lack of use. A tiny window, too dirty to reveal how dark it was outside. Another door, leading on to some further forgotten corner of the theatre. A battered wardrobe. Quinn found a lamp, and lit it. I found a chair and sat, and he lurked nearby. I spotted a dusty wicker basket near at hand, and dragged it towards me, and placed a pistol on it.

We only had a few minutes to wait. Then we heard footsteps in the corridor, and a figure appeared in the doorway.

'Well well', I said. 'Come on in, Erskine.'

79.

Humphrey Erskine stepped into the room like the whole place might be about to collapse around his ears. Which, given my track record, was fair enough.

'Gosh', he said, and he managed a nervous laugh. 'Delamere. I didn't…'

'I'll bet you didn't. No doubt you're wondering why I should have sent a message pretending to be an anonymous Latvian keen to discuss something Josef Sokoloff had told me.' I leaned closer. 'Just as I'm wondering why you responded to it.'

Again the laugh; again the nervousness. 'But I - No, I didn't… I'm just…'

'Save it', I said. Between him and Churchill I'd spent too much time stuck in sentences that were never going to end. 'You're a hell of a lad for the long-matured plan, but improvisation's not your strong suit, is it?'

He was distracted a moment by the ominous vision of Quinn stepping towards him, and round him, and closing the door.

After another alarmed glance at Quinn, and then at the pistol, he refocused on me. 'Whatever do you mean?'

'I knew an assassination had been in the works, thanks to my anarchist pals. I try to get to their meetings whenever I can; only way I can keep up with British politics - the things I know about the Coal Mines Act... Anyway, I also gathered from them that Jacob's mayhem at the Alhambra was a different plot, but coincidentally against the same target. While George Gardstein was trying to build up their strength and their funds and wait for the right opportunity, big Jacob insisted on seizing the initiative and making whatever noise he could as soon as he could. That's why you tipped me off about it, when you got wind something was up: you knew that Jacob's lunacy would disrupt your plan.'

Quinn had found another chair in the gloom, and pushed it into the back of Erskine's legs and he sat. 'My plan?'

'Strange thing: only the Assistant Minister was due to be at the ballet. The Minister only came at the last minute for a back-stage tour of his ballerina friend, and Churchill only came for the protocol of it. Likewise, when the bomb finally went off it was targeted at the same man: the flying enthusiast Russian, with your uncle. Who would want to kill one or both of those two, rather than someone higher-profile? Their deaths wouldn't do anything for the cause of international revolution. The only effect would be to stop your uncle pouring the family money into his eccentric enthusiasm, and the Russian's death in the same incident would have embarrassed the British government into steering clear of the company. With an explosion, they'd probably have blamed some fault in your uncle's new design. You may not care much about flying machines, Erskine, but you crave the lifestyle of the chaps who enjoy that sort of thing, don't you? And you craved it soon and you craved it while there was still money to enjoy.'

'This is - This is ridiculous. There are plenty of others who might benefit.'

'The Germans were snooping around the Erskine motor engine at Weybridge, certainly. Unfortunately for their man, so was Josef Sokoloff, doing his recce. The German either saw him, or was blocking his way out. Sokoloff was wild enough for anything, and one dead German spy was nothing. But precisely because their man was spying and getting knocked on the head, the Germans couldn't have been part of the bomb plot.'

The lamp made his frozen face more peculiar.

'And in the same way,' I went on, 'who would have wanted to kill poor Kyril, a man who lived only for his singing? Right from the start this business has been bound up with the wretched anarchists, and right from the start that's been wrong. You counted on your private benefit being buried in all their mayhem. But in truth they're rather shrewd calculators of their interest. Killing your uncle would have done them no particular good; killing Kyril Vassillev was distinctly bad.'

'And why the hell should I-?'

'Because Kyril had got suspicious when you started exploring your new found network of friends too enthusiastically. He got wind of the fact that you'd contracted Josef Sokoloff to build you a bomb. He couldn't know what you were planning, but he knew it had to be something far removed from the usual Bolshevik business. He knew that, whatever it was, you were going to attract enormous attention, more than the Latvians might normally. You were relying on precisely that, using their reputation as cover for your crime. Kyril knew you'd bring every policeman in London down on his community, his acquaintances... and his sister. He tried to warn you off. He threatened to blow the whistle. You had to act fast.'

I reached for the pistol on the wicker basket beside me, and tossed it into his lap. He couldn't have leapt more if I'd thrown his damn bomb at him. He let it lie on his thighs, untouched.

His mouth made an effort at a denial, a question, but he didn't have the oomph any more.

'As well as being pretty casually aimed, the firing squad rifles were casually allocated; Nina mentioned passing them round. And they weren't live-loaded; I had that from a man who had no reason to lie. With many of the cast on stage at that moment, you were one of the few people lurking back there. You'd had time to reckon the layout, and you knew the music. You wriggled your way into the shrubbery behind the firing squad, with that pistol, and with the noise of the music and the blank rounds in the rifles to cover your shot. Range couldn't even have been ten yards. A variation on the trick played by that policeman in *Tosca*, swapping the blanks for live rounds, but the effect was the same. You then had plenty of time to bury the pistol in the earth where you stood. I dug it up today. Couple of clear fingerprints on the stock and the barrel. And once they start looking, the police'll have no trouble placing you in Weybridge for the explosion.'

Silence. Humphrey Erskine was looking hunted, and sulky. 'You've been so frustrated for so long. Unable to enjoy the world you think is rightfully yours. Surviving on a thin allowance and a tedious administrative post. Watching life and the family fortune shrinking in front of you. And then you found yourself on the fringes of a world of truly dangerous men, and you saw a short-cut to wealth and independence, and you summoned your courage and you made your deal with Sokoloff for the bomb. But your scheme was chaos, and it trapped you, and you ended up having to kill a decent and innocent man; kind of man you might otherwise have appreciated.'

At last he touched the pistol. Looked at it accusingly. Uneasy, unsure, he found it was still loaded. 'Tempted?' I said. 'No, I think even you might find that too much to explain. But keep it as a souvenir by all means; police have no more use for it.'

He hefted the pistol in his hand, unconsciously. 'And now?'

'Now it's between you and justice, Erskine. None of my business.' I stood. 'You'll oblige me by giving me a couple of minutes. And then staying well clear. No more opera and ballet invitations, you hear?'

I stood, and Quinn and I watched him a moment longer. He looked small in the lamplight, the pistol on his lap large. He glanced at me for one last time: wondering, calculating, not sure what his choices and chances were.

80.

He was still staring at the pistol, not daring to look around again in case I changed my mind, when I closed the door on him for the last time and Quinn and I began to saunter towards the stairs and freedom.

I may not actually have heard the door inside the little room opening; I was listening hard for it. I certainly heard the voices: a man's shout of surprise, protest; a woman's fierce in passion.

'Guess Miss Nina will have heard your conversation, sir.'

'And this way we didn't have to meet today, and so she'll have kept a lower profile.'

'Bit of a surprise to get fingerprints, sir, after all that time in the damp earth.'

'I imagine it would be, yes.'

The voices had died away now. I could imagine Nina Vassilleva and Humphrey Erskine staring furious at each other.

'Sure this was the wisest course, sir?'

'No. But I doubt the police could have made the charge stick. Circumstantial stuff at best. And after all the chaos recently, I'd bet they'd rather keep the blame on the Bolsheviks.' We reached the end of the corridor, and I stopped and looked at Quinn. 'For me it was... unfinished business. His blood on me, and all that.'

He nodded. Quinn doesn't exactly approve of my sentimentality, but he recognizes it. And he knows a duty when he sees one.

The voices broke out louder again. I winced, and set off down the staircase.

'He might still have the advantage over her.'

'You've met Nina Vassilleva', I said over my shoulder. 'You don't believe that.'

As we came lower down the winding metal steps, I could hear the sound of the Act III crescendo rising from the orchestra and filling the great hulk of the theatre.

'Hasn't the grit to shoot a woman, you think sir?'

From somewhere above us: the unmistakeable crackle of pistol shots. Two, three, more. Quinn and I stopped, looked back up, exchanged a glance.

Then a scream: high, lost, ghastly. A man's scream, mortally-wounded, and immediately overwhelmed in the last surge of the music coming from below.

'Apparently she's still carrying that knife', I said. 'My opera knowledge as doubtful as ever: I may have swapped the live rounds in his pistol for blanks.'

Quinn grunted. We set off down the staircase again, to rejoin untroubled London society at the end of the show.

The execution was beautifully managed.

EDITOR'S NOTE

The Editor wishes to thank the present-day Philippa Tucker, who first suggested that it might be fruitful to explore Harry Delamere's investigation of a shocking killing which occurred during a theatrical performance in 1910 - one attended by her namesake.

We can, perhaps, excuse Delamere's ignorance - shared by most of his contemporaries - about the distinctions between Bolsheviks, revolutionaries and anarchists, not to mention the distinctions between Russians, Latvians and the other peoples of the Russian Empire. In the English language, 'Bolshevik' has rarely been used with any great precision. At this time they were technically still a faction within the Russian Social Democratic Labour Party, established after a split in the party in 1903 over the harder line proposed by V. I. Lenin: the nickname of his 'bolsheviks' simply derives from the Russian for 'majority'. The faction became a party in its own right in 1912-13, and seized power in the Revolution of 1917.

Although the British may have been hazy about the nuances of Russian politics and international radicalism, they had a strong if melodramatic idea of the real danger they were talking about. The Fenian dynamite campaign of the 1880s injured more than eighty people in London and elsewhere. Joseph Conrad's 1907 *The Secret Agent* drew on the true story of an anarchist's failed attempt to blow up the Greenwich Observatory, and on a growing trend for political assassinations and dynamite attacks. The novel's dark vision of London and the strange and dangerous ideals in its back-streets was adopted and adapted a year later in G. K. Chesterton's fantastical thriller *The Man Who Was Thursday*. The 'Tottenham Outrage' of January 1909, when two

Latvians with revolutionary connections tried to rob a factory payroll, saw a two-hour armed battle across north-east London involving among other things a tram chase, a shoot-out between the robbers and some duck hunters, astonishing intrepidity by the police and numerous members of the public including some local footballers, and the deaths of a policeman and a ten year-old boy as well as the eventual suicides of the two Latvians. London at this time was one of the world's great gathering places of humanity, and still relatively restrained in its policing, and thus a popular centre for international radicals. Indeed, the later stages of the 1903 Russian SDLP congress had taken place in London, making the city in effect the birthplace of Bolshevism.

This lurking threat acquired a further shocking reality for Londoners in winter 1910. Harry Delamere's account adds only some intriguing personal details to the generally-accepted version of events: the Houndsditch murders of 16th - 17th December, when a gang of Latvians led by George Gardstein were interrupted while trying to break into a jeweller's and tried to shoot their way out; the huge investigation that followed the deaths of the three unarmed policemen, Sergeant Robert Bentley, Sergeant Charles Tucker and Constable Walter Choat; the arrests and the eventual tracking of two remaining suspects to Sidney Street; the police and military operation to evacuate the street and besiege the flat, the gunfight and the fire, and the deaths of Fritz Svaars and Josef Sokoloff and District Fire Officer Charles Pearson.

Winston Churchill needs no introduction (especially not from Harry Delamere). But it's interesting to see him from the perspective of a contemporary following his career forwards rather than from the hindsight of his familiar greatness. His appearance on the spot at the Siege of Sidney Street was a perfectly Churchillian combination of intrepidity and vanity, and provoked considerable controversy. There was some concern about his recklessness; more about possibly inappropriate interference in police, fire brigade and military business. He was criticized in Parliament, and heckled by newsreel audiences. In 1913, by then First Lord of the Admiralty, Churchill learned to fly - the Royal Navy having been relatively early adopters of the new technology and accepted an offer of training from the Royal Aero Club.

The man due to become the first flying instructor for the Royal Navy was Cecil Grace, but he died before he could start work. Having successfully crossed to France on December 22nd 1910, he disappeared during the return flight. As Victoria Carteret learned, debris began washing up on January 6th 1911 - and eventually what may have been his body.

Harry Delamere had the good fortune - or misfortune, depending on one's taste for heights - to participate in the astonishing first decade of powered flight, a period when substantial leaps in technology and achievement were accompanied by terrible risk. Following the Wright Brothers' epoch-making flight in 1903, and their subsequent work on some of the critical problems of how to control a fixed-wing machine doing anything more than fly a short distance in a straight line in calm conditions, the Brazilian Alberto Santos-Dumont made the first public flight in Europe in 1906, and in 1909 Louis Blériot showed that flight had transformed the relationship between countries when he flew across the English Channel. From the start, there was an awareness that flying machines had significant military potential. As early as 1908, the Wrights won a contract to supply the U.S. government with a military aircraft; the contract acceptance trial flight led to the first fatality of powered flight, an American Army lieutenant travelling as Orville Wright's passenger. 1910 saw the first air-to-ground radio communication, the first simulation bombing and the first shots fired from an aeroplane, as well as the first commercial delivery flight and the first international discussion of air traffic control.

The Royal Aero Club began issuing Aviator's Certificates in 1910. John Moore-Brabazon was awarded the first, in

March; thirty years later he would serve as Minister of Aircraft Production, under Prime Minister Winston Churchill. The second was given to the Honourable Charles Rolls: the man who had launched history's grandest car marque in 1904 was an early enthusiast for balloon and then fixed-wing flight, becoming the first man to make a non-stop flight across the Channel and back in June 1910, and then becoming Britain's first powered-flight fatality a month later when the tail of his flying machine broke off mid-flight. Cecil Grace received the fourth certificate, and was dead before the end of the year. The British Royal Flying Corps was established by Royal Warrant in April 1912, and suffered its first fatal crash less than three months later. Following the deaths of Captain Eustace Loraine and Staff Sergeant R.H.V. Wilson when their monoplane dropped out of the sky, the station order later the same day from the Air Battalion at Larkhill established an enduring spirit: 'Flying will continue this evening as usual.'

The 1910 London to Manchester air race race gives some idea of the pioneers' zest, a series of wild short-hop flights as Louis Paulhan and Claude Grahame-White tried to keep pace with each other, involving crashing, running out of fuel, catastrophic wind damage, fierce rain, accidentally turning off the engine mid-air, and the world's first night flight - enthusiastically supported and occasionally obstructed by large crowds, marshalled by police, soldiers and boy scouts. Brooklands at Weybridge, so memorable to Harry Delamere, holds a unique place in the history of motor sport as well as flying: it is now a museum to both. Some of those first flying machines can still be seen in museums: their lightness and simplicity are astounding - and so is their fragility.

Harriet Vanstone soars out of Delamere's account as a rare and remarkable character. But she was by no means unique in the early history of flying. Sculptor Thérèse Peltier became the first woman to fly an aeroplane in 1908. Journalist and screenwriter Harriet Quimby was the first woman to gain an American pilot's certificate, the first woman to fly the

English Channel, and the first woman to be killed flying, thrown out her aircraft mid-air when it pitched unexpectedly. Given the lack of resources in Ireland at the time, the trouser-wearing, hunting-shooting-fishing sports journalist Lilian Bland had to design and build her own aircraft; the successful prototype incorporated an ear-trumpet for an engine hose, a whisky bottle as a fuel tank (presumably with something new inside) and bicycle handlebars for control. By the time of her death at the age of 92, she admitted that gambling was her only remaining excitement. Her death in 1971 came only ten days after that of Cheridah de Beauvoir Stocks, who lived into her eighties despite having spent six weeks unconscious after a crash in 1913.

Perhaps the most splendid was vicar's daughter Hilda Hewlett. Clearly an independent and intrepid spirit - 'I woke up from a narrow, conventional, stultifying childhood and first thought for myself', she said of a early trip to Egypt - she found her artistic training in woodwork, metalwork, and needlework handy for building and repairing aircraft. An early bicycle and motor-car enthusiast - she was twice fined for speeding within two months in 1905 - in her late forties she became the first woman to gain a Royal Aero Club Aviator's Certificate. While continuing to fly she also went into business, opening Britain's first flying school (at Brooklands) - her son has the minor distinction of being the first pilot in history to be taught to fly by his Mum - and building more than eight hundred aircraft for the British in the First World War. The character underpinning all this can be seen in her later decision to emigrate to New Zealand: 'The urge to escape from the three Cs, crowds, convention, and civilization, became strong.' Her husband's attitude, meanwhile - 'Women will never be as successful in aviation as men. They have not the right kind of nerve' - shows something of the social context for these extraordinary women, and something of why the Hewlett marriage didn't last. But he wrote historical novels, so what could you expect?

The historical record is patchy when it comes to some of the other figures who appear in this section of the Delamere papers. Vladimir Sukhomlinov was Russia's Minister of War from 1909 to 1915, when he was made a scapegoat for the country's military failures at the start of the First World War. Disgraced and imprisoned, at the end of the war he fled to Germany, living in poverty and eventually dying of exposure on a park bench one night. His Assistant Minister of War and eventual successor, Alexei Polivanov, was a reformer in the Russian system, whose enthusiastic engagement with Sir Malachai Erskine may have helped push the Russian Army to adopt aircraft at Corps level.

Information about the Latvian radicals is sketchy and sometimes conflicting. Sites such as Spartacus-educational have material on the likes of George Gardstein and Fritz Svaars. Through he'd been previously arrested for revolutionary activities and for attempted murder in Latvia, and clearly involved in the Houndsditch killings, there was not enough evidence to convict Jēkabs (Jacob) Peterss of murder or even conspiracy to commit burglary. He married an Englishwoman, before returning to Russia to take part in the revolution. When his English wife and daughter were invited to join him, they found that he'd already acquired another family and they themselves were unable ever to leave Russia. A victim of the Tsarist secret police, Peterss was briefly chief of their Revolutionary successors, the Cheka; but he was arrested in Stalin's Great Purge and executed in 1938. The body of Leon Beron was found on Clapham Common on New Year's Day 1911; he had been beaten and stabbed to death, and his face cut. Although a man was convicted of his murder, to this day we cannot be sure whether he was killed by the Russians, the Germans, the Latvians or someone else. Quinn's admirer Sara Trassjonsky, who had stayed with the dying Gardstein and was found destroying documents, was not convicted; her mental health was never strong, and she was eventually sent to Colney Hatch asylum. Nina Vassilleva was convicted of conspiracy to commit burglary, but this was overturned. She worked as a cigarette-maker, and lived on alone in the East End of London until the 1960s.

Much the greatest and the most enduring mystery surrounding the debacles in Houndsditch and Sidney Street concerns the man known only as Peter the Painter. His presence at both incidents was alleged, but not consistently. More bafflingly, despite much speculation there has never been any clear idea of who he actually was. Indeed, the strongest supposition has always been that he was merely the product of confusion and myth, and that no such man as Peter the Painter existed. Now, more than a century later, Harry Delamere's account enables us to answer the question of his existence at last, with a conclusive 'well, yes and no…'.

Ɗҽath
and thҽ
Ɗrҽadnought

A Dreadnought battleship dwarfs a man. And the man slumped at my feet, with his head bent up against the monster's keel, certainly looked small enough.

A shipyard, at night, was a damned odd place for a rendezvous. But Sinclair had insisted, and he'd seemed pretty het up, and he did owe me thirty guineas, and so I'd trekked across to London docks from the West End and spent twenty minutes stumbling around in the darkness until I'd bumped into the biggest latest thing in British naval warfare.

Cathedrals of the new century, and all that. Most advanced specimen of man's vision and engineering brilliance. And damned eerie if one finds oneself skulking underneath it in the small hours.

H.M.S. Thunderer was nigh on 600 feet long, a bit shy of 100 across. If St Paul's Cathedral were made of iron, Sinclair had said; more than once. And if St Paul's Cathedral had ten guns capable of firing one-ton shells to a distance of ten miles or more, and were an instrument of colonial rivalry designed to overawe Germany.

Not a very helpful comparison, all in. Sinclair's, not mine.

This was just the hull. The superstructure - funnels, guns,

bridge, portrait of the King and so on - was still to be installed; she wouldn't be ready to start overawing Germans until 1912. The crudeness made her immense bulk even more ominous in the gloom.

I'd not looked closely, but I was pretty sure it was Sinclair slumped at my feet. Against the keel of his beloved battleship.

He'd not given me exact directions, so at the gate I'd slipped the nightwatchman a shilling, and he described where the offices were, and shortly afterwards I was properly lost in the vast metal jungle of the shipyard. They left a few lights on at night, but all those did was hint at the shapes around them, and make the whole effect more ghostly. I walked past corners of large buildings, under the metal feet of enormous machines, through seas of shadow. My dress shoes splashed through puddles of unknown liquids that shimmered faintly in the gloom. Cranes and gantries loomed over me.

Eventually my wanderings through the wasteland of metal and oil and darkness brought me to the dry dock, and what I first took to be a wall: a blackness that closed out my vision and rose in front of me; but it rose and went on rising and back over my head and far up into the night, and instinctively my fingers reached for this mammoth and found the rough chill of iron, and I knew it was the *Thunderer*.

I seemed to have come at her from the river end, her stern. With a faint idea that the offices might be at the head of what was clearly the main area of the yard, I set off along those 600-odd feet of shadow towards her bow.

Tiny metallic echoes boomed in the ship, as the wind rolled a rivet off a plank, or a rat nudged a bolt and sent it plummeting into the abyss of the hull.

At the bow I'd found the body. There was a light strung quite near, and it caught the pale splashes of starched shirt and empty face.

Something was dark and glistening on the shirt front. Now I bent to the body.

It was Sinclair, alright.

Someone had stabbed him to death right under his battleship. The commission that he'd hoped would save his company had become his tomb.

Something gleamed faintly under his clenched left fist, and I picked it up: a cufflink, with a battleship design.

My fingers brushed at the knife still embedded in his chest.

At which moment the shipyard came alive with light, scorching the metal and blinding me and from behind there were shouts, and whistles, and boots converging on me.

For more on Death and the Dreadnought, *and other bits of historical chat, pop by www.robertwilton.com*

Death and the Dreadnought

'I've seen chaos in my time: the great bazaar in Constantinople; the retreat after Magersfontein; Frenchmen trying to put up a tent.'

London, 1910: Harry Delamere is wishing he hadn't agreed to a midnight meeting in the shipyard where Britain's newest battleship is being built.

Now the police want him for murder, the workers of Europe have declared him their enemy, he's hiding out with a burlesque dancer called Annabella Bliss and everyone's trying to kill him.

Murder, mystery, melodrama, skullduggery, derring-do, international espionage, dangerous liaisons, villainous foreigners, the British class system, a couple of sentimental music hall numbers, significant incidents on battleships, thrilling chases in motor cars, desperate escapades on railway trains, fights to the death armed with only a duck pâté sandwich, all in correct gentleman's attire.

Poison in Paris

'With flames and smoke billowing around us, and each dragging a Bulgarian railway worker by the scruff of the neck, we launched ourselves out into that arena of noise.'

When the British Government asks Harry Delamere to courier a secret document from Constantinople to Paris on the Orient Express, it seems such a simple way to cover a couple of months' rent and some outstanding bills.

But someone knows a lot more than he does, no-one trusts him, and pretty much everyone's trying to kill him.

Poison in Paris: All the glamour of the Orient Express, melodrama, excitement, sinister foreign gentlemen, exotic foreign ladies, bandits, revolutionaries, assassins, other exotic foreign ladies, interruptions to the regular timetable, surprises, disguises, explosions, outrages, breath-taking escapes from death and an unfortunate incident in a Viennese lavatory.

From the secret archive
of the Comptrollerate-General for Scrutiny and Survey
edited by Robert Wilton

Traitor's Field

1648: Britain is at war with itself. The Royalists are defeated but Parliament is in turmoil, its power weakened by internal discord.

Royalism's last hope is Sir Mortimer Shay, a ruthless veteran of decades of intrigue who must rebuild a credible threat to Cromwell's rule, whatever the cost.

John Thurloe is a young official in Cromwell's service. Confronted by the extent of Royalist secret intelligence and conspiracy, he will have to fight the true power reaching into every corner of society: the Comptrollerate-General for Scrutiny and Survey.

'*A new benchmark for the literary historical thriller.*' – Manda Scott, President of the Historical Writers' Association

Treason's Spring

1792: the blood begins to drip from the guillotine. The French Revolution is entering its most violent phase, and Europe confronts chaos. The spies of England, France and Prussia are fighting their own war, for a trove of secrets that will reveal the treacheries of a whole continent.

At the height of the madness a stranger arrives in Paris, seeking a man who has disappeared. Unknown and untrusted, he finds himself the centre of all conspiracy.

When the world is changing forever, what must one man become to survive?

'*A rare clever treat of a novel.*' – The Times

From the secret archive
of the Comptrollerate-General for Scrutiny and Survey
edited by Robert Wilton

Treason's Tide

1805: Britain is militarily weak, politically divided, unsettled by her rioting poor. A change in the weather will bring Napoleon's forces across the Channel and destroy the British Empire for ever.

Only a dead man stands in the way – Tom Roscarrock, unwitting agent to an obscure government bureau of murky origin and shadowy purpose. Behind the clash of fleets and armies, there is a secret world of intrigue, treachery and violence. His life in danger and his motives increasingly suspect, Roscarrock must pursue the conspiracy from England into the heart of Napoleon's France, there to confront the greatest mystery of all.

'Beautifully written, wonderfully clever, this is a triumph.'
– Daily Telegraph

The Spider of Sarajevo

1914: Europe is on the brink. As Britain's enemies grow stronger, the Comptroller-General must confront the man with whom he has struggled for a generation – a man he knows only as the Spider. In a desperate gamble, he sends four agents out across the continent, on a mission they do not understand…

The future of British intelligence – of the British Empire – is in their hands. Not all will return. Unique and resource-ful, hunted and deceived, they have embarked on a journey that will climax in Sarajevo on the 28th of June 1914.

'A learned, beautifully-written, elegant thriller.' – The Times

The Adventure of the Distracted Thane

'So we rode again into Scotland, Sherlock Holmes and I; only this time we came at the head of an army.'

A beautiful woman comes out of a storm to tell her macabre tale. And thus the legendary detective is confronted with his strangest case: the murder of King Duncan of Scotland, and the ascent to the throne of the haunted Macbeth.

Dr Watson's narrative reveals the untold story behind Shakespeare's play: a kingdom in chaos, a man possessed, and bloody murder. At last, literature's greatest detective gives his explanation for its most infamous crime.

The Case of the Philosophical Prince

A mysterious death. A castle of spirits and superstitions. A royal family of fierce and unnatural passions.

Prince Hamlet of Denmark believes his father was murdered, and he's determined that Sherlock Holmes will help him prove it.

But Holmes and Watson find the palace of Helsingør gripped by suspicion and fear. The spirit of the dead king lingers in unhappy minds, and rival interests are jostling as the new regime tries to settle. Holmes's investigations uncover buried secrets and betrayals, and Hamlet's increasingly deranged obsession is shattering the stability of his family. The royal court of Denmark is heading for a violent climax, and not everyone will survive.

'Was this an end to the blood and to the chaos?'
Holmes gazed at me. 'An end?' he said, and his voice was deathly. 'My dear Watson: it has not yet begun.'

The Silver Thread:
a journey through Balkan craftsmanship
by Elizabeth Gowing

From the mines in the cantos of Dante, to the prizes stolen in the wars of the 'nineties, follow the silver thread through Balkan history and culture to the new generation of crafts-women facing their uncertain future.

The Rubbish Picker's Wife:
an unlikely friendship in Kosovo
by Elizabeth Gowing

How can you find the best rubbish pastures for scavenging? How can you free children to go to school rather than to go out begging? Can mayonnaise deal with headlice? An account of an extraordinary charity, and the challenges and delights of finding your community a long way from home.

Edith and I:
on the trail of an Edwardian traveller in Kosovo
by Elizabeth Gowing

In 1900 Europe's last wilderness was explored by a stout, stubborn English-woman who travelled in her tam o'shanter across Albania's Accursed Mountains. One hundred years later, Elizabeth Gowing follows Edith Durham's trail into Kosovo, finding not only an Edwardian heroine but also a guide for today.

Two Summers:
Nixon and Trump by Greyhound Bus
by Tim Albert

In 1969 the 22-year-old Tim Albert spent three happy months travelling 12,000 miles around the United States on Greyhound buses. Half a century later to the day he set out to revisit his trip, armed with his original 30,000-word diary.

Mostly We Had It Good:
a baby-boomer's journey
by Tim Albert

Teddy Kennedy, EM Forster and Saddam Hussein: an idiosyncratic and insightful look at the second half of the twentieth century, combining recollections, family material and journalism.

Albania and The Balkans:
essays in honour of Sir Reginald Hibbert
edited by James Pettifer

A century of Albanian and Balkan history is seen from an unusual variety of perspectives in this collection of essays in honour of a man who parachuted into the country during the Second World War.

About the Editor

Robert Wilton was advisor to the Prime Minister of Kosovo in the years before the country's independence, Private Secretary to the UK Secretary of State for Defence, and acting head of an international human rights mission in Albania. He's co-founder of The Ideas Partnership charity, supporting the education and empowerment of marginalized children in the Balkans. Author of the prize-winning Comptrollerate-General series of historical novels, he also writes on history, culture and the failures of international intervention in south-eastern Europe, and translates Albanian poetry. He writes on and for film, and teaches film and literature. A practising life and writing coach, he divides his time between the Balkans and Cornwall. He is neither an adventurer nor a gentleman.

Visit www.robertwilton.com for free stuff, information, and a conversation about the curiosities of history

Printed in Great Britain
by Amazon